W9-BHZ-621

ST. MARTIN'S
MINOTAUR
MYSTERIES

OTHER TITLES FROM
ST. MARTIN'S MINOTAUR MYSTERIES

ZEN AND THE ART OF MURDER
by Elizabeth M. Cosin
BREAD ON ARRIVAL
by Lou Jane Temple
BIGGIE AND THE FRICASSEED FAT MAN
by Nancy Bell
MOODY FOREVER
by Steve Oliver
AGATHA RAISIN AND THE WIZARD OF EVESHAM
by M. C. Beaton
DEATH TAKES UP A COLLECTION
by Sister Carol Anne O'Marie
A MURDER IN THEBES
by Anna Apostolou
AQUARIUS DESCENDING
by Martha C. Lawrence
MY BODY LIES OVER THE OCEAN
by J. S. Borthwick
MURDER WITH PEACOCKS
by Donna Andrews
A COLD DAY IN PARADISE
by Steve Hamilton
CROSSROAD BLUES
by Ace Atkins
ROMAN BLOOD
by Steven Saylor

MINOTAUR IS ALSO PROUD TO PRESENT THESE MYSTERY CLASSICS BY NGAIO MARSH

BLACK AS HE'S PAINTED
GRAVE MISTAKE
LAST DITCH
TIED UP IN TINSEL

EXTRAORDINARY ACCLAIM FOR HOWARD SWINDLE'S

JITTER JOINT

"Delirium tremens turns to trembling fear in this fast, tense fiction debut . . . Swindle sweats his hero past multiple threats in a plot steeped in AA ambiance . . . without losing a suspenseful edge. . . . A credible story with an ending that points, happily, to a possible series."
—*Publishers Weekly*

"Brisk, confident, and funny."
—*Texas Monthly*

"A winner . . . Swindle manages to breathe new life into the serial killer genre . . . An explosive mix. This should be the start of a very successful series."
—*Library Journal*

"This is a good start, with a strong lead character, an active plot and plenty of violence."
—*San Antonio Express-News*

"The plot is strong, the writing is sure and clean, and the suspense palpable . . . This is a good book. The first of the year to go on my list of best first mysteries."
—*Deadly Pleasures*

Jitter Joint

Howard Swindle

St. Martin's Paperbacks

JITTER JOINT

Cover photograph by Ed Holub.

Library of Congress Catalog Card Number: 98-40558

ISBN: 0-312-97611-9

Printed in the United States of America

St. Martin's Press hardcover edition / March 1999
St. Martin's Paperbacks edition / March 2000

10 9 8 7 6 5 4 3 2 1

To Bill W. and the late Jerry Stephens for picking me up;
to Bob Mong for dusting me off;
and to my beloved Kathy for showing the way.

. . . Admitted to God,
to ourselves, and to another human being
the exact nature of our wrongs . . .

—Fifth Step, Alcoholics Anonymous

Acknowledgments

Agents don't come any smarter, shrewder, or more supportive than mine: Janet Wilkens Manus. And on those occasions when legalities threaten creativity, no attorney gets to the bottom line quicker or better than Justin Manus, Esq. Deeply, I'm indebted to both.

I also owe sincerest thanks to Bob Wallace, editor-in-chief of St. Martin's Press, and Kelley Ragland, an editor at St. Martin's, both of whom were willing to believe that a nonfiction writer could also be a novelist.

Through no fault of my own, I travel in excellent circles.

1

He plunked two ice cubes into the glass and submerged them with Johnnie Walker Black. The movement was rote, and he kept his eyes on the graying man sitting poolside.

"So what's it been, two years, three?" the old man asked.

"Two," he said, moving to the chair across the table. "It was in the courtroom. I'm not surprised you repressed it. You don't have a lot of experience with defeat."

The man with Johnnie Walker hoisted his glass in an eye-level toast, fixed his visitor with a stony glare, and downed the scotch. He spoke while the burn was still in his throat, and his voice came out raspy and short.

"Think I'll have another," he said, leaning forward in his chair.

"No, let me."

Behind the portable bar, the young man poured another Johnnie Black. Casually, just as he had practiced, he moved his hand from the pocket of his blue blazer over the glass. There was no fizz when the pills hit bottom, and he watched them dissolve almost immediately. Still, he gave it two strokes with a swizzle stick. He spotted a bottle of Jack Daniel's, but he fought off the urge. He poured himself a glass of soda instead, squeezing in a quartered lime.

"You know," he said, pushing the scotch across the table to the old man, "that's going to finally kill you."

"Not in your lifetime," he said. "That would give you way too much satisfaction. Cheers."

They clinked their glasses, never taking their eyes off each other.

The older inhaled the drink in two swallows. His brow wrinkled curiously as he guided the glass back to the table. His face flushed, and his eyes locked wide on his guest.

The younger man sipped his soda, savoring the shock in the man's eyes.

"You know," he said, "I've made this a lot less painful than you've made it for me."

The gray-haired man slumped forward in his chair, clasping both palms over his heart, his chin falling onto his chest. His gasps were from deep inside, and they shook his shoulders. A gurgling sound came from within his guts, and a faint bubble of spittle formed at the corner of his mouth.

Across the table, the young man marveled at the redness of the man's skin. His face and neck, even his hands, looked as if they been blistered by the sun. The reaction had been almost instantaneous, much quicker than he had anticipated, and he smiled at his own efficiency.

"You're a dead man," the younger one said. "You're dying just as surely and certainly as if I had shot you in the head. You need to know that so you can appreciate what I'm about to say. It's a final thought, one you can carry with you to hell."

He studied his prey as he spoke, watching the old man's chest heave and the muscles contort in his face. He'd never seen him vulnerable, ever, and now he was mesmerized by his helplessness. He had fought off the urge for a Jack Daniel's himself, and now, he realized, he didn't need it. He was soothed, uncommonly tranquil. The euphoria of killing was better than bourbon.

"This isn't about money," he said, realizing his message was about to be lost. "That's what you tell people, but it's *never* been about money. You know what it's about. You never accepted responsibility for what you did. Now, you see, you have no choice."

The young man in the blazer checked his Rolex and rose from the chair. He walked behind the gasping man, grabbed him roughly by the back of his collar, and pulled his torso straight in the chair. He reached over the man's shoulder and shoved a laminated card into his shirt pocket. He released his grip on the collar and the man's face fell hard into the table, knocking the empty scotch glass onto the marble deck and shattering it.

The young man walked alongside the cabana to the wrought-iron gate, fashioned, as were most things at the Highland Park estate, with the logo of an oil derrick bearing the name *Dora I*. He heard retching behind him, and he paused at the gardenia bush, leaning into it to take in its sweet fragrance. He snapped the stem on one of the white blooms, trimmed a few leaves, and guided the stem through the lapel in his blazer.

Then he headed around the house to the circular drive and the black Porsche.

2

Jeb Quinlin was a man without viable options. He had had no choice but to succumb to the conspiracy between Sarah, the estranged wife from the far side of hell, and Captain Bill Barrick, the warm-and-fuzzy, new-breed chief of Crimes Against Persons ten years his junior.

The pair had tactfully referred to the ambush in his own den as an "intervention," just two people who cared deeply about him and who wanted to see him straight and sober. They could call it anything they wanted, but truth was, Sarah had him by one testicle and the good captain had him by the other. Together, they had cracked his balls like walnuts. It was extortion, Quinlin knew, pure and simple.

The former was threatening divorce, which at that turbulent juncture in their marriage was neither here nor there. But Texas was a community property state; divorce meant that Sarah would walk with half his retirement. For the last several years, the pension was all that kept Quinlin playing the game. He had earmarked that money long ago for fifty acres and a log house in the remotest pocket of Deep East Texas he could find, as far from asphalt, skyscrapers, sociopaths, and assholes like Barrick as he could get.

The latter, the ever-sensitive Captain Fuzzy, had already

"temporarily" suspended him. He had relieved him of his badge and city-issue .357 Smith & Wesson and was hinting at outright termination.

Neither had bought Quinlin's argument that his so-called problem was actually just the residual debris from the meanest five months of his career in Crimes Against Persons, or CAPERS, as cops called it. He had had a high-profile, big-dollar insurance tycoon with a tag on his toe, and five heirs, including a trophy wife twenty years younger who couldn't keep her legs together, with millions of motive. Not to mention two business partners who wouldn't have pissed on the deceased if he were a human torch. Fact was, Barry M. Hawthorne was universally despised and had littered his road to success with the bodies of everyone with whom he'd ever shaken hands. Only hours into the investigation, Quinlin figured the only way the family could throw a funeral was with court-appointed pallbearers.

Hawthorne's murder was high-society intrigue, and it led the front page and ten o'clock news for weeks. *Inside Edition* had done a full half-hour on the wheeler-dealer, focusing on his Horatio Alger beginnings, following his conglomerate of far-flung insurance companies and ending, of course, with a grainy close-up of Hawthorne sprawled in his own blood beside his red Jaguar convertible. In the eleventh hour, under unrelenting pressure from the brass and the media, and just when Quinlin was about to offer up the insurance executive's daughter to a grand jury, he had closed the case with a totally different suspect.

An investor, scammed in an insurance deal five years earlier, had bought the murder weapon from a convicted felon. And when the ex-con gun dealer got upside down with the police for dealing guns out of his trunk, he gave up the juiciest piece of information he possessed to save his own hide. Quinlin knew his high-profile case had been a near miss. Had he offered up the got-rocks heiress, his career—and pension—would have passed before his very eyes.

In the aftermath, he had diluted the stress with booze, and some events of that particular period had become substantially woozy, Quinlin reluctantly admitted, but it was nothing a little R&R wouldn't resolve. Barrick, of all people, should have had some appreciation. Quinlin had managed to pull him from the dung heap, too, and leave him smelling like a rose. The captain had appeared coolly confident and professional at the press conference, making it appear for the cameras that he had known all along about the vindictive business partner Quinlin had discovered only twenty-four hours earlier.

Time, and a modicum of understanding, Quinlin pointedly had told Barrick and Sarah, and things would smooth out. They always had.

Quinlin's argument had fallen on deaf ears. Theirs was the only deal on the table. Nor did they offer any guarantees as inducement. He supposed that was the beauty of ultimatums. Only one side could issue one, which meant the poor bastard target with no leverage ultimately had to bend over and take it in his BVDs. He had worked the ultimatum himself a hundred times from the other side of the table, gouging suspects with evidence, even an occasional bluff, until they coughed it up and saw things his way.

There were no guarantees in his case, Sarah and Boy Wonder had made that crystal clear. The marriage and the job might or might not be there in twenty-eight days, the minimum he would have to spend in whiskey school. Yet, they claimed, his future was in his own hands. He had heard smarter strategies from speed freaks.

"I'll tell you this," Captain Barrick had told him, sitting in his own favorite recliner, "you have no chance whatsoever, not with the Dallas Police Department or apparently with your marriage, if you don't go to the hospital right now and take care of this, uh, problem."

They were accusing him of being a certifiable drunk, but they didn't have the guts to say it. They used euphemisms; he had a "problem," they said, a "situation."

"You say no to this, uh, 'opportunity,' and, well, both your options end right here and now," the captain said. "Your call, Detective."

Across the coffee table, Sarah nodded silently. They were in lockstep. Quinlin studied his boots momentarily, then abruptly headed for the master bedroom. He recognized the old feeling; he had to leave. He didn't know where he was going. It never mattered. He couldn't stay. He threw several pairs of Wranglers and a few starched shirts into a canvas bag, and grabbed a pair of tan Tony Lama ostriches. He was leaving. That was certain. But where? In the master bath, he threw his razor, aftershave, toothbrush, and toothpaste into the bag. He stopped at the front door on his way out. The decision was split-second.

"Call the hospital," he had said finally, locking on Barrick's eyes. "You can tell 'em I'll be there in the morning."

He saw Sarah out of the corner of his eye. She held her head in her hands, and he thought she was crying.

"All this talk about my personal welfare is pretty damned heartwarming, Barrick, and I'm sure Sarah thinks you're a real sensitive guy. But we both know it doesn't have a goddamned thing to do with what's going on here. I do my job. I'm there every day. And when the squad draws one that's going to cause you problems, one that'll show your ass or get you fried in the media, I'm the first one you come to.

"I stay alive by reacting," Quinlin said, "by reading people. I'm damned good at it, too. What I'm reading here is that you're a paper-shuffling piece of garbage. You're a brown-nosing bureaucrat who couldn't make it on the street. Bottom line, you're a phony bastard, Barrick. You're a three-dollar bill of a human being. Add that to your file."

Quinlin spent the night a quarter-mile from his house, holed up in a La Quinta with a bucket of ice and a fifth of Wild Turkey. He drank and listened to the highway noise and stared at the ceiling until the Turkey anesthetized him.

Quinlin's head was awash in turbulence, the self-induced, virulent strain that he felt even in the pit of his stomach where ethanol and acid apparently had rendezvoused to produce radiator flush. Cautiously, he had inventoried his symptoms in a cold shower: Weak knees, shakiness in his extremities, and a felony case of cottonmouth. The prescription was familiar: Just avoid abrupt movements, anything that would jar his head, and hold off on the black coffee for fifteen minutes or so. But self-pity and Wild Turkey, he was able to determine, were potentially lethal.

Circumstances considered, he felt he had pulled himself together relatively well until he opened the door. The early morning sun slammed him in the face like an iron skillet. Even through his Ray-Bans, he felt the lasers of pain all the way to the back of his skull, which he suspected was lined with aluminum foil. Blinking was masochistic. The turbulence in his cranium upgraded to a full-fledged typhoon. He squinted and retreated backward into the darkened motel room until he felt the edge of the bed against the back of his legs. Delicately, as if he had a stick of dynamite between his knees, he lowered his butt onto the bed and breathed shallowly, with his elbows on his thighs.

Ultimately, the walk through the parking lot in the fresh air was recuperative. He inhaled the late April crispness into his lungs, cautiously at first, and as the cool oxygen made its way to the pain centers, he could feel the muck clearing from his head and gut. Clear enough for habit to overtake common sense. Sensing the onset of a month-long drought, he turned the fifteen-minute drive to Cedar Ridge Hospital into three hours.

He detoured to a narrow, two-story brick building on the frayed southern fringe of downtown and pulled into a parking space beside the front door. When his eyes adjusted to the dark, familiar confines of the Probable Cause, he spotted a group of DPD stragglers from deep nights arguing affirmative action at a corner table.

"Miranda ain't shit, it's this quota crap that's ruining law enforcement," a white patrolman said, apparently winding up a dissertation on forced equality. "Until four years ago, this big-assed woman that's my sergeant was a fuckin' 911 operator. She can't cover your back, but she can damned well cover the front seat."

"And her mustache is heavier than yours," yelled someone to immediate guffaws.

Billy Earle Gibson, who had spent twenty-five years carrying a badge, had just finished san-o-flushing the women's john. He was appropriately aghast when Quinlin told him about the conspiracy.

"You tellin' me a man's wife and his needle-dick captain can get by with that kinda shit, just like that?" the barkeep asked, snapping two fat fingers. "Just pronounce a man an alcoholic and force him into a hospital? Even baby-rapers get due process. Hey, I'm glad I pulled the pin when I did. The department's more chicken shit every day."

They commiserated and dissected the dilemma every which way looking for a loophole. Periodically, Billy Earle reurged a course of action that entailed a baseball bat across the captain's kneecaps. In the duration, they oiled the conversation with four or five stiff Turkey and waters. Two hours later, when Quinlin went for his wallet, Billy Earle, in a charitable act unprecedented at the PC, held up an ample hand, palm out.

"No, these here are on the house," the old cop barkeep said. "I'll have one waiting on you when you get out."

Quinlin drove three blocks down the back alley to avoid

going the wrong way on a one-way and pulled into the drive-up window at Willie's Cut-'n-Run, where he bought a drive-time six-pack of Bud Lite.

Lost, more lost, and finally found, Quinlin ultimately made out a sign that said CEDAR RIDGE HOSPITAL—LONG-TERM PATIENT PARKING. He wedged the International Scout into a space so close to a yuppie Lexus that he had to extricate himself, his bag, and boots from the passenger side. He stood beside the Scout until he killed the lone surviving Bud Lite and pitched the empty into his aluminum recycling project on the back floorboard.

Once inside the lobby and finally—mercifully—out of the sun's glare, Quinlin followed the blue arrows on the floor to Admissions. A clerk, someone's long-haired, lithesome, nineteen-year-old daughter, performed a wallet biopsy and photocopied his insurance card. She produced a sheaf of paperwork, loaded it into a printer, and began typing on her computer. Quinlin noticed a pink, sticky note attached to the papers and reached for it. It said *Upon admission, notify Capt. Bill Barrick, Homicide Division, Dallas Police Department*. The bastard.

Quinlin watched the clerk's long fingers on the keyboard. The process reminded him of getting drafted, with a stranger asking him for personal information then typing for blocks of time, digesting his history without comment.

"And who should we notify in case of emergency?"

"Geneva Quinlin," he said, surprised at the defiance in his voice. He spelled his mother's name and dictated her address and phone number into the record. Sarah was a co-conspirator, and she could jam it. He wasn't sure she'd even answer an emergency call.

In the blank labeled PROGNOSIS, he watched her type in *305.*

"What's a 305?" he asked.

"It's just an insurance code," the clerk said. "Means alcoholism. Well, actually, *chronic* alcoholism."

Quinlin didn't realize he was crying until the young lovely shoved the box of tissues across the counter. Then he couldn't stop.

Down the sterile, high-sheen corridor and beyond the electronically controlled doors of Cedar Ridge Substance Abuse Unit, a nurse finally steered Quinlin through a solid white door stenciled in two-foot, red letters that said DETOX.

The room was barely the size of cells that Detective Jeb Roy Quinlin had used over the last seventeen years to deposit various of Dallas's most notorious and violent societal dregs. It was one of three detoxification rooms that faced a circular nurses' station, which appeared to be the hub of five wings that ran like spokes from the center. Collectively, according to the sign he saw on the way in, the five wings constituted the Cedar Ridge Psychiatric Pavilion. The complex was hidden in a clump of twenty-foot cedars behind the real hospital.

Pine-scented disinfectant hung in the air, burning the back of his sinuses and agitating the fresh batch of radiator flush in his gut. His eyes took in the cramped room, and he imagined himself trapped inside a mammoth cotton ball. The walls and ceiling were white, the floor was off-white, and the bed had white hospital sheets, but no spread. The white toilet was in a white-tiled cubicle with no door, and a walk-in shower was concealed by a white shower curtain. Except for the bed, a metal nightstand welded onto the bedframe, and a metal IV stand, also welded to the frame, the room was devoid of furniture. The premise was the same as a jail cell, Quinlin figured: There was nothing that could be grabbed and thrown. Outside the four vertical, rectangular windows was a pie-shaped courtyard that backed onto another spoke in the crazy hub. It didn't escape his notice that the wire-meshed windows had no handles. Not that it mattered. The windows were so narrow Tiny

Tim couldn't get through them.

Quinlin heard the door creak behind him and watched a colossal man the color of coal tar, wearing a bright white uniform, load his canvas bag and extra pair of boots onto a small cart. The attendant motioned at Quinlin and said, "Just step out of your clothes, your underwear, your socks, and your boots." Then he left him naked with a drawstring gown and a list of rules.

Coal Tar returned minutes later with a clipboard and wanted to know precisely when Quinlin had consumed his last drink. The attendant was not amused when Quinlin looked at his watch, grinned his crooked grin, and said dryly, "A good fifteen, maybe twenty minutes ago. Thanks for asking."

"You're an acutely funny guy," Coal Tar said without looking up from his clipboard. "Gimme your watch. You can keep the ring if you want."

Quinlin looked at his wedding ring and slipped it off, too. The technician dropped it into a brown envelope, sealed it, and wrote its contents on the outside. It was a lot like processing a prisoner.

The hulking man then went through a checklist of medications, wanting to know if Quinlin was allergic to any of them. Quinlin answered yes only to penicillin.

"How you know?" Coal Tar asked.

"Because it turns my skin the color of a spanked baby's butt," Quinlin said, "and my heart races like a scalded dog. Say, any chance I could get my smokes back?"

"Not until you get outta detox," Coal Tar said, turning to another checklist on family history. "Answer yes if any of the following apply. Any blood relatives suffer from cancer, heart condition, arthritis, asthma, chronic bronchitis, alcoholism . . ."

"Oh yeah," Quinlin said. "Father."

"He ever undergo treatment?"

"Yeah, he treated himself to everything he could get his hands on. Four Roses, Falstaff, Thunderbird, vanilla extract, rubbing alcohol, paint thinner, whatever was available."

"Prognosis?" It was a blank on the form.

"Roadkill. A *gen-u-ine* loss to humanity."

Coal Tar caught Quinlin staring sideways into the floor-length, metal mirror bolted to the wall.

"Lose your attitude, work the program, and get your act straight," the big man said, "and you won't look that way when you walk out of here next month."

The interruption rescued Quinlin from a curious thought that had appeared in the mirror from nowhere. The sixty graduating members of his tiny Central Texas high school had voted him the handsomest guy in class. In their early years together, Sarah had called him The Marlboro Man, and claimed he made the rugged model on the billboards look like a fairy. Quinlin shook his head at the mirror. The Marlboro Man was long gone. The reflection of the forty-three-year-old substitute, he had to admit, looked more like the deep-fried crackheads and street scum he put in jail. The image was a dramatic revelation. How, he wondered, had he managed to shave every morning and not notice his own demise? And who was twisted enough to put a floor-length mirror in a detox room?

Barefoot and reduced to the white hospital gown, Quinlin was six-foot, rail thin, and noticeably slumped. Salt had replaced much of the pepper in his mustache, a cancerous trend that had metastasized at his temples. Pulling the polo shirt over his head had left a cowlick at the top of his head, making him a ringer for Ichabod Crane's lip-dribbling little brother. Notwithstanding the three-inch scar on his chin, a tribute to the cold efficiency of brass knuckles, his sun-parched face was an odometer rolled over with rough miles. The blue in his eyes was still penetrating, but the pupils were surrounded by a network of bulged red capillaries that looked like a Rand McNally map.

Coal Tar was in the middle of the door on his way out.

"Your mamma must be awful proud," the big attendant said, "abso-fuckin'-lutely *proud* of your white ass."

Quinlin could hear him laughing down the hall long after the door closed.

Every six hours during the first day, a nurse appeared with a tiny paper cup of Librium, a tranquilizer, and, stunningly, a jigger of hundred-proof vodka. She had heard the question a hundred times. With the bored reflex of a flight attendant pointing out emergency exits, the nurse said, "You've got to detox slowly or you could go into alcoholic seizure. Occasionally, the seizures can be fatal."

The vodka was discontinued after twenty-four hours; the Librium continued. Quinlin missed the vodka, not because he had ever liked its taste or even appreciated its jolt. But it was his only remaining link with the real world. Everything else in detox was muted and blurred, unearthly artificial and sterile.

Periodically, nurses appeared with trays of food, and the green blobs in one compartmentalized part of the plastic tray tasted like the white and yellow blobs in the compartments next to it. There apparently wasn't a grain of salt in the whole damned hospital. Coffee and tea were mandatorily decaffeinated—the guards didn't want inmates trading one addiction for another—and except for the fact that one commodity was lukewarm in a cup and the other was lukewarm in a glass, the brown liquids were wholly indistinguishable.

Mostly, Quinlin dozed around the clock, a fitful, jerking excuse for sleep that kept him off balance and made him dread drifting off. Sleep wasn't an elective exercise, not with the Librium. He dreamed of floating on gauzy white clouds, then suddenly hitting a patch of blue and falling. He was swimming in sunlight, then drowning at the bottom of a pitch-dark pit.

He was walking down a street, then dodging bullets from places he couldn't see. He would awaken, sweaty and clawing at the sheets, and curse Librium. In his few lucid moments, when he had a memory, he craved a Wild Turkey and Bud Lite chaser. He cursed Barrick and Sarah, imagining them sweaty and sated in his own bed. Was that part of the conspiracy? Or was it Librium-induced paranoia? It was irrelevant. He cursed them anyway.

Depending on the shift, one of three nurses appeared at his bedside every two hours with a thermometer, a velcro blood pressure cuff, and a stethoscope that they apparently kept in the refrigerator. They were heavy into efficiency and devoid of bedside manner. If the nurses spoke at all, it was a perfunctory response to a question, and sometimes just a nod or a grunt. At some point on his third day, Quinlin confronted one of them, a particularly haughty, petite, and freckled redhead about forty.

"Tell me, Red," he said, leaning up on one elbow, "are you rude to all patients or just the drunks? Because if you're going out of your way to make me feel like a second-class cit—"

"Mr. Quinlin," she said, "I am a recovering alcoholic. Through the grace of God and the principles of AA, I haven't had a drink in fourteen years. As a matter of fact, most of the nurses, counselors, and attendants on this ward are recovering alcoholics. We're on this ward because we asked to be here. We believe in what we do."

"Well, I was just—"

Red wasn't through. "And the reason we don't say much to patients in detoxification is because we've learned that they're generally too deep into self-pity, denial, and paranoia to make any sense. Nothing I've seen about you makes you an exception."

"Well, I, uh, I . . ."

She left him in a frigid wake before he could complete the sentence.

At 2:15 P.M. on the fourth day, a Saturday, Coal Tar grabbed Quinlin by his right ankle and jarred him awake. The cart was beside the door, and it contained the clothes and boots Quinlin had worn into the hospital, along with his canvas bag and extra pair of boots. From a good four feet away, the huge attendant heaved a plastic bag of books at him, forcing a groggy Quinlin to shield his privates with one hand and deflect ten pounds of books with the other.

"You could hurt somebody throwing that crap," he yelled to no answer. Quinlin prowled through the bag, pulling out a blue, Bible-sized book with *Alcoholics Anonymous* written on the cover. "Camp Librium doesn't give T-shirts?"

Coal Tar wrote on a clipboard.

"I give up," Quinlin said, holding the blue book. "You get your voice back, maybe you could tell me what this is."

"It's the Big Book," Coal Tar said. "It'll explain how AA works."

"This is a hospital, right?" Quinlin said, propped now on his elbows. "Nobody said anything to me about AA. I came here for *medical* treatment, not a prayer meeting."

"Well, this just ain't your day, is it, cowboy?" the attendant said, tossing Quinlin's personal effects onto the bed on top of him. "Naw, see the deal is, we fresh outta magic shots in the ass that make you act like a human being. You're actually gonna have to do some things on your own."

The burly attendant told him to get dressed, gave him directions to the dayroom, and told him to wait there until he found him a room and a roommate.

By 3:00 P.M., Quinlin had located a coffeepot, was disappointed to learn it was decaf, too, and meandered into the dayroom with his possessions, which he piled on the end of a threadbare and badly stained couch. It was twenty feet from the nurses' station; he figured his bag and boots would be safe there.

Walking no more than fifty paces left him weak in the knees, and he stared at his hands, which were shaking uncontrollably. He'd never had the shakes while he was drinking, and he wrote off the twitching to withdrawal. How long, he wondered, would he have to put up with not being able to control his limbs?

He surveyed his new surroundings and caught a tanned pretty-boy in a blazer and khakis being buzzed through the electronic double doors. Quinlin made him for a doctor, probably a young resident, unfortunate enough to have caught weekend duty. He headed straight for the nurses' station. Quinlin couldn't make out their conversation, but he knew he'd misread the guy when the nurse jumped him like a coyote with hemorrhoids. Quinlin's cup was empty, and he headed closer to the nurses' station to the coffeepot.

"So, what, I'm ten minutes late?" the yuppie was saying. "It's not like I was in some bar or something."

"You know the rules about furloughs," she said, pushing a clear plastic specimen container and lid at him. "Have a seat right there. A male attendant will be with you shortly. You'll provide a urine specimen in his presence."

Quinlin caught the man's eye briefly and nodded amiably, but the man wasn't in any mood for pleasantries. He ignored Quinlin and moved to a nearby chair, slamming the specimen jar loudly onto a weathered end table. He methodically arranged the starched pleats in his khakis, pulled the sleeves of his blue shirt precisely a half-inch beyond the blazer's sleeves and stared disgustedly at the ceiling.

Vanity in men was a trait Quinlin couldn't tolerate. One of his wife's colleagues, an interior designer, bragged about owning one hundred pairs of shoes and seventy-five suits. The fop couldn't walk past a plate-glass window without stopping to admire himself. He didn't have a clue who Nolan Ryan was, but you couldn't spend three minutes at a party without him bragging about having once met Tommy Hilfiger. The pretty-boy in the chair was cut from the same cloth. A superficial popdick.

Across the cavernous day room, a TV was locked on a professional wrestling match that had the Russian Rogue and the Masked Marauder grunting and slapping each other. Six hundred pounds of sweating, tattooed flesh was knocking the edge off his Librium, and Quinlin set out to turn it off. He hesitated momentarily when he saw the hand-scrawled sign beneath the on-off button: DO NOT TOUCH THIS DIAL, but he pushed the control anyway, vaporizing the sweathogs just as the Rogue grabbed the Marauder in a phony stomach claw.

"That's not following directions!" The voice from behind startled him. "You've got to be honest or you'll be a lush for the rest of your natural life. This is an issue we'll deal with in group."

The woman stood in the middle of the room, one hand dramatically on her hip. She was tall, dressed in black leggings and a bulky black sweatshirt. Her dark brown hair was up in a ponytail, and she appeared fresh-scrubbed, without a trace of makeup. Her eyes were mischievous, and her lips were full and grinning. She was also the most gorgeous woman Quinlin could recall.

He rose from one knee, smiling. "I'm Jeb Quinlin."

"No, no, *no*," she said. "You're supposed to say, 'My name is Jeb. I'm an alcoholic.' No last name. It's the anonymous thing, don't you get it?

"Then, see, *I* say, 'My name's Madeline. I'm an alcoholic.' It's the way we do things here on the Road to Recovery."

Road to Recovery? Was she for real or being facetious? Whatever she was, she was trouble. Anyone that beautiful and with that kind of mouth had to be a pain.

"When I get to know you better, probably later this afternoon," she said, holding up a spiral notebook, "I'll share my list of top fifty ways my filthy rich husband has screwed over the American economy as we know it. It'll be a treat. We'll have fun."

A smart-ass, rich bitch, and probably, a castrating feminist to boot. He made a mental note to stay away from her.

The pretty-boy in the leather chair said something to Madeline, but Quinlin couldn't make it out.

"Not on your luckiest day," Madeline told the man, shooting him the finger.

Pretty-Boy managed a feeble grin that couldn't conceal his disappointment. Quinlin figured he wasn't accustomed to being rejected by beautiful women. Pretty-Boy was humiliated; score one for the willowy beauty with the wise mouth.

"So, tell me, Jeb Anonymous," Madeline said, returning her attention to the ward's newest patient. "You don't look like a developer or a banker. That's heartening, trust me on this. Let's see, what must you do in the real world?"

Quinlin saw her fixing on his boots. Slowly, her eyes went up his body, making him self-conscious: Wrangler jeans, hand-tooled belt with sterling silver buckle, and blue-and-white window-pane shirt.

"A blue-eyed cowboy?" she guessed. "No, there aren't any *real* cowboys anymore. That's way too romantic. C&W singer? I know . . ."

"Cop," Quinlin said. The game was already old.

"Like blue suit with a leather . . . ?"

"Detective," he said. "Homicide detective."

Quinlin couldn't be sure, but he thought her eyes softened. Momentarily, she didn't have a comeback, and they stared at each other awkwardly. He wondered why he told her he was a cop. It wasn't something he normally volunteered. People either asked fifty questions or sneered. And it certainly wasn't any of her business.

Madeline smiled faintly and resumed her trip through the day room. "So, Jeb Anonymous," she called back over her shoulder, "welcome to the Jitter Joint."

Jeb Quinlin followed Madeline with his eyes until she disappeared around the corner at the nurses' station. He was instinctive in reading people on first impression, a trait that had been invaluable when it had been just himself and a suspect in an interview room. And in a department with no shortage of substantial egos, even his colleagues frequently asked him to do once-overs with their witnesses just to verify or dispute their opinions about the witnesses' trustworthiness and motivations. Now, Quinlin had to admit, he didn't have a clue about the motivation of the mysterious, beautiful woman who had strolled confidently—or was it arrogantly—through his life in a matter of seconds. Clearly, she had come on haughty, but hadn't she softened at the end? When he said he was a cop? Why did it even matter? Preoccupied, Quinlin walked to the window and found himself staring into the parking lot.

Behind him, the man in the khakis and blue blazer watched, taking in Quinlin's every move. Only after the cop had stood idly at the window several minutes did Pretty-Boy head for the nurses' station. Leaning over the counter, he motioned the nurse to him.

"I really didn't mean to argue with you earlier," the man said. "It's just a misunderstanding, and I apologize. The urine test is no problem, I assure you. It won't show anything.

"By the way," he said, dropping his voice. "That guy over there? I haven't seen him before. How long has he been on the ward?"

The nurse had worked the alcohol ward more than ten years. She knew a con when she heard one, which was about hourly. She merely shrugged.

"Well then, darling," the man said, an edge to his voice,

"why don't you and I go take care of this urine test? You might actually enjoy your job."

Pretty-Boy returned to his chair against the wall and watched the man at the window.

3

Michael R., a computer software designer and Quinlin's new roommate, had warned him about Dr. Wellman Bergoff III from the beginning. But after four days of sessions, Quinlin knew how badly he had underestimated the psychiatrist who presided over group therapy. Michael's calling Dr. Bergoff "mean-spirited" was like calling John Wayne Gacy "misguided." Dr. Bergoff was a Machiavellian cheesedick.

Quinlin had gone through boot camp and, later, fourteen months in Vietnam. He knew that demeaning unpleasantries were sometimes necessary to condition human beings for survival. The theory was that humiliation neutralized ego and, therefore, made the mind more receptive to change. But Dr. Jackoff, as Jeb and the others affectionately named him, reveled in the psychic trauma he dealt. Quinlin could see it in the wry smirk when Bergoff set up a defenseless drunk to be pummeled senseless and left naked for everyone else in the group to ponder.

Dr. Bergoff's favorite tactic was what Quinlin came to call "Psycho-Gladiators," a devastating mental exercise in which the psychiatrist pitted one patient against another in a game neither could win. Demanding complete honesty and coercing the group of twenty drunks to plumb the depths of their souls for it, the coldly dispassionate Dr. Bergoff would randomly seize on an unsuspecting inmate and ask him a neutron bomb of a question like, "Joel, what is the one thing you did drunk that you're most ashamed of?"

Regardless of Joel's answer, the patient would be accused of "masking," of lying to himself and the rest of the group. Wounded and embarrassed, Joel would resurrect yet another horror story: "I screwed my sixteen-year-old sister-in-law while my wife was in the hospital getting a hysterectomy."

Jackoff would be in one of his grandiose poses, staring, perhaps, out the window with his arms folded regally across his tweeded chest. Without interrupting his gaze, the sublimely smug doctor would say, "Janice, my dear, we don't believe Joel, do we? How could we? That's clearly not the worst thing Joel's done drunk. Does Joel think we're intellectually inferior? Why, Janice, do you think he's telling us such an obvious lie?"

The tendency among patients, of course, was to empathize with those as unfortunate as they. But Dr. Bergoff conditioned his drunks like Pavlov's dogs. If Janice agreed that Joel had been utterly truthful, the shrink abruptly turned on her, making her the object of the group grope. Over time, members of Dr. Bergoff's group learned to say none of their colleagues was telling the truth. It was a sadistic game in which the weakest chicken always was pecked to death.

The session had been uncommonly therapeutic, the doctor seemed to imply, only when he and the rest of the group adjourned at the end of the two hours, leaving a sobbing, broken drunk alone at the long conference table. In the end, the group not only abhorred Jackoff, they frequently loathed each other.

Alcoholism, depending on whichever expert has the newest book, is caused by too much or too little of a chemical in the brain, bad genes, crappy childhoods or, maybe, moral defects. The latter is a possibility eschewed by the multimillion-dollar, alcohol-as-a-disease psychiatric industry because mere character defects aren't covered by Aetna.

Dr. Wellman Bergoff III had his own wrinkle, one that Madeline had unceremoniously dubbed the Bergoff Sack O' Shit Theory, or simply, SOS. Most people became alcoholics, according to Dr. Bergoff, because they chronically dodged the truth about themselves. They went through life deflecting various painful episodes and brutal self-truths without having the strength of character to deal with the associated traumatic fallout. Instead, they buried life's debris in some dark recess in their brains ("Think of it as a sack," Bergoff said), and anesthetized themselves with alcohol against the inherent pain of coping. The heavier the sack of unresolved psychic debris ("Think of it as shit," Madeline mimicked), the deeper into the bottle they slipped.

Hence the rocky journey to sobriety, the Road to Recovery, Bergoff maintained, had to be paved with unerring honesty. And that honesty had to be the gut-wrenching, dehumanizing kind that came from deep in the soul and allowed the patient to resolve his mental debris once and for all. Honesty was the enema that purged the sewage of the psyche.

In his counseling sessions, Bergoff bludgeoned horrible truths from drunks in the name of sobriety. "Empty the sack," he would say. "Lighten the load. For once in your life, just tell the truth."

Most in Quinlin's group, whether they'd ended up at Cedar Ridge voluntarily or mandatorily under court order, would have tried anything to stop drinking. In AA parlance, they were "sick and tired of being sick and tired." They were a guilty, earnest, and pathetic sliver of society who had watched their families, careers, and character ebb away from them. Quinlin figured they, like him, had to be on their last leg; it was the only way they could have withstood Bergoff's degradation.

There was a thoroughly inhuman dynamic to Bergoff's form

of therapy, Quinlin believed: Twenty self-conscious, scared men and women, bound only by their abuse of alcohol, thrown into a large, sterile room and told their only chance at survival was to probe honestly from deep within and to pry loose their most bizarre and embarrassing acts and feelings. They were to lay those intimate feelings bare so that strangers, some of whom they probably wouldn't even associate with in the free world, could comment and criticize and sit in judgment. And they did it under duress, at the hands of a dictatorial psychiatrist whom each of them despised.

The premise, Quinlin thought, was as goofy as going to Dallas/Fort Worth Airport, cornering a group of travelers between flights, telling them every shitty, booze-induced indiscretion he'd ever committed, then asking, "So, what do you think? Am I a piece of work or what?"

4

Quinlin was at the window in the dayroom watching pea-sized hail ricochet off the cars in the parking lot across the street. The clouds were battleship gray with gangrene tinges, an ominous sign that tornado season had descended on North Texas. The freshness of rain had crept into the ventilation system, and he realized for the first time in a week he wasn't smelling disinfectant.

The tap on his shoulders startled him, and he sloshed coffee on his boots. Coal Tar moved quietly for a big man.

"Your day in the barrel, cowboy," the attendant said. "Ten minutes to feedback time. Try not to take it personally, you hear?"

There were two feedback sessions at Cedar Ridge, one at approximately a week or ten days into treatment, the other on the day before discharge. According to the booklet he received in the plastic bag on his first fully detoxified day, the sessions "allow patients to review their records and ask questions of the therapeutic staff in order to chart their individual progress on the Road to Recovery." But on the wing, patients called the sessions "autopsies" and "gangbangs." Bergoff and the patient's counselor, Jerry Stephens in Quinlin's case, sat in the same small office watching the inmate read his file. If the inmate didn't ask questions, they did. There was no way to get out without a bloodletting.

"I'm gonna hate it if Jackoff tries to hug me," Quinlin said.

"He thinks you got a cute ass," Coal Tar said, escalating the banter. "You get that riding horses or humping goats?"

Coal Tar, Quinlin quickly discovered, was a deceptive giant of diverse propensity. AA meetings were outside the hospital at various groups scattered throughout North Dallas. Coal Tar drove the institutional drunks in a Ford Econoline, an unmarked vanload of wobbly, recidivist sinners headed against their better judgment toward salvation. Late every afternoon, Coal Tar counted the patients as they filed onto the van.

"I got eighteen drunks," he would say in his booming voice, "and the big man's gonna be mighty disappointed if he don't have eighteen drunks when he gets back. And, hey, trust me on this, ain't nobody wants to see the big man mad."

Quinlin hated the AA meetings, particularly if anyone asked him to talk, but he looked forward to the trips. He could look out the windows of the van and see *normal* people driving home from work or headed for drinks at happy hour. One afternoon on LBJ Expressway, he saw a family in a Buick in the next lane. Everyone in the car was laughing at something, and there was a picnic basket and an Igloo cooler on the back seat.

Quinlin nudged the guy next to him, an English professor named Rog, and pointed at the car.

"That car is a mobile sack of shit," Quinlin said in his best haughty imitation of Bergoff. "They've got to purge themselves of their concealed lies. Look, they're intellectualizing right now, see 'em? They'll never have a chance at happiness."

Everyone in the seat laughed. Quinlin returned to his silence, feeling uncommonly depressed.

Inmates on Coal Tar's van never got a choice in music. Coal Tar would plug in an R&B tape, then drown out the singer with his own surprisingly decent rendition. On occasion, if he was really wound, he would eject the tape and continue on without accompaniment, tapping the music with both hands on the headliner and wedging his sufficient gut against the steering wheel to keep the van in the road. His impromptu productions frequently drew genuine applause from the drunks in the back.

Rumor on the ward, confirmed by Stephens, was that Coal Tar had been drafted out of Texas Southern University in the third round by the Dallas Cowboys. As a rookie, he started four games at defensive tackle before he blew out a knee. Booze and cocaine, however, had not been an officially endorsed part of his rehab, and the Cowboys waived him the next year. Supposedly, Quinlin had heard, the Mammoth Man was working on a master's degree in social work at University of Texas at Arlington.

Only a few days into his incarceration, Quinlin had watched Coal Tar save a patient's life. Raphael, a legitimate world-class chef and gutter-hugging drunk of equal legend, went into an alcoholic seizure en route from an AA meeting. Coal Tar had calmly pulled Raphael's twitching, gagging body from a rear seat and laid him alongside the shoulder of the road. He fished around with one of his fat index fingers until he disengaged Raphael's tongue from his windpipe, then massaged his convulsing chest with hands the size of catcher's mitts. When Raphael's body still refused to participate, Coal Tar cupped the little chef's mouth open, bent over him, and breathed life into his body. While a panicked patient drove like a drunk to the emergency room, Coal Tar sat in the front of the van, holding Raphael in his lap like a baby. Over and over, he told him, "Breathe, you little muthafucker." And finally Raphael had, an occasion that elicited widespread cheers from the other drunks in the van.

The drum of the hail outside Cedar Ridge had transfixed Quinlin.

"Yo, it's showtime," Coal Tar said, bringing him back. "You gonna go peacefully or do I need to assist you?"

Bergoff and Stephens were drinking coffee on one side of the conference table, and Quinlin's file was laid out in front of them. The patient pulled out his chair and looked at them.

"These sessions normally take an hour or so," the psychiatrist said, "but you can take as long as you like. You can ask questions as they arise, or you can wait until you read the entire file. This process is part of your recovery. *If* you're interested in recovery, Mr. Quinlin, I know you'll have questions."

Always the psychic jab.

Quinlin's week on the alcohol rehabilitation wing had already produced an inch-thick file. Something called a Shipley-Hartford Scale listed his IQ at 116, not exactly Mensa, but high average. The test results, Quinlin would discover, were the only indications in the entire file that he was "normal." A battery of other tests made it sound like his personality had been run through a shredder. He had, according to the various reports in the file, "chronically high levels of tension and anxiety." He was "restless and agitated." He had an "inadequate repressive mechanism." He was "overactive, which contributes to impulsive behavior." His "impulsivity and inability to sustain effort may result in failure."

Those failures "are particularly difficult for his underdeveloped coping mechanism because he is an overachiever who sets unrealistically high goals for himself." He "contributes to tension and anxiety by allowing the opinions of others to determine his own worth." Ah, he thought, there's even a place in my file for the lovely Sarah.

Then the shrinks packed all the personality fragments into one wrecking ball of a bottom line on his psyche: "The patient is likely beleaguered by feelings of guilt, shame, obsessive condemnation, and depression." Quinlin translated: a certifiable wingnut; he figured he certainly wouldn't invite himself to any party he was planning.

When finally he looked up, it was to the stares of Bergoff and Stephens. They met his eyes and didn't waver. What the hell were they looking for?

Stephens, who had been relentless in private sessions with his questions about Quinlin's father, had done a cold kill on the written synopsis of his background. The counselor had filtered out Quinlin's trivializations and rationalizations and written only facts, some of which Quinlin didn't even remember volunteering.

Stephens's report noted that Quinlin was a third-generation alcoholic. Even with his booze-fragile genes, lifestyle hadn't dealt Jeb Quinlin a decent chance. Before age eleven, when Quinlin's mother, Geneva, divorced her husband and moved the youngster to her hometown in Central Texas, they lived in North Houston. It was a hope-diminisher of neighborhood, a white-trash enclave surrounded by creosote and cement plants and staggering crime. Home was a lean-to, four-room apartment built onto the rear of the family-owned "ice house," which was redneck code for beer joint.

Young Jeb's father, Bob, was a decent enough guy sober, but alcohol abuse, particularly on weekends, wired him into a wild-eyed, mean drunk. His violence was almost always directed at Jeb's mother, Geneva, a tiny but deceptively strong-willed country girl who was a teetotaler. Jeb's bruises, bloody noses, and broken arm came tangentially and only because he had interceded in his mother's behalf.

When Jeb was ten, his father, well over six feet and solid at two hundred pounds, beat his mother to the linoleum floor and was straddling her, choking her purple. Jeb slammed him diagonally across the forehead with a half-empty bottle of Four Roses, dousing both his father and mother in cheap whiskey and glass shards. The blow opened a gaping wound in his father's head, and he fell unconscious into his own blood. Jeb had never seen that much blood, but he wasn't remorseful. Believing he had killed his father, he threw a pair of clean underwear and a T-shirt into a brown grocery bag and ran. A police officer, answering a 3:00 A.M. disturbance call from the part-time janitor cleaning up the bar, apprehended Jeb ten blocks from home where he was hiding in a clump of bushes.

Quinlin, according to Stephens's background notes, claimed he was genuinely disappointed when the cop told him he hadn't killed his father. There had been, however, a silver lining to the blood bath. It had been the catalyst for divorce. In the six months it took Geneva Quinlin to save up the money and the courts to grant her divorce, the cop stopped by the beer joint two and three times a week. Just as regularly, he would take Jeb in his police cruiser to an all-night cafe where Jeb would eat banana splits while the cop took his break. Jeb was relieved to leave Houston and his father, but he hated leaving Officer Roy McQueen. The cop had even called him periodically once Jeb and his mother had settled in Comanche Gap, and he sent Jeb fifty dollars for graduation.

Bob Quinlin drank himself out of the ice house and died homeless in Houston while Jeb was hardscrabbling his way through the University of North Texas. The paternal side of his family, the few who hadn't disowned Jeb, told him that his father had died of throat cancer. Jeb knew better. His father had pickled his liver, and his pancreas probably looked like a football. He didn't go to the funeral. Funerals were to pay respects, and he didn't have any. He had never even looked up the gravesite.

"While the patient exhibits contempt for his late father," Stephens had written in the file, "he has extraordinary respect and devotion for his mother, whom he credits with saving his life and instilling strong and decent traits. Patient's belief that he has disappointed his mother is, in his opinion, the strongest negative impact of his alcohol abuse.

"Preliminary clinical data and testing suggest that this patient, a homicide detective, most likely suffers from Post-Traumatic Stress Disorder, the onset of which lies not in his combat service in Vietnam, but most probably in the traumatic childhood events that preceded his naval service."

Traumatic childhood events. Quinlin had conditioned himself over the years never to dwell on his childhood. It was debilitating and counterproductive, and the hatred seized him for days. Hungover days and neon nights. Now he couldn't stop himself. He saw himself at eight, lying awake in the back bedroom, listening for the knob to turn on the front door. He never slept until his dad was accounted for. They never talked about it, but he knew his mother was hostage to the same ritual in the front bedroom. Waiting in the dark. Listening for the hard, stumbling footsteps on linoleum. Sometimes, when he and his mother were lucky, there would be only a few footsteps and a heavy thud, meaning his father had made it to his favorite chair in the tiny living room where he would pass out. A lot of footsteps spelled trouble. He was headed for the front bedroom. The light would shoot down Jeb's hallway and then there'd be cussing and beratement. Jeb conditioned himself to move automatically at first light, flying barefoot up the hall on cold linoleum and appearing between his father and his mother's bed before his father could get out of the doorway. It didn't always work, but sometimes Jeb could steer him back into the living room, agreeing to sit and listen to him ramble drunkenly until he passed out. Most of the time, though, Bob Quinlin was too mean-drunk to fall for a child's diversion. Inevitably, that's when Geneva and her only child paid the price.

Even now, Jeb Quinlin wondered how a third-grade teacher could make him sit in the corner for falling asleep in class and not ask about the bruises on his face or the tan elastic bandage on his arm.

Quinlin's contact lenses had turned to sandpaper and his throat was cotton. He dodged the men's eyes in front of him and scanned the room for a coffeepot. Stephens anticipated him, and brought him a glass of water.

Bergoff's handwritten progress notes were the last entries in Quinlin's file. Quinlin wasn't surprised that they were psychobabble. They were stilted, sterile words that didn't make sense, not to him anyway. He could feel both pairs of eyes on him, and he scanned the reports as quickly as he could. He hated strangers knowing this much about him, and he wanted out of the room. Out of sight.

He slowed at one of Bergoff's last entries:

> Patient has difficulty differentiating between his personal and professional roles. Absent a positive role model in his father, he associated himself with perhaps the only positive male influence in his life, a police officer who reportedly befriended him at an early age. In response to question about what he was most proud of, patient responded: "I never hit a woman. Not sober, not drunk. Never. That's one thing Sarah can't say. I'm not like my father. And I'm a good cop." In response to question about why he became an officer, patient responded: "I'm not like my father. I help people." Session discontinued. Patient too emotional to continue.

Quinlin felt the water in his eyes as he closed the folder.

"We'll hear your questions or comments, Mr. Quinlin," Bergoff said.

"I'm up to my ass in questions," Quinlin said, "but you don't have the answers any more than I do. Frankly, I'm too tired to be jacked with."

It was Bergoff's play, and Quinlin had just raised the stakes. Quinlin was surprised when Stephens interceded.

"Go to your room," the counselor said. "You're beat. We'll talk later."

Quinlin made it as far as the dayroom. His legs were concrete-heavy, and his insides were skittering around like live electrical wires. Tired, wired, these were times when booze always helped. A straight shot, something to lighten the load and settle the insides. The first shot was the best: a burning sensation that shocked the back of his throat and warmed him as the Wild Turkey filtered down to his feet. It was as close to euphoria as Quinlin had ever known and more predictable than any friend. Magic in a bottle. Predictable.

He shifted mental gears, reaching instinctively for his left shirt pocket. His hands were shaking so badly he couldn't catch the Marlboro Light with his Bic. He steadied the side of his thumb on his chin, flicked the Bic, drew heavily, and felt the smoke in his throat.

Throat cancer. Maybe cirrhosis wasn't the only thing that punched his old man's ticket. He stared at the Marlboro. What if he were successful kicking the Turkey only to die of throat cancer? It was another fear he couldn't allow to linger.

Flashlight Larry moved like a cat on the ward, appearing every hour after lights went out at 10:00 P.M. He was a tall and lanky black man, gray and maybe sixty, and he wore hospital whites and white leather Reeboks. On nights like this when Quinlin couldn't sleep, he used Flashlight Larry's intrusions to count off the hours.

Flashlight Larry appeared stealthily in the open doorways to the rooms, directing the glare from his five-cell flashlight from one roommate to the other. If he didn't see a patient's chest or back rising and falling in a breathing motion, he moved closer, poking the light into their eyes until he was satisfied they were alive.

Administrators explained the hourly checks as medical precaution, merely to ensure patients hadn't gone into alcoholic seizures. Too, drunks were legendary for having inflicted a multitude of other self-induced medical problems associated with their intimacy with booze, the most fatal of which are blown-out livers, bloated pancreases, marginally functioning kidneys, and dicey hearts.

Drunks are cynics by nature, and those confined on the alcohol rehab ward at Cedar Ridge knew there were other, equally compelling reasons for the unannounced surveillance.

It wasn't without precedent, for example, for Flashlight Larry to appear silently at the door of a bathroom, illuminating a surprised patient with his five-cell just as the drunk pulled a bootlegged flask from his lips. Inevitably, the contraband came from the purse of a misguided visitor or in changes of clothes brought by well-intentioned family members, known derisively among staff as "enablers."

Flashlight Larry captured one ingenious drunk chug-a-lugging from a family-sized bottle of Listerine at 4:00 A.M. Cutty Sark had the same amber hue, the patient had figured, as Listerine, and he had placed the mouthwash bottle of scotch in his medicine cabinet in plain view. But he severely underestimated Flashlight Larry's olfactory senses. The patient was escorted to a nurse who locked him down in a detoxification room where he would begin anew his journey to recovery; it was an unfortunate event known among inmates as "recycling."

Among the patients who were committed to treatment by court order as a part of their probation, mostly recidivist drunk drivers and a few barroom brawlers, recycling could add another three or four weeks to their sentence. The staff seemed to cut more slack for the volunteers, apparently in deference to the fact they were trying to get straight on their own. And, Quinlin figured, because they knew most insurance policies maxed out at the $15,000 they were already paying for twenty-eight days in Club Bud. Court-ordered drunks wept and wailed at recycling. But it was amazing how resourceful they could be in finding money for the extra weeks in treatment when they knew it separated them from six months behind real bars.

Flashlight Larry also occasionally discovered empty beds. Sometimes the vacant beds signaled only an innocent trip to the dayroom or cafeteria, which were open all night. Other times, though, it meant a disenchanted drunk had managed to slip off the ward by mingling with a group of departing visitors. Cedar Ridge, the largest alcohol rehab hospital in Dallas, was nothing if not image-conscious. Escape, they determined, had a distinctively negative connotation too closely associated with jail; unauthorized absences were "elopements."

At least once during Quinlin's first week on the ward, an empty bed hadn't had anything to do with elopement or late-night movies in the day room. About 2:00 A.M. one morning, Quinlin had awakened to voices. The light off the high-sheen corridor was brighter than usual, and it appeared the lights were coming from the room next door. Quinlin walked past Michael's bed to the doorway and poked his head around the corner.

The room belonged to David, a lawyer currently facing disbarment for dipping into a client's trust fund, and Reg, a missile-systems engineer who had been indicted on his fifth drunk driving charge, a felony. In both cases, their attorneys had admitted them to Cedar Ridge, hoping that voluntary alcohol treatment would mitigate whatever a judge would do to them in a courtroom.

But the first voice Quinlin recognized from within the room was a woman's. It was unmistakably high-pitched and singsong, and it belonged to Kristin, a swimsuit model at the Apparel Mart. She was in Quinlin's novice therapy group, and she had been dry a week. According to her story in group grope, her mother had footed the bill for her treatment and personally delivered her to the hospital. Her mother claimed she was a slut. It was a bum rap, Kristin explained. The young woman would admit that occasionally—but only when her morals were eroded by prodigious amounts of Bacardi—she had been "kinda" promiscuous.

"I've got a substance abuse problem, okay?" Kristin had told the group. "It's not like I'm a nympho or something."

An obviously agitated Flashlight Larry was in David's and Reg's doorway, the everpresent flashlight at his side.

"That ain't my problem," the attendant was saying. "It's too bad you don't have your clothes, but you should have thought about that when you strolled down here naked."

The scenario presented a hell of a mental image: a machine-assisted, full-body tan, a waist tiny enough that you could reach around it with thumbs and forefingers, and a chest that stuck straight out like the models who advertised 900 numbers at the back of alternative tabloids.

Kristin emerged moments later draped in a sheet and protesting her innocence. Flashlight Larry escorted her a hundred feet down the corridor to her room at the end of the wing. The next morning, Kristin and Reg the Missile Man were confined to their rooms.

On most nights, Quinlin was aware of most of Flashlight Larry's intrusions into his room. Decent sleep didn't come easily. Pouring through his file had triggered a retrospective journey through the shrapnel in his life. The replays and questions started as soon as his head hit the pillow. What if he *had* killed his father? Would he have still ended up a drunk like him? He would have a juvenile record, which, even sealed, would mean he couldn't have been a cop. What would he have done with his life? Stayed in the navy after Vietnam? Would Sarah have been any happier as an officer's wife, moving over the globe every three years, with him at sea for months at a time? He probably wouldn't have even met Sarah if he'd stayed in the navy. Maybe Bergoff was right. He *couldn't* separate himself from being a cop. Quinlin the cop was real; Quinlin the person was a coward who ran from himself.

Quinlin was lying on his side, his back to the door, when he heard hurried footsteps. He turned to see a pair of nurses join Flashlight Larry at the door across the hall and watched them rush in.

He walked to the door across the hall. The staff members were crouched over the bed by the wall, and he could see pant legs protruding from the huddle of white uniforms examining a man's upper body. The detective sensed something was catastrophically wrong. He didn't remember walking into the room, but he felt Flashlight Larry's palm on his shoulder.

"You need to get back to your room," he said. "We can handle this."

"What's wrong?"

"Willard passed away."

5

Detective Paul McCarren knew the scenario had all the potential of blowing up in his face. Meddling in another man's personal affairs—even if that man had been your partner for two years—was tricky, particularly if you didn't know his wife all that well, which McCarren didn't. Still he had tried for two days to check on Quinlin by phone, and finally figured he'd have more success trying to get through the CIA's switchboard. Cedar Ridge wouldn't even confirm Quinlin was a patient.

On impulse, the detective headed for Quinlin's house after an unusually long shift. Sarah Quinlin, he knew from random comments Jeb had made recently, had been on him hard about his drinking. Well, now Jeb had committed himself to quitting. That'd make her happy, right? He'd just stay long enough for an update on Jeb, maybe slip in a couple of comments to make things better between his partner and his wife, and be on his way.

McCarren saw the dome light go off a block from Quinlin's house. The car was parked at the curb, and by the time he pulled beside it, the detective could make out the outline of a man in the dim glow of the porch light. The silhouette was halfway up Quinlin's walk, and the man didn't turn to look at the car passing slowly behind him. As McCarren drove past the car at the curb, he checked his rearview mirror for the front plate of the Crown Victoria, and made a mental note.

At the end of the block, McCarren turned left, went a half block, and made a U-turn. Twenty feet from the intersection, he pulled to the curb, made sure he could see the car in front of 1109 Grassyknoll, and killed his lights and engine. The tree-lined neighborhood was well-kept middle-class, maybe twenty years old, with rear-entry garages accessible through back alleys. The houses were mostly one-story, brick traditionals with an occasional contemporary or Spanish tucked in to break the mold. At 9:00 P.M., there were walkers, joggers, and a couple of kids on skateboards and bikes.

An hour passed, and the car was still in front of 1109. McCarren got out of his car and walked to the alley that ran behind the south side of Grassyknoll. Quietly, he made his way to the fifth house from the end. Like all the others, Quinlin's had a six-foot-high, wood privacy fence. He squinted one eye and peered between the spruce slats. The back of the house was virtually all glass. The miniblinds to the den were open, and he could see images on a TV, but he couldn't make out anybody in the room. There was four feet of brick, and to the right of the den, the drapes to the master bedroom were pulled shut. The lighting was dim and the drapes were lined, but he believed he saw movement in the bedroom. He couldn't be certain. Nor could he stay around to make sure; a dog's bark touched off a chain reaction of others. Briskly he made his way back to his car.

Another hour and twenty minutes, he saw light pour onto the porch at 1109. The front door was recessed, and he couldn't see anyone. But apparently there was some lingering conversation in the open doorway, because it was a couple of minutes before he saw the outline of a man emerging from the house and heading down the walk.

McCarren started his engine. Without turning on his lights, he backed alongside the curb, out of the line of sight of the man walking from Quinlin's house.

When the white Crown Victoria pulled from the house and turned right onto Alamo Drive, the man hidden in darkness gave him a two-block lead, then fell in behind him, still without lights.

6

Willard Beane died on the most humiliating day in all of his sixty-six years. As word of the retired stockbroker's death spread through D wing, several of his colleagues in the advanced therapy group claimed the painfully quiet, deeply introverted man almost certainly had committed suicide. In animated conversations between roommates, in clusters of patients in the hall and in the dayroom, they openly blamed Dr. Wellman Bergoff III for leaving Willard no choice.

"A psychiatrist's supposed to know a patient's limits, and if he forces him beyond a point where he doesn't care about living, that isn't suicide," said Bart W., a CPA who had sat by Willard in the group session earlier in the day. "Bergoff knew what he was doing. Hell, he dogged Willard unmercifully. My opinion, that's murder, pure and simple."

Indeed, Bart, a chronic drunk who lost his career for falsifying the financial condition of a notoriously corrupt and failing savings and loan, spoke for the majority. Others in Willard's group told of watching an uncommonly impatient and frustrated Bergoff singling out the meticulously dressed stockbroker over the last three days, browbeating him and taunting him until he snapped.

"You're not leaving here in twenty-eight days, Willard," Bergoff had yelled. "You're going to stay here indefinitely until you acknowledge what you did to your grandson."

Willard's face flushed and his eyes fell to the floor. Around the large table, other members of the group glanced at each other curiously. The whole premise of therapy was that the *patient* searched his soul and volunteered information. It was a rule, wasn't it? Willard hadn't said anything about a grandson. What was Bergoff doing?

The psychiatrist's unrelenting pressure—"You ready to tell us about Nicholas, that's your grandson's name, isn't it?"—went on for two days. Never talkative even before he became Bergoff's whipping boy, Willard had retreated deeper into his shell.

"Are you ready yet, Willard, to tell these good people why your own wife, daughter, and son-in-law forced you into this hospital?" Bergoff had asked. He was a prosecutor, not a therapist; he was unyielding, asking variations of the same question over and over again. Meanwhile, the stooped stockbroker sat at the table silently, occasionally shaking his head, but never taking his eyes off the white tile floor.

"We have time, Willard," Bergoff had said resolutely. "We'll sit here quietly while you inventory your thoughts and review your actions. You know what you did. Say it. Get rid of it! It's weighing you down."

The angst, embarrassment, and tension had been too much for everyone in the room. Willard, like a car-struck, writhing dog in the street, was too pathetic to look at. The awkward patients fixed their stares on the floor, walls, and the window.

On the third afternoon, the final day of Willard Beane's life, he appeared at group therapy in the same clothes he had worn the day before. The normally crisp, starched white shirt with razor-sharp creases was as wrinkled as if he'd slept in it. The back of his hair was flattened from his pillow, and his face bore a crop of gray stubble. Eyes transfixed like a zombie, Willard slumped into a chair at the other end of the table from Bergoff. Overnight, Bart W. recalled, Willard had gone from a distinguished, handsome former executive to a slovenly homeless man who looked eighty.

"Tell us, Willard, why you're here," Bergoff asked as soon as his target had settled into the chair. "It'll make you feel better."

Surprisingly, Jackoff's prey finally responded.

"Because my family is going to the police if I don't." The voice was distant and lifeless. It was a barely audible monotone.

"Why's that?"

"Because they say I molested Nicholas."

"How old's Nicholas?"

"Seven."

"Tell us what you did to Nicholas."

"Noth—I drank a fifth of vodka that day. Every day. I don't remember."

"You're lying." Bergoff was staring at Willard, smiling. He sensed a breakthrough. The psychiatrist walked to the end of the table and stood behind the beleaguered patient. The stockbroker's eyes were on the floor, and he hadn't seen the psychiatrist move. He was startled when Bergoff spoke.

"Was Nicholas asleep?"

"Yes."

"Tell us what you did."

"I was drunk. I don't remember. Nothing."

"A stockbroker deals in trust, doesn't he? You can trust us, Willard. You pulled his pants down, didn't you? What'd you do after that? We're waiting, Willard."

Willard tried to suppress a sob, and it came out like a hiccup. His forehead fell into his hands and his body shook quietly. Bergoff bent within an inch of Willard's right ear. "You're a pedophile, Willard," the psychiatrist said in a raspy whisper. "Isn't that right? That you're a pedophile?"

Halfway down the long table, Mary Alice B. bolted from her chair.

"Leave him alone," she screamed. "My God, can't you just leave him alone?"

"Be seated, Mary Alice," Bergoff said, returning his stare to the man in front of him. "I wouldn't want to see you recycled after all your wonderful work."

The airline reservationist turned on her heels toward the door, her trembling right hand over her mouth.

"I don't care," she said. "I can't do this. I won't."

The room was quiet and motionless except for the hiss of the pneumatic arm at the top of the door that kept it from slamming.

"I put my hand in Nicholas's pants and touched his genitals." Willard Beane had raised his head from his hands and was staring at the table. His pronouncement stunned the patients, each of whom avoided looking at him. He spoke dispassionately, trancelike, as if he had taken sodium pentathol.

"I touched his penis and I masturbated," Willard said. There was no more crying or embarrassment, just the lifeless monotone. "I don't know what happened. My daughter came in. Began screaming and beating me on my face and back. They despise me, even Nicholas. I love Nicholas. I would never hurt him."

The man looked up at Bergoff with distant eyes. "I'm through," Willard said simply. "I have nothing left."

Dr. Bergoff had had his breakthrough; no psyche was invulnerable to his techniques. He adjourned the session. As the group filed out without saying anything or looking at anyone, the psychiatrist called two attendants to escort Willard to his room. Not surprisingly, Willard had skipped dinner. His roommate, an air traffic controller everyone called Sky King, said he told him he was too ashamed to face anyone.

Mary Alice, summoned to Dr. Bergoff's office minutes after

group session, had to stand in the hallway outside while he finished a phone call. She stood beside the open door a good five minutes while he made reservations for two at The Mansion, Dallas's only five-star restaurant. Then he told her he was recycling her. Her disruption of therapy, he said, would cost her another week.

Jeb Quinlin was still in Bergoff's junior therapy group for rookies, but members of the senior group were more than willing to pass along the saga of Willard Beane. Big surprise that the shrink could coax a guy onto the roof, then badger him into jumping. And apparently his success had triggered a five-star appetite. As he dozed off, Quinlin imagined Bergoff choking to death on forty-dollar prime rib.

At breakfast the next morning, Quinlin cornered Coal Tar for details. Willard's family had asked for an autopsy, scheduled for later in the afternoon in the medical section at Cedar Ridge. Willard's background sheet showed a history of minor heart ailments and he was on medication for his blood pressure. There were "medical indications," the attendant said, that Willard's death was due to natural causes. Besides, the body was unmarked and there were no obvious signs of suicide.

If the psychiatrist felt any moral hangover in the aftermath of Willard's death, it wasn't apparent when Quinlin's group of fresh drunks met at ten o'clock. If anything, Quinlin thought, Bergoff was even more arrogant and sanctimonious than usual.

"As I'm sure you're aware, one of your fellow patients died overnight," he said. "I'm told that perhaps Willard suffered a coronary. He was a deeply troubled alcoholic and he resisted to the end our attempts to help him in his recovery. Guilt, as we've discussed, is a powerful stressor. Honesty, the unflinching self-analysis we attempt to practice in our sessions, salves guilt. So perhaps there is a lesson, albeit tragic, for all of you in this man's unfortunate demise."

Dr. Bergoff reached into his briefcase on the floor and produced a white legal pad. He pulled a Waterman pen from the breast pocket of his brown tweed sports coat. He fixed on the unsuspecting swimsuit model seated midway down the table.

"So tell us, Kristin," he said, watching her flinch, "how did you feel walking naked down the hall to Reg's room? That was part of the thrill, was it not?"

By late-afternoon, as patients were about to file onto the van for the AA meeting, Coal Tar pulled Quinlin aside. Willard's death had suddenly become more curious. The autopsy wouldn't be finalized until a toxicological study came back in a week or more. But when morgue technicians were undressing Willard's body to send it to pathology, they found an AA card tucked inside the front of his briefs.

"In his underwear?" Quinlin asked.

"Yeah, beats me, too."

"What kind of card?" Quinlin asked.

"One of those they give out at meetings, you know, the laminated kind that opens up into four sides," Coal Tar said. "Got the AA preamble, the Twelve Steps, all the stuff, you know. And check this. The line from the prayer, the one that says 'Courage to change the things I can'? Well, that was underlined on Willard's card. What you think that's about?"

"It could mean anything. Have they called the police?"

"Naw, are you kiddin', dude? This is Cedar Ridge. That'd be bad for the image."

When the van pulled into the parking lot of the Genesis Group, an AA chapter in North Dallas, Quinlin found a pay phone in the lobby. He called Paul McCarren, got his voice mail and left a message. "Hey, it's me, Jeb, at the monastery. You hanging it up early without me there to watch you?"

Quickly, knowing he had sixty seconds on the message tape, Quinlin ran down the basics on the death of Willard Beane for his partner at CAPERS.

“Sounds like the guy couldn’t live with being a weenie-wagger,” Quinlin said, wrapping up, “and left the card as a suicide note. But these smug bastards out here know they should have phoned it in. Shake ’em up a little and let me know what happens.

“And McCarren. Tell Barrick he can kiss my sober ass.”

7

Sarah Quinlin was sitting at the end of the couch, staring aimlessly through the window into the parking lot. Jeb hadn't seen her in a week and a half, not since the confrontation with her and Barrick in his den. Watching her across the dayroom, he sensed their first meeting wouldn't go well. Jerry Stephens had prepared him for as much. Sarah, the counselor said, had elected not to participate in marriage therapy, a part of his treatment program. It was a sure sign, Quinlin knew, that she believed there was no marriage to save.

He closed the twenty feet between them, searching her face for nuance. All he saw were the reasons he had fallen in love with her in the first place. She was barely two inches over five feet, a flowing, natural blond with huge, vulnerable brown eyes that instinctively made him want to put his arms around her and protect her. As petite as she was, Sarah's tiny waist only accentuated a disproportionately large bust. It was an anatomical disparity that caused her grief in finding dresses; if the waist fit, the chest didn't. Hers was a body that attracted second glances even though she routinely tried to conceal her bustline with loose-fitting tops and blazers. Today, though, she wore an outfit Quinlin had never seen, navy pants snug over her butt and a tan turtleneck that left nothing to imagination. A vague feeling of loss swept him as he pulled a chair close to her. There was no mistaking the distance when he bent over to hug her.

The burden of conversation fell to him, and he tried to avoid the flashpoints guaranteed to trigger all-out hostility. The talk was civil enough, but meaningless. Yes, she was doing all right and, yes, she had remembered to put out the trash on Tuesday and Friday. She had forgotten the car payment, but it wouldn't be more than a day late. His mother and McCarren had called to check on her. Work was fine. The silence were awkward before he could muster another superficial question. Conspicuously, she didn't ask about him.

Bergoff's SOS theory had rubbed off on Quinlin more than he had realized. He was frustrated by the inconsequential charade and desperate for answers. He cut to the chase.

"Part of learning to live sober is making amends to those we've hurt," he said, looking her in the eyes. "I know I've hurt you, Punkin, I didn't mean to, but I did. I have to live everyday with what I've done. Alcohol was a major part of it, no question. It wasn't all of it. I'm trying to learn how to deal with it. My counselor says I may suffer from PTSD, a problem getting over my childhood and my father. I'm trying hard. It's not easy. But over time, I hope you can forgive me."

Sarah's eyes turned back to the window, and her silence confirmed everything he already knew.

"So you're pulling the pin on us?" he asked, finally. Her eyes were still on the window and she didn't say anything.

"Look," he said, "I intend to stay sober when I get out of here. What I'm saying, Sarah, is that you and Barrick were right. That's not easy to admit. But believe it or not, I'm learning some stuff about me. I honestly wish I had come here earlier. I'm going to try. . . ."

"The road to hell is paved with good intentions," Sarah said. Her tone was sharp and angry, and it slashed Quinlin like a knife in the throat. "I can't stand the pain any more."

"I guess I can't blame you. You don't mind my asking, uh, do you still feel anything for me, or have I screwed that up, too?"

"I don't know where I am, Jeb," she said, looking him square in the eyes. "I just know I've got to move on with my life. I can't depend on you. Actually, I guess, I never could. I've got to do what's best for me."

He reached for her hand on the arm of the couch, but she pulled it into her lap and gathered her bag and sunglasses.

"What do you think is best for you?" he asked.

"Not you."

It was a deep cut. He didn't know what to say, and he knew he'd have trouble saying anything with the lump in his throat. He lost track of time in the silence. Sarah was standing before he realized it.

"Take care of yourself," she said. "I wish you well, Jeb. I really do."

He watched through the window as she appeared in the parking lot, walking briskly, he knew, toward a life that didn't include him. Only then did he realize she had been dry-eyed throughout the meeting. The woman who once cried over a dead deer beside the highway, cried each of the six times she had seen *Terms of Endearment*, cried even when she was happy. He admired her and despised her now, and he wondered if he'd ever see her again.

Michael was lying on his bed reading the sports section. He asked how the meeting went, but Quinlin walked quickly past his roommate without saying anything. The cop fell face-first onto the bed and pulled the pillow over his head.

On occasion, the Bergoff-induced hostility between patients spilled over even after the sessions had ended. The animosity would be understandable among normal people, Quinlin figured, but among a group of shaky, self-centered, and paranoid drunks, uncontrolled anger was as inevitable as beer and belching. And sometimes, it turned violent.

Quinlin, preoccupied with his depressing meeting with Sarah, was standing in the evening buffet line behind a bald computer engineer who was in Bergoff's other counseling group, the "senior class" of drunks nearing graduation. A large woman Quinlin knew only as Zoe Zowie, a wino who also dabbled in amphetamines, appeared from nowhere, grabbing the little man in front of him in a headlock.

The engineer let out a startled groan, and the big woman's weight carried them three feet into the steam table where she plunged his face into a vat of bubbling chicken à la king. Zoe held him there, his face submerged in bubbling chicken bits and peas, until Quinlin managed to pry him from her grip.

The victim, an indefatigable complainer who claimed, among other things, to have developed the world's tiniest zip drive, came back from the emergency room two hours later with his face swathed in gauze bandages. Through scorched lips, he lamented that he was destined for cosmetic surgery and promised to sue Zoe's fat ass for everything she owned. Within minutes after he retired to his room, the engineer's screams again electrified the ward. Zoe, ostensibly restricted to her room while administrators figured out what to do with her, apparently had heated her curling iron into a torch and tried to cauterize his left ear as he lay wacked out on Demerol.

Two white-suits showed up from the psycho lock-down wing next door to haul off Zoe Zowie, and Quinlin was surprised when members of her group defended her. Actually, Zoe was a teddy bear, docile and caring, even shy, they claimed, until Dr. Bergoff coerced the engineer into humiliating her in group grope a day earlier. A guy named Walt, a heavyset sporting goods salesman who had the worst jokes on the ward, said that if anyone should be locked up in the wingnut ward, it ought to be Bergoff.

Meanwhile, rumor on the ward was that Myron S., a slip-and-fall lawyer with a half-page ad in the Yellow Pages, supposedly had gotten to a phone and tried to recruit Willard Bean's widow in a malpractice suit against Dr. Bergoff. As Jeb made his way to his room, he saw Myron at the computer engineer's bedside, yelling his spiel into the little man's good ear.

Quinlin played Dr. Bergoff's game. To a point. He had surprised himself in a group session by admitting to a brief but intense extramarital affair two years earlier. It had been an on-duty indiscretion that he had shared with no one, not even McCarren. Her name was Holly Doyle, and she was a stripper. Holly had discovered her older sister, Jerri, butchered and raped when she returned to their apartment on a Sunday afternoon. The sisters were roommates and worked together at the Moondust, an upscale "gentleman's club." The sisters were all that each other had, their parents having been killed in a car wreck when the girls were teenagers. Quinlin had been spending time with Holly and at the club looking for suspects. The affair had been spontaneous and unplanned.

One night, after too many drinks at the Moondust and when Holly brought up suicide, Quinlin said, he had tried to console her. "I was just trying to help," he told the group, "and things got out of hand. I knew it was wrong—it made me feel like hell in a way—and I ended . . ."

Quinlin was in the midst of trying to explain the only indiscretion in his marriage when Dr. Bergoff saw his weakness and seized on it. The psychiatrist accused him of "intellectualizing."

"What you're really saying, aren't you, Jeb, is that you used your position of authority, your badge, in effect, to coerce sex from a victim you knew to be distraught and vulnerable?"

"No, it was wrong, I knew that. It made me feel guilty. But

I felt sorry for her. I cared about her. She had just lost the only living relative she had. At that point, she was threat—"

"Actually," Bergoff said, "that's what criminals do, isn't it? They sense opportunity and they exploit it for their own benefit. Morally, what's the difference between you and the criminals you pursue? *Is* there any difference?"

"It was over in a week. I ended it," Quinlin said. "*I* ended it because it wasn't right, and it was dangerous, and it made me feel like shit, okay?"

Bergoff's allegation was a slap in the face. Here he was admitting in front of a group of strangers one of the most embarrassing and complex chapters in his life, and the truth wasn't enough. Bergoff deliberately skewed the facts, like defense attorneys did when they got him on the witness stand. Holly wasn't just about sex. Sex wasn't even the impetus, though Jeb thought better of trying to explain his motivation to strangers. Holly was alone and afraid, feelings Quinlin sometimes had even when he was surrounded by people. What was the Merle Haggard line from "Misery and Gin?" Sitting at a table with my friends, talking to myself. What happened with Holly, strange as he knew it would sound, was about decency and caring about another human being. And maybe, he knew, it was just as much about him as her.

"So the difference would be what, Jeb?" Bergoff said, pulling him back in the dark hole. "Between you and criminals? That you're not an opportunist?"

"The difference between me and scum is that I don't cheat, steal, or kill," Quinlin shot back. He was about to explain that he had found Holly a secretary's job in the district attorney's office, that she'd never set foot in a strip joint since, that he had introduced her to a friend in Auto Theft, and that she was engaged. He held his tongue; he'd be accused of rationalizing or intellectualizing. Bergoff's mind was made up.

"What do you think, group?" Bergoff was smug, knowing

he had found the pressure point.

"Fuck all of you!" Quinlin shot back. "I don't give a shit what any of you think about me, particularly you, Bergoff. This is all a goddamned talk show with you. You love it. You'd do it for free because you're a dickwad."

The group fell quiet enough to hear a flatulent gnat. Quinlin strode to the door and tried to slam it, but the hydraulic hinge caught the impact, making a slow hiss. He walked deliberately past the nurses' station to his room and fell into his bed with his boots on.

Nothing about Jeb Quinlin's painful, volatile revelation escaped the handsome young man seated halfway down the long conference table. Dressed in a collarless, gauzy shirt, pleated linen pants, and Gucci loafers, he looked like he was headed for a country-club brunch instead of a group therapy session. He alone had pushed his chair a comfortable distance from the table and crossed his legs, careful not to unduly wrinkle the creases in his pants.

While other patients winced and fidgeted under Quinlin's embarrassing confession, the confident onlooker studied the detective's weary face for every nuance. Only when Quinlin exploded at Bergoff and bolted from the room did the man lean back in his chair and relax.

His smile was unmistakable.

Quinlin was still seething when Coal Tar appeared at his closed door, which, by hospital rules, had to remain open at all times. Jerry Stephens had summoned him to his office.

Stephens, a retired marine who never got over it, was the toughest counselor on the ward. There wasn't a touchy-feely tendency in his soul, and what he lacked in interpersonal skills, which was legendary, Stephens made up for with no-bullshit bluntness, a trait Quinlin actually admired. Stephens, according to those on the ward who professed to know, had been a lieutenant colonel and had flown F-4s in Vietnam, another resumé item Quinlin found acceptable.

The adjustment to civilian life had not gone well for the retired colonel. Selling life insurance had bored him, and he couldn't make himself act like he gave a damn about his clients. An already substantial daily alcohol habit turned gradually into binges, three-and four-day reprieves from the civilian treadmill in which alcohol transported him back to the sixties and 'Nam.

As the story went, Stephens's last overt, booze-enhanced act had been a precariously close simulated bomb run over the FAA tower at Love Field in a Beech Bonanza. Stephens himself was an alumnus of Cedar Ridge, where his wife had committed him long enough for a lawyer to plea-bargain him out of a federal criminal record. Stephens spoke from experience, not textbooks.

"You're a vet and you're a cop," Stephens said after Quinlin settled into the leather recliner in front of the counselor's desk. "You know the drill, you know the program. You let Bergoff get to you. You showed your ass. By your actions, you made him a winner. You're the loser."

Quinlin didn't like the personal attention. He ran his hand over the back of his neck and stared at the institutional carpet. He was still light-headed with rage and his hands were shaking, but he said nothing.

"Smoke 'em if you got 'em," Stephens said. "You'll be kicking the walls if you don't."

The counselor scratched his flattop and stared at the patient notes Bergoff had personally delivered only minutes after group grope.

"Says here that you're 'uncooperative, uncommitted, and hostile.' Intellectualizing, too. That's what your therapist says. What he also says is that you need to spend an extra week here in our fine institution to work on anger control."

"Bergoff hasn't seen anger," Quinlin said, drawing deep on the Marlboro Light. He was thinking of walking, an option everyone had after seventy-two hours of detoxification. He had voluntarily committed himself, on paper at least. He could check himself out.

"It won't work, Quinlin," Stephens said, knowing where Quinlin's mind was going. "If you let Bergoff run you off, your supervisor's going to be waiting outside to punch the ticket on your career."

"Screw both of 'em."

"Your marriage still mean anything to you?"

"She can get screwed, too," Quinlin said. "Probably already has."

"This isn't about them," the counselor said. "It's about you. They don't make you drink, and they can't keep you from drinking. You're the one who does that."

"Maybe I just give everyone what they want," Quinlin said, not looking up. "Maybe I give Sarah her divorce, give Numbnuts his badge. And maybe I just knock Bergoff on his turd-cutter on the way out."

"You having fun at your pity party?" Stephens asked. "Look; you've been here barely more than a week. Nothing's changed except you don't have booze running through your system. And that's only because you can't get your hands on any. But you sure as hell want it. You're pissed off, and you want a drink. You always drink when you're pissed. You drink when you're happy. You drink when it thunders. You get it, genius? You drink because you're a damned drunk."

The counselor stared hard at Quinlin while he digested the words. The cop's eyes stayed on the floor.

"There's only two guarantees," Stephens said. "A: You walk out of here right now, you'll be drinking before dark. Here's B: Alcoholism is a progressive disease. Then you die."

* * *

The nurse intercepted Quinlin three feet from his first cup of morning coffee, steering him from the coffeepot to a deserted spot near the windows in the dayroom.

"Registered mail for people in here is never good news," she said, handing him a glassine-windowed envelope and a ballpoint pen. "It's registered so you've got to sign for it."

Quinlin scanned the return address— Dallas Police Department—as he signed his signature on the green postal card. "Probably not a big deal," he said, more to himself than her. "They're probably notifying me that I'm officially on medical leave. DPD has an official cover-your-ass form for everything."

He headed back for the coffeepot, opening the envelope as he went and dodging a couple of patients en route to the TV for headlines on *Good Morning America.* The first paragraph in the letter stopped Quinlin in his tracks. The nurse had made it back to the nurse's station, but she was still watching him. She saw his jaw tighten and his eyes narrow.

"Well, kiss my ass," Quinlin said to no one in particular. He started over at the top of the letter, momentarily immobile in the middle of the dayroom with people walking around him and giving him curious stares.

> "You are hereby advised that thirty days from receipt of this letter a Civil Service Commission hearing will be held to determine why you should not be terminated from the Dallas Police Department. According to a duly-filed complaint, you have violated the following provision(s) of the Dallas Police Department Code of Professional Responsibility, to wit, dereliction of duty, use of alcohol during on-duty hours, and general incapacitation to perform professional duties due to chronic alcohol abuse."

Quinlin scanned the rest of the letter quickly. It was legal boilerplate that he already knew: He was suspended with pay pending the outcome of the hearing, he could be represented by a lawyer, he could call witnesses, and he could address the hearing officers in his own behalf.

And none of that, he knew, would protect his pension or the log cabin in the woods. Civil Service hearings were a farce. Two of the three hearing officers were senior cops and the third was an arbitrator paid by the city. Cops took more hits than Mohammad Ali.

Quinlin saw an empty chair and fell into it. Only then did he notice the staple at the upper left corner and turn to the second page. It was a sworn affidavit, signed by Captain Bill Barrick, that listed six dates in which Barrick claimed that Quinlin was either hungover or smelled of alcohol. Then he noticed the date Barrick had signed the affidavit—the same day Quinlin had admitted himself to Cedar Ridge.

"Protect my marriage and job," Quinlin said cynically. "Rotten, lying sonfabitch."

"Who?" Jerry Stephens was standing over him.

"Fuckin' everybody, near as I can tell," Quinlin said. "But Barrick, the good captain so concerned about my welfare, well, that bastard's at the top of the list. 'Just take care of your problem,' he said, 'and everything's going to be just fuckin' peachy.' On the same goddamned day I check in, he fills out the papers to fire me. He's a lying piece of . . ."

"Control the things you can," Stephens said firmly. "Sit in that chair, whine, feel sorry for yourself, and you don't have a chance. At anything. Not the job or Sarah either. It's like I told you yesterday. Work the program, do it for yourself, and you build a good case for maybe keeping both. The battle's not over unless you convince yourself it is."

"They both lied," Quinlin said. The bitterness dripped like battery acid.

"Yeah," Stephens said, "but you're an honest drunk, right? You never lied to anyone, did you? Spare me the righteous indignation, okay?"

The counselor turned to leave, then stopped abruptly.

"You want to write me off, too?" Stephens asked. "Fine. I don't have time for anyone who won't help himself. But you got the balls to try, I got the patience to help. Otherwise you're wasting my time."

8

The Alcohol Treatment Unit was, in effect, a minimum-security prison. ATU was a self-contained, self-sufficient wing, intentionally designed to accommodate long-term residents and to limit their ingress and egress. Three meals a day were prepared in the hospital's main kitchen and transported in thermal-insulated carts to a dining room where the food was deposited in steam tables and served buffet style. Snacks, an institutional coffeemaker, and a tea dispenser were accessible around the clock.

In a room off the dayroom, behind unlocked, accordion panels was a Laundromat with three washers, three dryers, a coin-operated detergent dispenser, and five wall-mounted ironing boards with irons. It wasn't uncommon for recovering drunks, particularly as they were weaned from their daily dosage of Librium, to become insomniacs, or "night prowlers," as the staff called them. And though it undoubtedly complicated Flashlight Larry's accounting ritual, patients frequently put in loads of wash at all hours of the night, then walked across to the dining room to drink decaf coffee and eat Oreos while their clothes washed or dried.

Luke T. was among the most notorious of the night prowlers. He was in Quinlin's group, and if anyone should have problems sleeping, Quinlin figured it was poor, beleaguered Luke. Until three months earlier, Luke had been a Catholic priest. He was from Ireland, which was the genesis of a heavy brogue that was both charming and difficult to understand, and his life had collapsed like so many dominoes stacked on end. Shortly after the Brothers of Holy Charity had assigned him to the Dallas Diocese three years earlier, Father Luke had fallen in love with a parishioner, a twenty-something divorcée with two sons. Though their relationship was unconsummated, the ensuing guilt from the emotional violation of his vows had plunged him into the bottle.

Twice the diocese had packed Luke off to a remote New Mexico retreat to get help for his alcoholism, but never, Luke confided to the group, had he acknowledged the real reason he drank—because he had committed the sin of lust in his heart. When the monsignor confronted him after he had delivered a mass drunk, Luke reluctantly resigned from the priesthood and asked for forgiveness. He borrowed $10,000 from a benevolent parishioner and showed up at Cedar Ridge on his own, trying to redeem his life.

Madeline Meggers had been at Cedar Ridge two weeks before Quinlin checked in. He was in only three sessions with her before she moved up to the advanced counseling group. Most of what he picked up about her came parenthetically during conversations they had at dinner or in the dayroom. Discreetly, he hoped, he had asked others about her, too.

Despite his initial reservations, Quinlin and Madeline had become almost immediate friends. Her room was two doors down from his, on the other side of the hall. As long as the lights were on and the doors were open, men and women patients could visit in each other's rooms before 10:00 P.M. After classes and sessions, Quinlin and Madeline routinely sought each other out for coffee in the dayroom. She peeked her head in his door, and they walked to the Living Sober classes together. They migrated to the same table at lunch and dinner.

They were night prowlers, too. Finding her alone at a table at 2:00 A.M. one morning when he couldn't sleep, Quinlin made it a habit to show up after midnight, grabbing a cup of decaf and sitting with Madeline well into morning. The meetings became unspoken rituals, their talking while Luke, whom they dubbed "Saint Luke," burned off nervous compulsive energy and obsessive guilt by cleaning and rearranging the coffee shop and periodically refilling their cups.

Madeline had never known a detective, and she regularly called Quinlin "Officer." He had never met anyone as classy as she, and he was surprised at how she could be so down to earth.

"The only smart thing I ever did drunk was file for divorce," she told Quinlin early in their dark-hours meetings. "It should be final by the time I get out of here. I'm taking my full share of his money and I'm investing it legitimately. The bastard owes me that. You married, Officer?"

The conversation was vintage Madeline. There was no transition between thoughts, as if her mind didn't have time to finesse her thoughts before her mouth said them.

"I truly don't know," Quinlin said with a grin. "Can they serve papers in this place?"

"Do you want to be married?"

"I don't know that either. Never looked at things this sober this long."

"As institutions go," Madeline said, "marriage sucks even more than this place."

Beneath the veneer of her flamboyance and facetiousness, Madeline was sensitive, deeply moral, and, Quinlin suspected, a bona fide pollyanna. She and Beau Meggers were from middle-class backgrounds and they married after graduating from Southern Methodist University. He became a custom home-builder, and Madeline, with her degree in accounting, kept the books. Over time, the way she explained it, her husband's ambition—she now called it greed—no longer could be contained by reality. Or, apparently, legality.

Beau Meggers became a developer, and his projects were bigger and bigger—whole subdivisions, gated condominium communities, and even a new, high-rise hotel near D/FW Airport. Quinlin vaguely knew the name. He had seen the distinctive black diamond logo with *Meggers Group* written inside in gold.

"Meggers Group," Madeline said, her voice dripping sarcasm. "Let me tell you about the *group*. Beau is a front. His ass and his money belong to a bunch of guys who fly into Dallas every once in a while in a private jet. I don't know where they're from, but they barely speak English. They're crude and rough, but they wear these thousand-dollar suits and alligator shoes, and they don't go anywhere without these hard-bodied cretins surrounding them."

Quinlin pictured an entourage with heavy gold necklaces, pinkie rings, and forty-weight hair.

"A week or so after every visit," Madeline said, "Beau's bank account balloons. We're talking seven zeroes here."

"Sounds like ol' Beau ought to rename his company the Meggers Cartel," Quinlin said.

The arrangement, Quinlin surmised, put Beau Meggers butt-deep in dirty money and gave his subterranean buddies a way to funnel their illicit funds into legitimate, tax-paying pipelines. Drug money in South America became bricks and mortar in Dallas. Meggers's new hotel venture was a nice added touch. Money launderers love hotels, casinos, and car washes, or any other business whose traffic is virtually impossible to measure. Who's to say a hotel's occupancy rate isn't consistently ninety-five percent, or that six hundred people a day didn't pump seventy-five cents in quarters through a three-bay car wash?

Traditionally, a crooked banker gets a dime for every dirty dollar he launders. A construction magnate building hotels not only cleans dirty money, he sets up a perpetual money laundry, complete with tax deductions and depreciation.

"Nice gig," Quinlin said. "What, you don't like money?"

Madeline Meggers was not amused. Dallas worships success, and the gaudier the better. And Beau Meggers became the biggest overnight icon of materialism since Jerry Jones flew in from Arkansas to commandeer America's team and paint his new Highland Park mansion pink like the EverReady bunny. Indeed, when Madeline checked herself into Cedar Ridge, she listed a home address exactly four blocks from Jerry Jones's compound. She also could have listed addresses in Aspen (which Beau liked to call "the ski house"), New York ("the Central Park condo"), and West Palm Beach (simply "the West Palm house").

"When his PR people told him that *Fortune* was considering a profile on him, he pulled out his checkbook and wrote major contributions to the Crystal Charity Ball," Madeline said. "He lobbied to get me on the board of the Cattle Baron's Ball, and when I told him he was a goddamned hypocrite and I refused to do it, he stopped speaking to me. Anyway, he ended up in *Fortune* and got offers for four board appointments the next week."

Along the way, there were confrontations—violent ones, the way Madeline told it—and ultimately their marriage became as dead as his ethics. He rededicated himself to greed; she did a swan dive into a bottomless vat of high-dollar Chablis.

As intriguing as her story was, Quinlin had to force himself to pay attention. Madeline mesmerized him. It wasn't just her long lashes, high cheekbones, and wisp of brunette hair that habitually fell over her left eye. Her voice was raspy, like a lounge singer's, and when she laughed, which was frequently, it was from deep within and was contagious. Nothing about her was pretentious. Beau Meggers, Madeline's new friend determined, was a fool.

Down the hall, Saint Luke pitched two-thirds of his earthly belongings into a washer and headed for the soap dispenser. At the end of the row of washers and dryers, he abruptly dropped his quarters onto the floor and screamed, "Sweet Mary, Mother of Jesus!"

Wedged between a washer and the wall was a lump of flesh and hair that appeared to be a woman. She was naked, sitting with her legs pulled up in front of her and her head collapsed onto her knees. Long, flowing brunette hair cascaded over her knees hiding her face, and her arms lay limp at her sides.

The erstwhile priest looked around; he was helplessly alone. Quinlin and Madeline had gone to their rooms an hour earlier. Flashlight Larry appeared momentarily, along with Red, the nurse. Gently, the male attendant cupped his hand beneath the woman's chin and pulled her head up. Her eyes were open and squinted at the corners. It was Kristin.

Not until attendants from the main hospital pulled the nude swimsuit model from her crypt in the corner could they see her abdomen. Scrawled and smeared, the message in red lipstick was from the First Step of AA: *Our lives had become unmanageable.*

9

Begrudgingly, Jeb Quinlin had to admit that maybe hospitalization, or group therapy, or—more remotely, he thought—his surprising AA-induced belief in "a power greater than ourselves," was working. On the worst day of his mandatory treatment, when he knew thoughts of Sarah would haunt him all night, he had silently recited the Serenity Prayer over and over again:

God grant me the serenity
to accept the things I cannot change,
the courage to change the things I can,
and the wisdom to know the difference.

Maybe he had learned acceptance, or maybe he had just given up. Maybe it was too subtle a distinction for him to know the difference. But after talking to Madeline in the coffee room, he miraculously had slept like a newborn.

Until Coal Tar jerked the pillow from beneath his head a few minutes before 4:00 A.M. The big man was agitated and not making a lot of sense.

"Strange shit's goin' down 'round here," he said, grabbing hold of Quinlin's shoulder. "You got visitors waiting on you in the dayroom. You need to move your ass."

Quinlin looked at his Seiko. Visitors? A puzzled Quinlin brushed his teeth and combed his hair, leaving the shaving until later. He was almost to the dayroom in yesterday's clothes and socks when he realized he hadn't put on his boots.

Paul McCarren had a styrofoam cup of coffee and had obviously been rolled out in the middle of the night, too. There was no trademark coat and tie, and he had made no attempt to knock down the overnight stubble. Captain Bill Barrick was near the nurses' station talking on a cell phone. They motioned him beyond the station to Stephens's office.

Quinlin, Barrick said pointedly, had slept through a homicide: Kristin Williamson, white female, twenty-six, five-foot-eight, one hundred twenty-six pounds, twice divorced, no children, model, no physical signs of violence on the body, and a murky message in lipstick beneath her tanned breasts that screamed ritual murder. Not to mention the new dimension Kristin's death added to the demise twenty-four hours earlier of Willard Beane, whose body also bore no evidence of violence but carried a similarly cryptic message.

McCarren reported that he'd responded immediately to Quinlin's voice mail from a day earlier, appearing in the administrator's office at Cedar Ridge after regular working hours. Hospital officials reluctantly had summoned the administrator back to hospital. While McCarren hadn't found any indication of foul play even after a trip to the hospital's morgue, the young detective nonetheless had bludgeoned the hospital bureaucrat, per Quinlin's suggestion, with multitudinous threats of criminal exposure for not calling police in the first place.

"Mr. Beane died in a hospital under the care of a physician," the administrator had said, appearing smug. "Surely you're aware the law does not compel us to phone a coroner or police under those circumstances."

"I know this," McCarren had responded. "Your patient died with a card on his dick that should have indicated to a reasonable person that maybe his demise wasn't entirely natural. Now if you want to play this out, I can just cordon off Mr. Beane's room with some yellow tape and hold it as a crime scene for a couple of weeks."

McCarren had left Cedar Ridge believing that a distraught Willard Beane probably had offed himself. But he also ordered the suddenly agreeable administrator to hold Beane's body, pending completion of an expedited toxicological scan, the results of which were due in four or five days. Given Kristin Williamson's bizarre demise, McCarren was now doubly glad he had kept Beane's body on ice.

Roused unceremoniously from one of the few decent nights since he'd been at Cedar Ridge, Quinlin, without benefit even of decaf coffee, was having trouble keeping up. Kristin was dead, but no marks of violence?

"So you didn't hear anything?" Barrick asked. "What time did you go to bed?"

"If I'm a suspect, Mirandize me," Quinlin said, eyeing his boss coolly.

"This is embarrassing, that's all," the captain said, making no attempt to conceal his agitation. "A homicide detective fifty feet from a murder and he's asleep. That'll look great if the reporters pick it up."

Quinlin held up his right wrist and pointed to the clear plastic identification bracelet issued by the hospital.

"I'm not a cop," he said pointedly. "I'm a patient. Actually, I'm a drunk, and even if I'd been a cop last night, my supervisor wouldn't have believed I would have been capable of doing—"

"Save your trash," Barrick said. "Until we know differently, both these deaths have to be treated as homicides. And clearly, if they are, other people are at risk, maybe even yourself. I am assigning McCarren here as the primary investigator on these cases."

Quinlin could see Barrick was avoiding his eyes.

"You are in a precarious, ah, situation with the department and your medical situation, but all that aside," the captain said, "I'm assigning you to help work this case. I'll talk with whoever's in charge here, and we'll figure out a way you can communicate with Paul. Some of the staff will have to know what you're doing, but I don't want any of the patients knowing. I want you to pick up whatever you can from them."

McCarren anticipated his partner, and lunged between Quinlin and Barrick before Quinlin could throw the punch.

"It's not worth it, Jeb!" McCarren yelled, shoving his partner backward two steps.

"You lying bastard!" Quinlin yelled. "You led me to believe that I'd keep my pension if I came here. On the same goddamned day, you try to get me fired. You put me on medical leave, you sign the complaint, and now you're telling me I'm assigned to a homicide investigation? You want it both ways, goddammit. Why should I?"

"Because I'm ordering you to," Barrick shot back. "You know the job. You're a cop twenty-four hours a day, on-duty, off-duty, or in this goddamned hospital or anywhere else. Your shit's already in the toilet, you want to flush it yourself?"

Barrick pitched him the cell phone he'd been using and a beeper.

"Use the 8711 number," the captain said. "It'll be set up directly to McCarren. I want you two talking twice a day, minimum. McCarren will keep me posted. And he better tell me you're busting your ass."

Barrick left McCarren behind to work out the details and headed for the electronically controlled door, glancing at his wristwatch. He had enough time for a shower and shave before his 8:00 A.M. commander's briefing with the chief.

* * *

Not until the door buzzed and Barrick was safely on the other side did Paul McCarren head for the coffeepot. He poured two cups, delivered one to his partner, and fell heavily onto the couch, sloshing himself with a few drops from his own cup. He ignored the spill and rubbed his free hand over his face.

Quinlin knew his battle with Barrick had made his junior partner feel awkward. But Quinlin was too angry to apologize. They had been partners for more than two years, ever since McCarren transferred in from uniforms. They were living proof that opposites attract, even complement. If Quinlin, in his everpresent Wranglers and cowboy boots, was state fair, McCarren, a suspendered Brooks Brothers poster boy, was savoir faire. McCarren was thirty-one, single, and held a master's degree in criminology from the University of Texas at Arlington. He jogged six miles before showing up every morning in the bullpen, and his desk was loaded with enough vitamins and health-food supplements to restore a third-world country.

McCarren was by the book, one-hundred-percent cop. In his off hours while he was still on patrol, McCarren had once programmed his laptop to assimilate the data from twenty-seven rapes that spanned seven months and occurred predominantly in his district. Using software he had adapted himself, he predicted the two most likely places and times the serial rapist would next strike. McCarren's dubious lieutenant, a computer illiterate who had been to rookie academy with Quinlin, forwarded the information to Sex Crimes. Borrowing troops from the Major Case Unit, Sex Crimes staked out two apartment complexes, and on the third night, they caught one of the most prolific rapists in Dallas history. The arrest was McCarren's ticket to detectives.

Quinlin was as set in his ways as McCarren was innovative.

The veteran detective was the last in CAPERS to learn to use the computer, and only then because a sergeant had forbidden the secretary from doing it anymore. More than two years later, Quinlin still typed in the information with his index fingers and used a handwritten cheat sheet that included only the most basic commands. While he was a technological dinosaur, a distinction he wore like a badge of honor, no one in the squad had more street savvy or contacts. It was why the sergeant had assigned McCarren to work with Quinlin in the first place.

"Don't be misled by his good ol' boy bullshit," the sergeant had told the rookie detective. "Just keep your mouth shut and pay attention. People talk to Jeb. It's a gift in detective work. You can learn it, all right, but with Jeb, it's instinctive."

Working with Quinlin for two years, McCarren had appreciated the sergeant's advice. Quinlin was a man for all seasons. Prostitutes and barmaids trusted him, McCarren suspected, because it was clear Quinlin didn't make value judgments. Not to mention that they admired the rogue scar on his chin as much as the Wranglers and boots. Judges talked to him because Quinlin didn't ask unless it was important, and he never gave up sources. Quinlin called it integrity.

But nowhere, McCarren discovered, did Quinlin excel as a detective more than in an interview room. Hard cases, crying and remorseful ones, construction laborers or insurance salesmen, they all gave it up after a few hours with Quinlin. He didn't threaten, most of the time; he just talked. Constantly. Chain-smoking, cup after cup of coffee, and talking. No matter the suspect or his background, Quinlin found middle ground. No value judgments and no condemnation. He told jokes, commiserated, and once, when McCarren happened to look through the one-way mirror, he saw Quinlin on his knees, holding hands with a suspect, and praying.

If he could tap into his partner's intuitive knowledge about people and master his savvy in questioning, McCarren joked, he'd be chief in five years.

"Don't worry about this crap with Barrick," Quinlin told him. "Whatever's going to happen is going to happen."

"You realize if you do this assignment, and we catch this turd," McCarren said, "they *can't* pull your badge. That'd be service above and beyond. It'd destroy every argument Barrick's got for firing you."

"I don't know, Mac," Quinlin said. "The train's moving pretty fast. Sarah's gone. She . . ."

"I've got to talk to you about that."

The younger detective appeared to be fidgeting under some indecipherable weight.

"About Sarah? You got to talk to me about Sarah?"

Two days earlier, McCarren explained sheepishly, he had gone by Sarah's, thinking he could get an update on Jeb's hospitalization.

"Jeb," McCarren said, "I don't know if I'm doing the . . ."

"Put it on me, Mac. What is it?"

"One of our unmarked Crown Vics was parked in front of your house," McCarren said. "I couldn't make out the guy, but the plates belong . . ."

"To Barrick," Quinlin said, finishing the sentence. "The plates checked to Barrick, am I right?"

The junior partner looked away and said nothing.

"Just because you're paranoid," Quinlin shrugged, "doesn't mean they're not out there trying to get you."

10

LouAnn Shields had seen the man earlier on her way into the funeral home. She had walked between his black sports car and a pickup truck. He was in the driver's seat, reading a folded newspaper. Before she got to the porch, she turned—discreetly, she hoped—for a second, admiring look.

There were maybe twenty people in the viewing room for a man named Clyde Shields, LouAnn's late uncle. Uncle Clyde was a retired brakeman for the Santa Fe Railroad who had succumbed daily and painfully to emphysema, the final fruits of forty years of unfiltered Camels. When the handsome man from the parking lot appeared in the doorway, LouAnn pointed him out to Aunt Bess. Bess Shields had other things on her mind, to be sure, but she couldn't recall ever seeing him before. Yet the handsome stranger passed solemnly by Clyde Shields's open casket, mouthed what LouAnn took to be "God bless," and filed past. Near the door, the man shook hands with two of Aunt Bess's friends, and walked into the hall. The pair of family friends couldn't place him either.

By the time LouAnn made her way out of the viewing room, she saw him at the far end of the hall, peering through a barely opened door. She watched him hesitate, then disappear into the room. She went back to Uncle Clyde's viewing room, hoping to bump into him before she left.

A half hour later, LouAnn, having dutifully paid her respects, headed for the room at the end of the hall. A stooped man, gray and wearing a name tag with the Garrison & Sons Funeral Home logo, emerged from the room as she neared.

"Oh," LouAnn said, embarrassed and awkward. "I was just looking for someone."

"If you're looking for someone in there," the funeral attendant said, smiling, "it's generally too late. That's the preparation room."

She walked to the entryway and glanced through the paned window, just in time to see the black sports car turning from the parking lot onto Routh Street.

11

It took nearly ten minutes for Quinlin to return Paul McCarren's call. Quinlin wore a beeper beneath his shirt, on vibration mode. He had to go to his room, retrieve the cell phone from his shaving kit, and close himself in the bathroom.

"You been lying to me about what a tough place Cedar Ridge is?" McCarren asked good-naturedly, hoping there wasn't residual debris from their conversation a day earlier. "The ME says both Beane and the lovely swim lady had booze in their blood, less than .10, but booze in the alcohol ward nonetheless."

"You've got to be kidding," Quinlin said. "That's at least a couple of stiff ones apiece."

Certainly bootleg booze in the ward wasn't unprecedented, but what were the chances of both Willard and Kristin imbibing before they died? McCarren didn't give Quinlin time to digest the information.

"I promise not to make this a habit," the younger partner said, "but I've got more bad news. The ME's people don't know jack about what killed Beane or Williamson. Berryman said he'd normally rule congestive heart failure on the guy. And the woman, well, she's a dice roll. Not a clue."

Mark Berryman was the youngest medical examiner in the country and, in Quinlin's opinion, the best. Quinlin was relieved that Berryman had saved the cases for himself.

"He's ordered toxicological scans," McCarren continued, "but you know the story there. You'll be retired before they come in."

"Nothing shaking here either," Quinlin said. "I've tried to talk to all the drunks, particularly Willard's and Kristin's roommates and the people on either side of their rooms. No one saw anything. Everyone has a theory, but no one knows anything."

"What about staff?"

"You talked to Flashlight Larry and have his statement," Quinlin said. "I figure him for a working mope just getting by. Seems decent enough. Coal Tar's the only one I trust around here. He was off duty and out of the hospital when both bodies were found. I haven't gotten to him yet. I'll get him before he leaves tonight. Any word on records?"

"Went the way we figured," McCarren said. "The administration's wormy. Called their attorney who gave us the regular runaround about doctor-patient confidentiality. At this point, they're not even giving us *last names* for the patients. They were magnanimous enough to give us the ex-priest, Sean Luke Tarrant, but only because he was a witness."

"That's par for this place," Quinlin said. "Fine, we'll do it the hard way. Badge them for the names and personnel files of every goddamned staff member who works or has access to the alcohol ward. That's not doctor-patient privilege. Nurses, technicians, orderlies, and I want Bergoff's, too. They had as much access as the drunks. More, actually."

"No problem, but we're still screwed on the patients," McCarren said.

"I'll get the files," Quinlin said.

"How?"

"I've got a plan. Trust me. I'm shoving this one up Barrick's ass. Whatever it takes."

* * *

"If I still had a badge, I'd show it to you and make this official," Quinlin said. "We need to cut to the chase. I need your help. Confidentially."

Since Quinlin had checked in two weeks earlier, Coal Tar had matched him tit for tat in cynical wit. It was an evolving game of one-upmanship, and a quiet camaraderie developed around it. Now, with just the two of them in Jerry Stephens's office, the big man appeared ill at ease and not up for games. Quinlin wasn't just a drunk any more; he was a cop who wanted to see him alone.

The attendant's name tag identified him as Robishawn.

"I don't even know your first name," Quinlin said, trying to put him at ease.

"Winston," he replied, shifting his weight in the chair. "My mamma smoked Winstons."

Quinlin grinned. "Good thing it wasn't Virginia Slims."

The detective relied on his instincts and a few key comments Winston Robishawn had made over the last two weeks. No question he had character; Quinlin had seen Coal Tar's intensely personal reaction when he saved Raphael's life. The detective figured the cynicism came from his having to take a technician's job after his fifteen minutes of fame with the Cowboys. It was like 'Nam, Quinlin thought. A sharp, decent guy taking orders from dipshits when Winston Robishawn knew he could do it better.

Most important in this context, though, and critical to Quinlin's plan, Coal Tar hadn't been bashful about badmouthing his employer. From a few parenthetical remarks, it was clear he viewed hospital administrators as being more concerned about the hospital's image than its patients or murder investigations.

Quinlin approached Coal Tar cautiously.

"We wouldn't be having this conversation if I didn't trust

you," the detective said. "But by a similar token, I don't want to do anything to jeopardize your job. Or your ethics. So when I finish talking, if you hear something you don't like, you just get up and leave the room. No hard feelings. All I ask is that you don't tell anyone we talked. Fair enough?"

"Deal is," Winston Robishawn said, "this job's been fine for me, but it's not the end-all, you understand what I'm saying? I'll be quitting pretty soon anyways, 'cause, see, well, I've kinda been working on another degree that'll take me somewhere else. Give me a chance to do some other things. So I'm still listening to you, all right?"

"That keyring on your belt there," Quinlin said. "Those keys fit just about everything on this ward, right?"

"Yeah," Coal Tar said, reading Quinlin immediately. "So where you want to go?"

Quinlin had noticed that individual patient files were maintained by counselors in their offices, except on Friday afternoons when they were forwarded to Bergoff so he could update counseling notes. There were four counselors for all the patients on the wing.

"When you leave here today," Quinlin said cautiously, "you go to a locksmith and have copies made for the keys to all four of the counselors' offices. Tomorrow, you hand them to me. You don't need to know anything from that point on."

"Well," the big man said, grinning, "we could do it that way. But you'd still have to get around Flashlight Larry. And it'd probably take you a month of Sundays to copy all them files. Try this on. How 'bout I have you copies of everybody's file by tomorrow afternoon when we load up for the AA meeting? Now, you the big-time *dee*-tective, but me, I think I got a better deal."

"How are you—"

"Guess you don't need to know nothing from this point on." Coal Tar grinned, revealing the whitest, straightest teeth Quinlin had ever seen.

12

Geneva Quinlin was seventy-six, older than her son figured he'd ever be, and notwithstanding some brutal miles in her past, she still routinely passed for sixty. Not long ago, when Quinlin and Sarah had taken her to Luby's Cafeteria after church, the cashier actually questioned whether she qualified for the senior citizen's discount. Geneva, in a jaunty, navy blue pantsuit and frilly white blouse, had gushed and hugged the woman.

Quinlin knew his mother would show up. She always did in a crisis. He had had to tell her about the hospital. He routinely visited her at her house in East Dallas two or three times a week, so his absence would have been obvious. She knew his whereabouts anyway. In the same phone conversation, she told him that Sarah had phoned. She also said that Sarah had filed for divorce.

Quinlin, currently undergoing treatment for alcoholism, soon to be a defendant in a divorce, and potentially unemployed, was embarrassed seeing his mother in the dayroom. But she wouldn't have any of his self-pity. She had brought a pound cake, his favorite.

Geneva Quinlin never gave advice, at least not in declaratory sentences. She asked questions.

"Don't you think everything's for the best?" she said, an obvious reference to the divorce. "You're here getting things straightened out, and who knows the good that'll come of it? It's an opportunity to move past some bad things in your life, don't you think, Jeb?"

Move past some bad things? God, had she been comparing euphemisms with the diabolical duo?

"I don't like to lay blame," she said, "but I'm not sure that Sarah ever appreciated what you go through with that job. It's an important job, but there's not a day of my life that I don't say a prayer for you. Do you think the worry just got to be too much for her?"

"Mother, this isn't just about my job," Quinlin said. He had been schooled in studying honesty; it was tough to practice it. "This is about why I'm here. I'm an alcoholic. Just like my father was."

He caught himself. His mother's experience with drunks had been limited to one violent man.

"I don't mean that I got drunk and beat Sarah," he said. "I'd never do that, Mama. I've never hit a woman, drunk or sober. But I have the same disease he did. I can't control my drinking, and my drinking ruined my marriage. What's happening, well, it's not Sarah's fault. It's my fault. I messed everything up, and now this is the price I have to pay."

He felt his lower lip quivering, but he had to get it out.

"I had to stop," he said, feeling the water welling in his eyes, "or I was going to end up just like him. I've done bad things, Mama, and I hate myself for them. I can't take them back. I'm trying to deal with them."

The truth hurt, but he knew he couldn't stop.

"I . . . I hate the bastard for what he did to you. I'm forty-three years old now and I, uh, I'm just like him. I hate him and I turned out just like him. I hurt Sarah. Whatever she's doing, it hurts, it hurts bad, but I forced her. Don't blame her,

Mama. This is me; I did it. I deserve whatever I get."

"I may be old, sweetie, but I'm not stupid," Geneva Quinlin said. "You think after all these years I don't know what a hangover looks like? I've known you had to fight the same problems your father fought. But you're nothing like him. I knew you'd reach a point where you'd dealing with your drinking. You care too much. That's one of your problems, son.

"And it's one of the reasons you and Sarah fought over children. Because you care too much, maybe expect too much of yourself."

Quinlin was stunned at his mother's mention of children. The issue had been the most fractious in his marriage, even more so than his job. But he had never discussed the issue with his mother. Sarah wanted children desperately. He always had an excuse—his job, money, the fact that both of them had professions, whatever he could come up with, except the truth.

"Mama, I could never bring a child . . ."

"You were afraid you couldn't be a good father," she said. "You were afraid you'd be like your father. I've always understood that. It's like I said, son. You care too much."

He was crying and spent, and he laid his head on his arm on the table. At some point he felt his mother's hand on his, patting like she had done when he was a kid with earaches. It was silent and soothing, and he didn't feel like he had to talk.

Red was the duty nurse, and she told him he could walk his mother to the parking lot. The nurse hugged Mrs. Quinlin at the electronic doors.

"Your son's doing real good," Red whispered out of Quinlin's earshot. "He wants to do the right thing. We're going to help him. Don't you worry about him."

The last twelve years of Quinlin's career had been spent in CAPERS. His first two years out of uniform, he had been assigned to the Sex Crimes Squad. As desperately as he had fought to become a detective, Quinlin knew he couldn't cope with a prolonged career of rapists, window-peepers, bicycle-seat sniffers, and sundry other perverts.

There was the stereotypical assortment of lowlife dregs, but he also arrested a CEO, four preachers, a psychiatrist, an EMT, and a variety of so-called white-collar, family men on rape charges. Anybody with a whanger he assumed to be a potential rapist.

Inevitably during interviews with rape victims, Quinlin found himself apologizing and feeling guilty on behalf of the entire male species. He took his cases home with him, agonizing mental replays that made him detached and distant. Sarah had been compassionate and understanding at first, but ultimately Quinlin was taking lurid crime scenes into his own bedroom. Days filled with victims of forcible intimacy made nights of voluntary closeness impossible with the woman he loved.

Their sex life gridlocked; he was impotent. The distance meant she went to bed at a decent hour, and he was in the den drinking. It was the only way he could sleep. For the first time, Quinlin feared alcohol. Not that fear stopped him. It only made him feel guilty. He knew better.

Peddy Freddy had been the last straw in Quinlin's career in Sex Crimes. Fred Mullweeney was a bald dweeb of a man who wore a black clip-on tie and a white short-sleeved shirt every day of his life as a salesman at a women's shoe store. On average of once a week, his fantasies overcame him, and he broke into women's apartments.

At gunpoint, he rubbed their feet, *ped à la Fred*, with baby oil he carried in a small shaving kit. Then he rummaged through their closets for the sexiest pair of heels he could find, and made them wear the shoes while they masturbated him.

A victim and former customer at the mall shoe store recognized Fred's voice through the ski mask, and Quinlin confronted him in the stockroom of the shoe store. It was an instantaneous confession: nasal, whiny, and rationalized like most sex offenders. When Fred claimed that victims actually enjoyed the massages, that the masturbation was actually just quid pro quo, Quinlin committed the only case of police brutality in his career.

He ground the cuffs as tight as they would go around Fred's wrists and, as he shoved him into the backseat, Quinlin "accidentally" banged the pervert's head into the roof of the car. It was July and the temperature at midday was one-hundred-five degrees. Quinlin rolled up the windows in the squad car and let Peddy Freddy sauté for an hour while he ate a hamburger and drafted his transfer letter on a table napkin at Chili's.

A medical retirement two weeks later created an opening on the Homicide Squad. The early years in Homicide resurrected Quinlin's marriage; the transformation wasn't a mystery, not to Quinlin. Rape victims, the fortunate ones, were still able to tell their traumas, notwithstanding all the psychic devastation that usually entailed. They were emotional and vulnerable, and they sapped the life from him.

But the beauty of corpses was, well, they didn't talk. In the 246 homicide investigations he had conducted over ten years, Quinlin had never encountered a victim he had known in life. They were strangers and therefore there were no memories. Looking at a body sprawled on the floor, Quinlin sometimes caught himself trying to imagine how he or she had appeared in life. Pleasant, maybe, judging from the laugh lines around a mouth. Or maybe stern and unyielding if there were wrinkles above the brow. His take, he knew, was abstract, something he conjured up in his own mind.

The crime scenes were frequently grisly, enough to tax the imagination about what one human is capable of doing to another. Guns and knives, of course, were everyday occurrences, but over the years, Quinlin had also seized as murder weapons ropes, tire chains, arsenic, lug wrenches, matches and gasoline, barbells, claw hammers, a trained rottweiler, a chainsaw, and a frozen Long Island duckling. Whatever the means, the results of that violence were lifeless, as inanimate, an old homicide dick once told him, as meat on a rack. Quinlin appreciated the detachment.

Murder, the supposed ultimate crime, actually wasn't about death, not the way Quinlin saw it. It was about lost potential and unrealized dreams. He had seen it in Vietnam—mere fuzzy-faced boys in body bags who would never be husbands, fathers, or welders or rocket scientists. Man might fail at his ultimate undertaking, but that should be attributable to his own incompetence or lack of ambition. For one human being to premeditatedly deprive another of *opportunity*, that was truly the ultimate crime.

McCarren thought Quinlin's theory was quirky rationalization that allowed his partner to escape the gory reality of homicide, but he couldn't deny that Quinlin, however quirky his philosophy, was uncanny in his clearance rates. Six of Quinlin's erstwhile suspects sat on death row at the Ellis I Unit of the Texas Department of Criminal Justice. Captain Lawrence Louis, who had headed Homicide before he retired, used to call Huntsville's death row the "Quinlin Wing," a tribute to the fact that Quinlin had put more men in line for the lethal needle than any other detective in Texas.

The transfer to Homicide had also given Quinlin more prestige, at least in Sarah's eyes. She had once confided that she dodged people's questions about the kind of detective her husband was.

"What am I supposed to say, Jeb—that you hunt down window-peepers?" she told him. "You've got a college education, and you lurk around alleys trying to catch voyeurs while they're whipping off? Wow."

Quinlin could imagine the conversation in Sarah's office. She was a senior associate at L'Elegance, an interior design agency whose clientele included CEOs' wives and contributors to the Cattle Baron's Ball.

Sarah had come a long way from the night-school student Quinlin fell in love with at the University of North Texas. Privately, he preferred the uncertain, spontaneous blond in tight Levis and halter tops to the demure designer who consistently tried to get him to swap his boots and Wranglers for Hugo Boss. He couldn't tell her that, of course, without it appearing to be bitter grapes, especially since she made twice what he did.

Any improvement in their marriage attributable to his transfer from Sex Crimes was momentary. They both realized the problem, but it was Sarah who made it an issue. One of her silk-stocking clients had a condo in Hawaii and offered it to Sarah for three weeks. On the night before they returned to Dallas, minutes after they had made love on the balcony in a light tropical mist, Sarah said, "We're not even going in the same direction, are we? It's not just about your being a cop. You don't have any ambition. You could be a captain now if you'd taken the tests. Maybe deputy chief.

"And then what?" she asked, knowing the answer. "You want to live like a hermit, drag me to some backwater place with log cabins and pine trees, and that's supposed to make me happy?"

Sarah's exposure to the rich and famous had sucked her in, twisted her goals and warped her values. That's what Quinlin saw. A Lexus, more clothes than would fit into a walk-in closet the size of a bedroom, and client lunches at chic restaurants, the names of which he couldn't even pronounce. He'd seen the change and hoped that she'd see the superficiality of it all. It was yuppie materialism crap. After Hawaii, he knew she'd never go back to the jeans and halter tops. Or to his dream house in the country.

Quinlin also knew he couldn't change his agenda if he

wanted to; and he didn't. In the hundred thousand years that man had been a species, not one of them, save maybe Jesus, had failed to die. Prestige, even wealth, didn't make a damn in the grand scheme. He believed in the bumper sticker stuck to his desk: LIFE IS A BITCH, THEN YOU DIE. The cabin in the piney woods was his only mitigator. His life's motto, fittingly, he thought, came from a beer commercial: *You only go around once; grab for all the gusto you can.* The cabin was an opportunity, the payback, however brief, for the bitch of a life he shared with sociopaths.

In the three years since Hawaii, Sarah had recommitted to her career. Jeb Quinlin saw the fork in the road was getting closer. In between bodies, blood, and perpetrators, when he fantasized about his cabin, he saw only himself.

13

Cyrus McKay's embalming days had long since passed. The arthritis and osteoporosis had left him stooped and painfully slow. But the Garrison brothers, heirs to Garrison & Sons Funeral Home, were smart enough to keep the old man on the payroll. McKay's age—he was a year short of three-quarters of a century—and his frailty were actually pluses, particularly in the casket room.

Moving slowly in his stooped shuffle and wearing his weary, compassionate undertaker's half-smile, Cyrus McKay led the bereaved through the maze of boxes, starting with the cheapest, which he always deemed "adequate, I reckon." He ended up at the high-end, $20,000 caskets which were always "the one I 'spect I'll end up in when the good Lord calls me home."

"Yessir," the old man would intone, knocking his skinny knuckles on the box to produce a deep metallic sound, "this one here's the one I put my sweet Rosalee in when she passed in 'seventy-six. God rest her sweet old soul."

The result averaged $14,557 a trip, the commissions of which, when figured with the ten percent stake in the business old man Garrison personally had given him, totaled more than $100,000 a year for Cyrus McKay. When he wasn't upgrading customers into luxurious boxes, he came in early or stayed late, sometimes sleeping overnight, depending on the Garrison brothers' schedules.

McKay slept over the night of May 1. There were three bodies laid out in the viewing rooms, and the last family stayed until nearly midnight. He made his rounds after they left, turning off the coffeepots, killing the lights in the empty embalming room, locking the doors, and forwarding the phones to the small apartment at the back of the renovated turn-of-the-century mansion.

By 6:30 A.M. on May 2, McKay was reversing the ritual from the night earlier, starting with the lights and the coffeepot. Six hours of sleep wasn't enough, and his body told him so. He vowed to talk to the Garrisons about cutting back on the overnight tours. He saw the open door to the embalming room as soon as he turned the corner. The old man could have sworn he'd closed it the night before, another reason, he surmised, that he needed to cut back on his hours. He pushed his hand through the door to the light switch on the wall, following it in.

McKay was in midstep when the light illuminated the woman on the cement drain table and he was so startled that he fell, hearing the bone in his right wrist snap like a string of uncooked spaghetti.

He had seen hundreds of corpses in his career, but he had never seen anything like this. The woman was nude and lying on her back with her hands folded prayerlike over her breasts. Each leg dangled off the side of the table, and at the base of her vagina was an arrangement of red carnations with baby's breath.

Cyrus McKay wondered if the fall had made him hallucinate. The elderly man moved closer to the slab and knew the corpse was real. The woman's eyes were locked wide open, staring at the huge fluorescent light over the table as if she had seen something horrific in it. Crimson lipstick was smeared a good inch beyond the lines of her lips, painting a grotesque clown's smile beneath the startled eyes.

Whoever had left her that way had also used the lipstick to scrawl a message across her lower belly, just above her pubic hair. Cyrus McKay didn't take the time to make it out. He realized his right wrist was broken when he tried to pick up the receiver on the wall phone. He tucked the receiver in the crook of his neck with his left hand and punched 911 with his left index finger.

The old man was flustered and grew impatient quickly.

"Yes, dammit, murder," he repeated to the dispatcher. "Of course, this is a funeral home. But I'm telling you it isn't one of *our* bodies. What I'm saying is, I guess it must have happened *here.* Last night, I s'pose. Do you understand what I'm trying to tell you?

"Young woman, get me somebody I can talk to."

14

The copier stopped, and the unanticipated silence made the big man swing around from the documents stacked on the floor. The red light on the control panel was pulsating; the toner cartridge was empty.

Winston Robishawn cursed beneath his breath and scanned the room for supplies. Subbing on the overnight shift hadn't been a problem. He owed Greg Gaines a shift, and Gaines had jumped at the chance for a three-day weekend. Robishawn had checked earlier. The head nurse, actually one of only two on the overnight shift, was Patty Werner. She was cool, laid-back, and working on a new potboiler, which meant she'd spend most of the shift reading in the coffee room.

Even so, Robishawn had had a close encounter with the second nurse, who had wanted him to help her do a random audit of the medicine closet. The pill check was done mandatorily at the end of every month; procedure called for two random checks in the interim. Robishawn begged off, claiming that Jerry Stephens had asked him to do some filing on the patient records. The random pill checks, the big attendant said, could be done any time.

"You know how Stephens is," he told her. "He hates paperwork and pawns it off on everybody else. And you also know you don't want to piss him off."

The nurse, once the unfortunate victim of a Stephens confrontation, bought the story, and he was relatively certain she wouldn't mention anything to Stephens.

Robishawn found a cartridge, but didn't have a clue how to replace the old one. Fifteen minutes studying instructions with type so tiny it hurt his eyes, and he finally resurrected the copier. He stuck the final five files on the automatic feed and turned his attention to reassembling files he had already copied.

Surreptitiously copying forty-two sets of files was a pain in the ass, as Robishawn had known when he volunteered. The fact that he offered at all surprised even him. When he first saw Jeb Quinlin, the big black man figured him for another drunk redneck. The cowboy boots, the Wranglers, and the Texas twang you only perfected in racist pockets of small-town Texas.

Aggravating the formula, Robishawn figured, was the fact Quinlin was a cop. He himself hadn't had any run-ins with good-ol'-boy cops, but they were legendary for racism, even in a supposedly enlightened city like Dallas.

But there were cracks in the stereotype Robishawn originally built for Quinlin. The cop was the only inmate off the van who had come up to him after he kept Raphael from gagging on his tongue. Quinlin had been genuine when he called him a hero, even if it embarrassed him. And unlike some of the yuppie assholes on the ward, Quinlin hadn't asked him for special favors or tried to treat him like an orderly or manservant.

Quinlin was at Cedar Ridge under duress, just like about everyone else. But, Robishawn noticed, the cop appeared to be genuinely working the program, even if he pissed and moaned about it. Quinlin's confrontation with Bergoff was legendary on the ward, and Robishawn admired anyone strong enough to take on the pompous psychiatrist.

Besides, he knew Quinlin couldn't be a racist when he befriended Lem Buffey. When he had left Cedar Ridge a few days before, Buffey, a black Vietnam vet who owned a small courier service, was facing revocation of his probation, if not a new set of charges, for drunk driving. This one would be a felony, which meant prison time. Buffey was a quiet, shy, sincere guy with two kids at home and a daughter in college. He also presided over a self-made business that was in deep financial trouble. Robishawn had helped Quinlin make an unauthorized call in Buffey's behalf, and he had overheard Quinlin's side of the conversation.

Quinlin didn't know Buffey's probation officer, but he knew a friend of a friend who knew the P.O. A week later, Buffey was notified that his probation would remain intact if he successfully completed alcohol rehab; there would be no additional charges. Buffey never knew Quinlin made the call.

Robishawn knew there was yet another reason he had volunteered to help Quinlin. The thought of a killer walking the halls scared absolute hell out of him.

15

Anne Marie Ingram, fifty-one years old, twice divorced, and twenty-five pounds past prime, had been discharged from Cedar Ridge less than forty-eight hours when Cyrus McKay discovered her on the embalming slab.

Uniformed officers answering the 911 call at the funeral home also discovered Anne Marie's clothes, a yellow-and-green flowered, scooped Mexican dress with puffed sleeves, a pair of pantyhose, bikini panties, and a 38-D bra folded neatly beside her sandals on the front porch of the mortuary. The neckline of the dress smelled distinctly of fresh bourbon.

The clown face and the carnations, coupled with the way the body was displayed on the drain slab, made her death the most dehumanizing and macabre thus far, a clear indication to McCarren that the killer was escalating in his frenzy. But more important, Anne Marie Ingram was found *outside* the hospital, which meant the killer had unlimited mobility; a hospital staff member, perhaps, or a patient who had been discharged recently.

Ingram's body, like those of Willard Beane and Kristin Williamson, bore no physical trace of violence. The killer's personalized message this time said, *The weak and pitiful perish.*

As soon as he saw the message on her abdomen, Paul

McCarren phoned Cedar Ridge for Dr. Wellman Bergoff III. The psychiatrist, irritable and condescending, reluctantly agreed to meet the homicide detective at the medical examiner's office to identify the body. In actuality, Anne Marie Ingram's identity was confirmed well before Bergoff arrived at the morgue. A computer comparison matched the dead woman's fingerprints with those of Ingram, who had been arrested three times over the last eight years for drunk driving.

Having heard Jeb Quinlin's horror stories about the infamous Bergoff, McCarren wanted to see how the psychiatrist reacted to Anne Marie's body. Not to mention that the computer had also given him an ace in the hole. And he couldn't wait to play it.

The detective told the morgue attendant to take his time rolling the body into the viewing room. A year earlier in the same room, McCarren had gotten a stunning confession from a man he didn't even consider a prime suspect. As the attendant rolled in the sheet-draped body of his late girlfriend, the man began pacing, sweating, and running his hand over his forehead.

"I'll tell you what happened," he had blurted out, "but just don't make me look at her. You can't make me look at her!"

Relieved, the man calmly admitted to beating his girlfriend with a claw hammer until her face was unrecognizable. A jury sentenced him to life without parole.

McCarren had added the suspect-in-the-viewing-room scenario to his growing repertoire of investigative techniques. It was a left-handed way of unofficially interviewing suspects and, at the same time, gauging their reactions to the victims' bodies.

Bergoff was disinterested. He sat in a straight-backed chair, one of the few pieces of furniture in the spartan, cement-floored room. Fastidiously, the psychiatrist adjusted his tie and coat, and glanced frequently at his watch. The detective didn't see nervousness. What he saw was a vain man who was bored and obviously considered himself far too important to be spending his time in a morgue identifying someone he didn't give a damn about.

McCarren tried to engage him in conversation, but Bergoff was wholly unresponsive. Twice he declined the detective's offer of coffee. He didn't take the bait on the weather or his work. Maybe the corpse would jar him, but McCarren wasn't holding out a lot of hope. The guy was ice.

When finally the attendant appeared and pulled the sheet down to Anne Marie's waist, McCarren was disappointed to see the body had been cleaned, apparently in preparation for autopsy. He knew the impact would have been stronger with the killer's handiwork still intact. He positioned himself for an unobstructed view of Bergoff.

McCarren noticed that Bergoff actually had to suppress a yawn before nodding and saying, "That would be the late Ms. Ingram. Are we through at this point?"

"This would be the same woman who was in one of your therapy groups at Cedar Ridge Hospital, Doctor?" McCarren asked for the record. "And that would be the basis for your identification?"

"Yes."

"If I told you that Ms. Ingram were found on an embalming table, her face painted, naked, carnations placed against her vagina, and a lipstick message left on the body," McCarren said, studying the doctor's face, "what would that mean to you? That would obviously be a symbol of something, right?"

"It would have some profound significance to her rather tragic background," the doctor said. "However, I should tell you that I am not comfortable discussing this patient's history until I have had the opportunity to consult with the hospital and its counsel. Now, is that all?"

McCarren played his hole card. A stickler for routine, the detective had already run Bergoff through TCIC, the Texas

Crime Information Computer, and NCIC, the corresponding national network. He had been surprised when he got two hits on this great savior of mental health and sanity. Now the smug bastard wanted to be cute.

"Have it your way," McCarren said. "Certainly, I want you to be comfortable, Doctor. You don't want to talk about Ingram, that's fine. For now. But you and I have plenty of other things to talk about.

"Like your wife's lipstick. I figure you'll be more comfortable talking at the station."

Dr. Wellman Bergoff III had been arrested two years earlier on charges of criminal trespass and violation of a restraining order. McCarren's computer showed that the charges, both misdemeanors, had been dismissed "in the best interests of justice," a garbage legal euphemism that meant the victim declined to pursue charges or some slick defense attorney concocted a sweetheart deal. Simultaneously with the filing of the charges, according to civil records, the psychiatrist had been sued for divorce.

Claire Bergoff had called police to the couple's fashionable North Dallas house, according to the original offense report, shortly after she returned home in the evening from her antique studio. At the time, according to civil court records, her estranged husband was forbidden by a restraining order from being on the premises, pending completion of court-ordered marriage counseling. When Ms. Bergoff walked into the master bath, she said, she found her makeup drawer open and two tubes of lipstick lying on the counter. Across the mirror, someone had used the lipstick to scrawl *Adulterous slut.*

"Complainant Ms. Bergoff says there is no doubt her husband was the intruder," the investigating patrolman had noted in his report. "She recognized his handwriting."

Five hours after the first call and before uniformed officers could locate her husband, a frantic Claire Bergoff phoned police again. She told them she had heard her name called from the study. She recognized her husband's voice, and when she peeked around the door into the room, she found him sitting naked in a leather chair, his feet propped on the desk. He smiled at her and continued masturbating. Ms. Bergoff fled in her robe to the garage, left in her Mercedes, and called police from her cell phone. Dr. Bergoff was gone when police arrived, but the officers had no reason to doubt Ms. Bergoff's story. According to the police report, there was pool of what appeared to be sperm in the chair.

Claire Bergoff filed for divorce two days later. She restored her maiden name, Smith, and when the divorce was finalized, she moved back to New York. McCarren had managed to locate her divorce attorney, who explained that his client had been happy to drop the criminal charges in return for an uncontested and lucrative property settlement in the divorce. The good doctor, according to the divorce attorney, had taken a three-month leave of absence from Cedar Ridge to undergo counseling, a perfunctory move designed to keep his medical license intact and to keep his staff position at the hospital.

Bergoff, still angered at being driven downtown in McCarren's unmarked car, was impassive now as he sat in Interview Room 2 on the third floor of Central Headquarters. All three interview rooms were empty, but McCarren chose Room 2 because it was the most starkly depressing of the lot. The stench of body odor and nicotine hung in the pale green, peeling paint, and except for dumping the butts and cleaning obvious debris off the metal table in the center, the cleaning crew had long ago given up on Room 2. It was the room where Captain Will Fritz and Detective Gus Rose had sweated Lee Harvey Oswald, and old-timers swore it hadn't been painted in the thirty-five ensuing years.

"Are you required to inform me of my rights?" the doctor asked smugly.

"Only if I consider you a suspect," McCarren said. "Right now, I'm merely conducting an interview of possible witnesses in a murder case. You knew the deceased. You might have information that would help me. Should I consider you a suspect, Doctor?"

The psychiatrist merely glared.

"So about this lipstick message on your wife's mirror," McCarren said, making no attempt to limit his questions to Anne Marie. "So why didn't you just leave Claire a letter? Why the lipstick?"

"Divorces, if you haven't been through one, Detective, can be very acrimonious," the psychiatrist said. He scanned the room as he spoke, disgust registering on his face. "Events are misconstrued, even fabricated, all to the end of distorting the truth for personal gain and vindictiveness. Innocent people often are harmed in the process. Perhaps, Detective, you've noticed that same phenomenon in your investigations here."

"Actually, no," McCarren said. "Nine out of ten people I bring into this room are guilty as hell. They're not about innocence. More about killing and lying."

The detective was on comfortable turf. His visitor, he noticed, kept his manicured hands in his lap, apparently too appalled with the filthy table to risk touching it. McCarren smiled and opened the manila file in front of him.

"I've gone over your original charges," the cop said, "and they're actually pretty depraved, I would think, for a man of your background."

McCarren leaned back in his chair and put his Bostonians on the desk, continuing the smile. He flipped through the file in his lap.

"Say, do you know what Quinlin calls you?" McCarren said. "I mean, he's got a nickname for you."

"I'm sure I wouldn't know," Bergoff said dryly, "but I anticipate you're about to tell me."

"Funny thing," McCarren said. "At first I thought it was just a takeoff on your name."

The detective pulled a single sheet from the file and held it up.

"And now I find out reading your file my ol' partner may be clairvoyant," McCarren said. "He calls you 'Jackoff.' Now how would he know that without this file? You think our friend Quinlin is a genuine clairvoyant or what?"

"What your friend is a desperate alcoholic in substantial need of clinical therapy," Bergoff said.

"Your ol' lady didn't already hate you enough?" McCarren said, pushing the pressure point. "You had to choke your chicken in front of her? Spooge in her chair? So, Doctor, what was that all about?"

"I'm late for a staff meeting," Dr. Bergoff said, rising from his chair. "You've said I am not a suspect. Good day."

"I'll be at the hospital later this afternoon," McCarren said. "Do the real shrinks out there know you're a twisted puppy yet?"

The door slammed hard. The young detective opened it and saw Bergoff repeatedly punching the elevator button.

"Would you like a uniformed unit to take you back to your Mercedes?"

Bergoff stared, saying nothing.

"Have a nice day, Doctor."

McCarren didn't tell him the elevator was for authorized personnel only and that it required a key to operate.

Amid a hospital ward rife with pathetic backgrounds and abysmal failures, none approached the depravity of Anne Marie's. Indeed, her grotesque demise on the cement embalming table was wholly symbolic of the tortured life she had endured since her years as a preadolescent.

Quinlin began piecing Anne Marie's background together from inside the hospital as soon as he was alerted to her death by McCarren. Jerry Stephens reviewed the former patient's file, including Bergoff's own therapy notes, and passed the information to the detective.

Anne Marie never volunteered anything about herself. Virtually everything in her file had come from therapy sessions in which Dr. Bergoff had browbeaten her. Anne Marie had actually been in Bergoff's advanced group twice, having suffered some kind of psychiatric meltdown during her first stint. The "episode," as it was referred to in the file, had necessitated her transfer to the psychiatric lockdown ward for about three weeks. While there, Anne Marie had tried to hang herself with her bra on a shower rod. A psychiatrist on that unit prescribed a strong antidepressant and, after observing her for a week and a half, transferred her back to the alcohol rehab ward.

Anne Marie was the only child of a respected, small-town undertaker who owned three funeral homes in East Texas. From the time Anne Marie was seven, her father had forced sex on her. The first time, she reluctantly admitted in group therapy, she kept her sanity by fixating on a bouquet of red carnations while her father ravaged her. When she was young, she believed he molested her in the embalming room because it was a good place to hide from her mother. But as a teenager, she realized the cement embalming table was an integral part of her father's sexual ritual.

When she was fifteen, she bought a five-gallon can of gasoline, doused the embalming room in the middle of the night, and tossed a match inside. It didn't do any good. Her father continued to rape her until she ran off a year later to live with a cousin in Dallas. She said she knew she was an alcoholic when she swallowed her first taste of wine. It soothed her and, temporarily at least, she didn't think about the embalming room. She didn't drink socially; she drank by herself to get drunk. She was unrepentant, and she admitted herself to Cedar Ridge only because she had suffered painful, organic damage to her liver. And nobody knew better than she that her chances of living alcohol-free were virtually nonexistent when she walked out of the hospital.

16

Clint Harper's cubicle was in a dead-end corner, the only one that had a window. The window faced north, overlooking the only square block of greenery preserved in downtown Dallas. But the city's forefathers finally screwed that up, too, digging up a two-hundred-year-old live oak by its roots to build a circular fountain in the middle. Once a week, city parks employees dumped enough chlorine into the fountain to turn the water cobalt blue, an electric hue that reminded Harper of Tidy Bowl and which prompted gawking tourists from Omaha to gouge each other appreciatively in the ribs. The window was a begrudging concession to the *Dallas Register and News*'s only Pulitzer Prize winner.

Harper sipped his third cup of black coffee and reread the offense report, which had been left in his chair by the night city editor. The DPD report had a yellow sticky attached: *FYI: We only got eight graphs in the ayem paper. Rookie on night cops can't find his ass. Good sty here if you can find it. Want to help us out? Kim.* Kim Wester was the best editor on Metro, and she had earned Harper's respect over a decade of plane crashes, natural disasters, political scandals, and breaking crime. Wester also had a keen eye for the offbeat. Harper had read the eight graphs that made the inside of the metro section (WOMAN'S

BODY FOUND IN NW FUNERAL HOME) and shared Wester's reaction: Somewhere beneath this shit was a pony.

The offense report was filed by uniformed officers and didn't show that a detective had been assigned. He spun the worn Rolodex to Jeb Quinlin's number, dialed the phone, and was surprised to hear Paul McCarren's voice on the other end. He was even more surprised at the young cop's evasiveness about his partner's whereabouts. The reporter had known McCarren only since he had transferred to CAPERS two years earlier, but he and Quinlin went back years to Harper's drinking days. McCarren wasn't operating by the unspoken cop-reporter code—Quinlin trusted Harper and therefore McCarren should trust Harper. The reporter bludgeoned him into meeting him for lunch at the Farmers Market. He knew he could get the answers in person.

"I called Quinlin," McCarren said as soon as they slid into the worn vinyl booth, "and he told me to go ahead and lay it out for you."

The veteran reporter listened silently, occasionally sipping his iced tea, while the detective told him about Quinlin's mandatory hospitalization, the impending civil service hearing to terminate him, and his divorce.

"That's crap," Harper said, "but I knew it was a matter of time if he didn't hang it up. Being good isn't good enough. Not any more. DPD's changed. The *Register*'s changed. Image is more important than results. If I hadn't quit, I'd have been shitcanned three years ago. I saw the writing on the wall. But, I'll tell you, cold turkey was the toughest thing I ever did."

Except for an infrequent lunch to exchange rumors and, occasionally, a telephone call to swap information, Harper hadn't seen much of Quinlin since he quit drinking. The reporter hated sanctimonious recovering alcoholics who preached sobriety, and he checked himself whenever he had been tempted to talk to Quinlin about his drinking. Harper hadn't made any secret of the fact he was on the wagon, but neither had he appeared on the doorsteps of his former drinking buddies like some Jehovah's Witness with a personal road map to individual salvation. Three years without a drink, he was still fighting the urge daily.

The quiet conversation in the booth was interrupted long enough to appease a harried, persistent waitress. McCarren ordered a chef's salad and a cup of homemade potato soup. Harper opted for the Farmers Market specialty, chicken-fried steak and cream gravy, with sides of mashed potatoes, black-eyed peas, and mustard greens. Since he quit drinking, he ate anything that didn't bite him first, a habit that expanded his belt by a notch and now threatened to make his thirty-four-inch pants extinct.

Over lunch, Harper steered the conversation back to the reason he had called in the first place—Anne Marie Ingram. Hers was death with a twist, the bizarre kind of story that attracts reporters like lawyers to car wrecks. A funeral director opens up and finds a mysterious corpse on his embalming table that didn't belong to him. The eight graphs in the morning paper hadn't mentioned the flowers left at the base of her crotch or the smeared message written across her abdomen, and when McCarren casually mentioned them, Harper reached inside the breast pocket of his blazer for his reporter's notebook and pen.

The reporter made a mental note to look up the cops' names on the report when he got back to the office. They were ratfuckers. The *Register* hadn't mentioned the flowers or the message because the cops hadn't included them in their report. It was a cat-and-mouse game that cynical cops, or more likely senior police brass, played with the media. Knowing a crime had elements that would create media scrutiny and cause them discomfort and realizing that cop reporters thumbed through every offense report, police simply omitted those pertinent parts of the crime scene.

McCarren saw the reporter's reaction.

"It wasn't the beat cops," the detective said, reading his reaction. "Barrick told them at the scene to leave out the evidence when they wrote their report."

"What's it to Barrick?" Harper asked, his instincts kicking in. "Ingram wasn't the mayor's girlfriend and she wasn't off the Highland Park social register. BFD."

"The big fucking deal," McCarren said, leaning across the table and dropping his voice, "is that Anne Marie Ingram isn't the only stiff we got with the same MO. There's another one for sure and maybe a third."

Harper stopped writing in his notebook.

"How'd Barrick hide the other two?"

"Easy. They were found at Cedar Ridge, literally just a few feet from Quinlin," McCarren said. "The first one, a guy, the hospital tried to pass off as a natural causes or suicide. The other one went straight to supplemental."

The Texas Open Records Act required all original police reports to be released to the public. However, supplemental, or follow-up reports were the exclusive internal domain of the cops. Public release of those reports, the cops' lobby had convinced the legislature, would reveal "investigative techniques" and impede ongoing investigations.

"But, hey, there's more than just the bullshit messages left on the body," McCarren said. "All three were at Cedar Ridge for alcoholism. Ingram had only been released a couple of days ago."

"Same causes of death?"

"Don't know yet. There's not a mark on any of 'em. Berryman's pulling his hair out."

Clint Harper spent the next ten minutes reassuring the detective his name would never be connected to the story.

"I'm telling you," McCarren repeated, "Barrick would have my ass in the same barrel with Quinlin if this comes back to me. But Jeb, well, he told me to run it down to you. Says your story will be a two-fer, that it'll jar Cedar Ridge enough to make them cooperate and it'll cause Barrick to suck his balls into his throat."

"Not to mention what it might stir with the *pre*vert killer."

Quinlin had always understood the media, Harper in particular. An honest reporter, one you could trust, reached 700,000 members of the public on an average weekday morning; on Sundays, that audience went to about a million. A trustworthy reporter was as effective to police work, Quinlin knew, as a good partner. Better sometimes. More like an insurance policy. Quinlin and Harper had used each other, mutually, knowingly, and beneficially, for years. Each had helped the other to the summit in their respective professions. And along the way, they had killed a couple of boxcar-loads of Budweiser's best.

Harper waited for McCarren to get out of the parking lot. He used his cell phone to leave a voice message for Kim Wester, whose shift didn't being until three P.M.

"I found the pony," he said. "But it'll take two, maybe three days to round him up."

Clint Harper trusted McCarren's information, but before it could ever see print, he'd need a second, corroborating source. Well before The *Register & News* adopted its two-source policy for anonymously contributed information, Harper had made it a personal practice to have a minimum of two people saying the same thing before it appeared under his byline. While the policy hadn't kept him from being sued eleven times in ten years, it had ensured that the white-collar thieves, drug smugglers, and sociopaths and their lawyers hadn't been awarded a single red cent in libel damages. Harper knew where he could get his second source, and he headed for SWIFS.

The Southwest Institute of Forensic Science was a spartan,

cement-gray afterthought at the end of the circular artery that fed the emergency room of Parkland Memorial Hospital. The relationship between SWIFS and Parkland's ER, one of the best and busiest trauma centers in the country, was one of convenience. On any given night, under the pulsating strobes of red and blue emergency lights, a substantial number of the gut-shot, stabbed, and bludgeoned victims pulled unconscious from the ambulance would defy the best human and medical skills inside the ER. After the synchronized high-tech trauma teams exhausted their bag of code blues, tracheotomies, and electric heart paddles to no avail, the controlled chaos abruptly stopped and rote resignation took over. Orderlies paid by the hour disconnected the electrodes, tubing, catheters, and bags, and offloaded the remains onto black vinyl-and-steel gurneys. Pausing to drape the gurney with a sheet, they delivered the fresh corpses down the long dim corridor with the maze of Pavlovian right angles to SWIFS. Before dawn, Berryman and his troops would remove the bloody sheets and cut, drain, probe, measure, weigh, and analyze to pinpoint the precise reason why the body in front of them was no longer among the living.

It wasn't the dead, but the living that made Harper routinely dread the trip to the ME's office. He had never made a trip to SWIFS without encountering victims of the deceased in the cramped outer waiting room. On this day, a Hispanic family claimed a corner of the room, apparently awaiting the release of a nine-year-old boy who had drowned in a flooded gravel pit in West Dallas. In his early years on the cop beat, Harper had seen a hundred similar families huddled together in ME's offices. He hated the intrusive but mandatory interviews with SODPs, reporters' shorthand slang for "survivors of dead people."

Dr. Mark Berryman's secretary rescued Harper quickly and granted him five minutes with the ME—the only slack, she said, in his schedule. Berryman was legendarily gun-shy of the media, but Harper, the notable exception, had standing entree. For the record, Berryman had nothing to say. He did, however, pitch a manila envelope of photographs—"slab shots" of Williamson and Ingram—on his desk so that Harper could get the exact wording of the messages left on their bodies. Off the record and not for attribution, the doctor noted that toxicological screens had been ordered which, hopefully, would provide the causes of death.

"Otherwise, your guess would be *almost* as good as mine." The doctor grinned. In their undergraduate days in Alpine at Sul Ross State University, he and Harper had delivered pizzas and, for a semester, had shared the same student crash-pad apartment.

From SWIFS, Harper made it to the Dallas North Tollway and was at the administrator's office at Cedar Ridge Hospital in twenty minutes. He never got past Raleigh Waymon's secretary. He hadn't phoned for an appointment, she explained cordially enough, and Mr. Waymon had meetings all afternoon. Over her shoulder, Harper could see a man's arm, a phone, and an ear.

"I understand," Harper said, raising his decibel level. "Would you tell Mr. Waymon that I'm writing a story about two deaths in the alcohol ward at Cedar Ridge? I need any comment he might have by three P.M. tomorrow. Otherwise, I'll just put him down for a 'no comment.' "

Harper nodded to the picture of two girls on the secretary's desk as he laid his business card in front of her. "Those are beautiful girls," he said. "You've got to be proud."

17

The "Twelve-Step Murders," as Jeb Quinlin had taken to calling them, were precisely the reason Mark Berryman had become a forensic pathologist. Long before he knew how he'd spend his adult life, Berryman was consumed as a kid with riddles, crosswords, and logic problems. Nothing—not the girls attracted to his fresh-scrubbed, boyish handsomeness or high school football, at which he had excelled as a quick, elusive tailback—motivated him like a good mystery. In the two decades since he had graduated third in his class at Texas A&M Medical School, Berryman had carved out a national reputation as one of the most painstaking, thorough professionals in forensic medicine. Annually, his expert testimony amounted to mid–six figures, well beyond the salary he earned as medical examiner for Dallas County. He stayed at the Southwest Institute of Forensic Science nonetheless, despite his annual budget battles with penny-pinching commissioners and killer schedules, simply because he thrived on the intellectual diet.

Dr. Berryman regarded the human body as the consummate crime scene, the site of empirical evidence too pure and irrefutable to argue. Fingerprints and polygraphs depended on human interpretation; eyewitness testimony was skewed by fear, prejudice, deceit, or simple human defect and was therefore frequently worthless. But skin, tissue, bone, blood, and urine were immune to the vagaries of human nature. As the clean-shaven, bespectacled pathologist routinely told detectives, "You can wish all you want; it either is or it isn't. The body tells the truth."

On this day, though, the expert's summation to the two detectives seated at the ME's conference table wasn't what they wanted to hear. Captain Barrick, feeling the pressure building in the investigation, had pushed for the meeting even though McCarren, who already had debriefed the ME, told him there weren't any answers.

"Everything I've done," Berryman said, "is inconclusive. Actually worse. I cannot identify the mechanism of death. Obviously, I haven't spent as much time with the Ingram woman as I would like. It is apparent that she, like the two from the hospital, died of acute congestive heart failure, but I still am unable to determine the mechanism that triggered the heart into collapsing. What we've got here, gentlemen, is a scenario of cause and effect. The effect is obvious—a blown-out heart. What we don't have yet is the cause, or the catalyst."

There were other similarities in the deaths, to be sure. Each of the bodies had elevated blood-alcohol levels, a curious finding considering two of the victims were locked inside an alcohol treatment ward at the time of their deaths, but the amounts were medically insignificant. Country-music star Keith Whitley had died of alcohol poisoning with a .35 alcohol blood level, as had a University of Texas freshman who was force-fed bourbon during a fraternity initiation. But all three of the victims in Berryman's morgue were below .10, the legal limit for drunkenness in Texas. Each had fatty deposits in the liver, a clear, organic indication of alcohol abuse, but not nearly enough dystrophy to have killed any of them. All three had an uncommon pallor about them, particularly so considering the nominal amount of time before their bodies were discovered.

Beane had a history of minor cardiovascular problems, but neither Williamson nor Ingram had suffered from preexisting heart conditions. The routine toxicological scans, which monitored the presence of commonly abused drugs from barbituates to amphetamines and cocaine and heroin, were negative. Likewise, there were no traces of the more unusual but not unprecedented poisons, such as arsenic, strychnine, or potassium cyanide.

Berryman sensed the impatience and frustration between the captain and his investigator.

"I have examined the bodies for some of the more unusual causes of homicide, too," he said, "such as insulin. In fact, I've gone over the first two bodies with a magnifying glass, looking for needle punctures. I'm finding nothing."

Even as he spoke, two technicians were probing Anne Marie Ingram's armpits, the quicks of her finger- and toenails, and the skin between her toes and her scalp for hidden injection marks.

"We're early into this," Berryman said. "We will find the mechanism of death. But at this point, I would tell you that it's something truly exotic. I would also tell you that the killer is not anybody's fool. He or she is obviously smart and sophisticated. Forensic psychiatry isn't my bag, but our killer's got to be feeling pretty good about himself. Success breeds success. All of us have our work cut out for us."

Fantastic, Barrick thought. The *Register & News* had carried Ingram's murder inside the metropolitan section. It was only a matter of time, he knew, before reporters discovered the two from Cedar Ridge, which undoubtedly would move the story to the front page. The thought of even more bodies made him cringe. Then he'd have a full-scale media circus on his hands.

"It goes without saying," the homicide captain said, "that we're not confirming or denying anything to the media."

Neither of Clint Harper's conspirators said a word.

18

For Madeline and Quinlin, the truth lay somewhere beneath the surface, heavy and unspoken. Neither was confident enough to risk honesty, so the conversation in the dayroom was awkward and superficial.

"What are you going to do when you leave here?" Quinlin asked.

"I'm going to lie in a Jacuzzi for two hours," Madeline said, "and *maybe* that'll soak the disinfectant out of my pores. No more *eau de Cedar Ridge.* Then I'm getting a haircut, maybe even get it colored. As we both know, I'm way too young to be getting gray hair. This place has sped up the aging process."

Quinlin didn't notice her grin. He was still on the Jacuzzi. He had certainly never seen Madeline naked, but he had fantasized enough to feel sufficiently guilty. The Jacuzzi gripped his mind, and he wondered if his face was giving him up.

Quinlin and Madeline had known for two days she would be discharged on Tuesday morning. A night earlier, he had tossed and turned, rehearsing the things he wanted to tell her before she left. All of it sounded feeble now. But in just two weeks, she had captivated his thoughts, and in a rarity in his world, she had made him look forward to the next day.

She also had made him a pendulum. One moment, he believed she felt something, too. She had taken to lightly touching the back of his hand when they drank coffee late at night and squeezing his shoulder when they went their separate ways. He thought even Saint Luke had noticed, too. Occasionally, for a split second, the couple's eyes locked on each other and he thought he saw genuine affection. Then he talked himself into knowing better. Madeline was rich, and when her impending divorce settlement came through, she'd still be worth millions. She looked, moved, and dressed like a Neiman Marcus model. Back on the outside, she'd have to fend off the yuppie studs with pepper gas. He couldn't picture her at The Mansion or Star Canyon at a table for one. Quinlin didn't kid himself. His eyes had cleared, a steady diet had added skin tone and eight relatively well distributed pounds to his lanky frame, and the stoop was lifting, which restored an inch back to his height, but he knew he was still no bachelor of the year, not in the circles in which Madeline moved. Their differences would be more pronounced than even his and Sarah's. Sarah was a wannabe; Madeline was genuine, by God, wealthy. And he was a forty-five-thousand-dollar-a-year cop who probably wouldn't even have that when he walked out of Cedar Ridge.

Now, looking at her, he was certain he had misread everything. If he had appealed to Madeline, however briefly, it was simply because they were locked behind the same walls. Quinlin figured any bond between them was like the old line from Darrell Royal, the University of Texas's legendary football coach and oft-quoted philosopher: *Ol' something looks better than ol' nothing.* Another axiom, one often repeated by Jerry Stephens, had also ricocheted through his mind as he tried to sleep a night earlier: *Don't make any major life decisions for the first year; you're too screwed up to make a decent decision.*

"I'm scared, Jeb," Madeline said. "I don't know what's going to happen."

"You mean about drinking?" he asked. "Naw, you're tough; you'll make it."

"I'm scared about everything," she said, ducking her brown eyes toward the table. "I've got an appointment tomorrow with my lawyer. Beau's offered a settlement. Last thing he wants is this to go to a jury. But if there's a problem with the divorce, a delay or something, I don't think I'm going to make this sobriety thing. I'm just real scared right now."

"Well, if he wants to settle, what could go wrong? It isn't a fair settlement?"

Madeline laughed bitterly.

"Oh, it's going to be a hell of a lot fairer than he thinks it is," she said. "Mr. Meggers doesn't have a clue what's about to happen to him."

Madeline read the curiosity in Quinlin's face.

"Beau is trying to make me think he's being magnanimous by giving me two-point-five," she said.

"I'm assuming we're talking in millions, right?"

"Yeah, but when it's all said and done, it'll be closer to six-point-five. And here's the part I really like: He'll be looking at the world through bars."

"Admittedly, I don't have a lot of experience with that many zeroes," Quinlin said, grinning. "I don't get it."

Nor did the detective fully understand when Madeline explained. What was crystal clear was that Beau Meggers, money-laundering mover-and-shaker that he was, had severely underestimated his estranged wife's intelligence and moral outrage, and, equally important, her lawyer's resourcefulness.

Meggers's $2.5-million offer was based on his legitimate set of books, and it represented, as required by Texas community-property statutes, approximately half his lawful assets. Madeline's lawyer, Aaron "Red Dog" Cullens, in all his negotiations with Meggers and his lawyers, had appeared pleased with the settlement, even complimenting them on their fairness.

What Beau Meggers didn't realize was that Madeline, when she still kept books for his construction company, had secreted away thirty bank and trust account numbers for a dummy corporation that was ostensibly a Meggers affiliate. Those accounts, the numbers of which Madeline collected from wire transfers, were scattered from Tacoma to Tampa. The accounts were controlled by a banking consultant who split the profits with Meggers, and they were repositories for roughly $26 million in illicit, South American drug money yet to be laundered through Meggers's construction and hotel management companies.

Red Dog Cullens was a gut-puncher of a divorce lawyer and legendary for being as mean as he was big, a foreboding profile considering he was a Caucasian Sonny Liston with flaming red hair and beard. Quinlin had heard that Cullens wouldn't touch a divorce unless the undivided estate totaled in the seven figures.

"Cullens has made an agreement with the IRS," Madeline said. "As soon as the divorce is final and Beau's check clears, the IRS shows up to grab the twenty-six million. I get fifteen percent of that for telling them where to look. The taxpayers get the rest. Beau goes to jail. How's that for justice? A nice bow on the package, don't you think?"

Quinlin's brow wrinkled.

"Don't let the math hurt you," Madeline said. "That comes to another three-point-nine million, roughly."

"I wasn't doing math," the detective said. "I was wondering what Beau's going to do to you when the feds show up on his doorstep and haul off the cartel's money."

"Cullens is taking care of that," she said. "The feds will make it look like it's coming from a different direction, like maybe the financial consultant, because they're going to arrest him, too. Besides, Beau will think I'm too naïve to figure this out."

"But it's not just Beau I'm worried about," Quinlin said.

"It's not Beau's money."

"Money isn't the issue, Officer," Madeline said, looking him intently in the eyes. She flashed her seductive grin. "How could one person, maybe even two, spend six-point-five million? That'd be obscene."

Maybe even two? There was no mistaking her intent this time, was there? He had hoped for something this obvious, a real signal that she cared, but he was too concerned to follow up. Not now.

"You're right, Madeline. Six million dollars is obscene," he said. "So take the two-point-five and leave this other garbage with the IRS alone. Take it and don't look back. I don't like . . ."

"You don't understand," she said, urgency in her voice. "I can't start my life over living with his filthy little secrets. I wouldn't stay sober. I know me. I wouldn't be good for anybody else.

"I'm not scared about the IRS or drug money," she said. "I just don't want any delays in getting my life back. Beau suffocates me, makes me want to run. Even the thought of being married just on paper makes me crazy. I know I'll be drinking. Without the divorce, I'll never make it."

Quinlin hated seeing her vulnerable, and he put his hand on top of hers. She rolled her hand over, palm up, and squeezed his.

"You're a lot stronger than you give yourself credit for," he said. "If you weren't, you wouldn't be here."

"I won't live like this ever again," Madeline said. "I want a life."

Quinlin winced; it was the same thing Sarah had told him before she left.

Coal Tar appeared at the table, smiling at Madeline.

"You," he said, putting his huge hand on her shoulder, "are holding up the system. Your counselor is waiting to discharge you. Got to get your ol' bed ready for another drunk so we can produce us another modern miracle here. 'Less, o' course, you wanting to stay 'cause the food and the fellowship's so damned good."

Coal Tar turned to Quinlin, the smile vanishing, and leaned down beside the detective's ear.

"Your records are in a white laundry bag," he whispered. "I'll put them in the van and take them to the AA meeting tonight. Be the last one out of the van."

None too soon, Quinlin though, particularly on the heels of Anne Marie's murder.

When the technician was out of earshot, Quinlin spoke fast.

"We don't have much time, so just listen," he said. "Anne Marie was found murdered yesterday, same MO as Willard and Kristin."

"But she just got . . ." she faltered, disbelieving.

Quinlin saw the shock and sorrow on Madeline's face. She didn't need more stress now. There was so much to say and no time.

"Listen, you've got to be careful out there," Quinlin said, taking both of her hands into his. "I'm damned serious about this, Madeline. If anyone should contact you from the hospital—patient or staff—you stay away from them. Then you call me ASAP. Will you do that?"

"Why would—"

"I don't know," the detective said, shorter than he intended. "But whoever's killing people knows them intimately. And Anne Marie was on the outside. So please, just do what I ask you."

He realized how tightly he was holding her hands. He pulled his hands back to the edge of the table and stood.

Madeline walked to him and hugged him tightly, burying her head beneath his chin.

"Everything's all jumbled up right now, Madeline, but

there's something I need to say," he whispered. "I don't know how . . ."

"I know," she said. "Not now."

He felt damp eyelashes on his neck.

"I'll have a new number," she said. "I'll call you and let you know."

"When I get out, can I . . ."

"Yes," she said. "Oh, yes."

She looked up at him. Her kiss was lingering and her arms were wrapped tight around him. Abruptly, she turned and headed toward her counselor's office. She walked quickly, and he watched her until she disappeared around the corner.

Paul McCarren's white Ford was parked in an angle space fifty feet from the Dallas North Chapter of Alcoholics Anonymous when Coal Tar pulled the van into the lot of the small strip shopping center. Quinlin was the last out, and lingered around the van while Coal Tar herded the grousing drunks into the building.

Quinlin reached into the front floorboard and retrieved the laundry bag. By the time he had it, McCarren was standing beside him.

"Barrick's trying to spring you from the joint," McCarren said, taking the bag. "Ingram's death makes it a new ballgame. We need you on the outside. Your counselor apparently is out of the hospital today, so it'll probably be tomorrow before Barrick can get the details worked out."

"Does Bergoff know?" Quinlin asked.

"Hell, no," his partner said. "What we're going to do is get Stephens to claim you checked out voluntarily. Barrick's also going to put out the word that you've been fired, which will be the reason you checked yourself out."

"Bullshit," Quinlin said. "I'm not going for that. The bastard will really do it. I wouldn't trust that bastard as far—"

"You better get inside," McCarren said.

There were maybe twenty-five people in the room, and Quinlin spotted Madeline immediately. She hadn't wasted any time. Part of the program was doing "ninety in ninety," ninety meetings in the first ninety days after discharge. There were fifteen AA chapters in Dallas, and Dallas North was the "chapter of the week" for Cedar Ridge. Madeline knew that, and he hoped she hadn't chosen it for mere convenience.

There was an open chair next to her, but a scraggly guy in his early twenties fell into it as soon as Quinlin spotted it. The guy was a wet drunk, and he could probably count his sobriety by the hours. Quinlin got a cup of coffee and sat two rows back where he could see her. Ten minutes into the meeting, Madeline turned to the back of the crowd, spotted Quinlin, and winked.

His heartbeat quickened, and he felt like a sophomore.

The sun was setting when the meeting broke up, and the western sky was a stunningly brilliant orange with purple clouds. Quinlin was waiting on the sidewalk, three drags into a Marlboro Light, when Madeline walked out. She flashed her mischievous grin, grabbed the cigarette from his hand, and tossed it nonchalantly over her shoulder. Shrugging, he guided her by the arm away from the milling clumps of recovering drunks.

"Beau's being an asshole about the divorce, but I'm all right," she said, anticipating his question. "It's gonna happen, probably tomorrow."

"Great," Quinlin said. "We don't have any time. Listen, I may be getting out tonight or tomorrow. Barrick thinks he needs me on the outside."

"Is that a good idea?" she asked. "Can you stay sober . . . ?"

"Don't know," he said, looking past her shoulder and scanning the crowd. It was instinct. "Call me at Homicide with your new number. If I'm not there, leave it on the machine. Gotta run."

She pulled him back to her, kissing him full on the mouth and pushing her body against his. The intensity and surprise left him lightheaded.

"Please be careful, Officer," she said.

"You too," he answered.

Quinlin headed for the van, watching over his shoulder as she got into her BMW at the curb. He didn't see the man staring intently from the black 928S Porsche.

19

Detective Paul McCarren felt his heart quicken as he scanned The *Register & News* through the Plexiglas in the newspaper rack. Clint Harper's copyrighted story dominated the top of the front page, unreeling over all six columns beneath a headline that said SERIAL KILLER STALKS RECOVERING ALCOHOLICS. The underline: *Three dead in so-called 12-Step Murders.* It was obvious Harper had talked to Quinlin; his partner was the only person he'd heard use the "Twelve-Step Murders" tag. McCarren quickly shoved two quarters into the slot, grabbed a paper, and headed briskly for his unmarked cruiser. It was 5:15 A.M., still dark, and he flicked on the dome light to read the story.

By CLINT HARPER

> A serial killer who apparently targets recovering alcoholics has killed three people during the past week, leaving macabre messages on their bodies, according to police reports and interviews.
>
> The bodies of Willard Beane, a 65-year-old retired stockbroker, and Kristin Williamson, 26, a model at the Apparel Mart, were discovered in the alcohol treatment ward at Cedar Ridge Hospital

where they were undergoing treatment for alcoholism, sources said. A third victim, 52-year-old Anne Marie Ingram, a real estate agent, was discovered Thursday on an embalming table at a Northwest Dallas funeral home. Sources said Ms. Ingram had been discharged from the same hospital less than 24 hours before her death.

Both women victims were found nude, sources said, and all three of the victims bore messages "relating in some manner to Alcoholics Anonymous," said one source who asked to remain unidentified. While the victims bore no traces of violence, according to sources close to the investigation, lab tests showed that all had alcohol in their systems, forcing investigators to rely on pending toxicological tests for a cause of death.

"I can neither confirm nor deny that the deaths are related at this point," said Captain Bill Barrick, head of the Homicide Division. "I'm not going to say anything that would jeopardize our investigation."

Raleigh Waymon, vice president of administration at Cedar Ridge Hospital, had no comment.

The *Register & News*, however, confirmed through family members and friends that all three victims had been patients at Cedar Ridge . . .

Harper's story was intricate in its insider detail, and it jumped to another thirty inches of copy inside the paper. It quoted verbatim the wording of the messages left on the bodies and mentioned that all the victims' psychiatrist was Dr. Wellman Bergoff III, who also refused to comment. As he read the story, McCarren grinned, imagining Barrick's and Bergoff's reaction when Harper showed up with questions. The detective read the story to the last paragraph, and took a deep breath.

There was nothing to indicate he had been the leak. Besides, the information could have come from several places—the medical examiner's office, the hospital staff, families of the victims, maybe even someone else in CAPERS. He wasn't the exclusive proprietor of the information. That was what he was prepared to tell his captain if he asked.

"I wouldn't give you a ghost's chance in hell," Jerry Stephens said heatedly. "You walk out of here after barely two weeks, and you're going to drink. Sure as hell. Even after twenty-eight days, the odds of drinking again are fifty-fifty, maybe sixty percent if you go to AA every day. You prepared to bet your life on odds like that?"

Captain Bill Barrick didn't give Quinlin a chance to answer. The captain had arrived at Cedar Ridge agitated and mad. He didn't have to read Harper's story; the deputy chief in charge of detectives called him before 5:00 A.M. and read it to him.

"He's a cop," Barrick said. "We got people dropping like flies, and his job is to stop it. Now the media is on it. Quinlin knows this place, he knows the victims, and he may even know the killer. And we all know there's going to be more bodies if we can't pull this freak off the street. I understand I put Quinlin in here. That was then, this is now. He can come back after we clear the case."

"Jeb's worked hard and made some progress," Stephens said, trying to use reason. "But he's a long way from being healthy enough to be on the outside. There're still unresolved issues about his father and his guilt over—well, that's between him and me. He won't make it out there, I'm telling you that right now. You said you put him in here because he couldn't handle stress, and now you're burying him in stress."

The discussion embarrassed Quinlin, particularly in front of his impassive junior partner. People were talking about him in the third person like he was some mental misfit traumatized at potty training who wasn't capable of speaking for himself.

"I seem to be repeating myself," Quinlin said, taking the conversation back. "Right or wrong, I have my own reasons for wanting to be on the outside, so I'm going to go ahead and play along. But the only way I'm doing it is if you call the deputy chief and let me hear it from his own mouth that you're suspending the hearing against me. Spin the dial or I'm staying."

Barrick's assurances that Quinlin's show-cause hearing on termination would be postponed indefinitely, witnessed by his counselor and partner, had burned up an hour. Quinlin still wouldn't budge. Finally, angrily, the captain conceded, and put in a call to Deputy Chief Jon Abrams.

The captain briefed the chief in charge of detectives and passed the receiver to Quinlin.

"So you're assuring me that the show-cause hearing is indefinitely postponed?" Quinlin asked. "Paranoid? No, chief, I'm not imagining anything. I'm serious as a heart attack."

Quinlin locked eyes with Barrick.

"I'm standing here looking at my captain, the same sonofabitch who put me in the freezer here and who wrote up the charges against me," Quinlin said. "I didn't trust him then, and that was *before* I found out he spent last Thursday night screwing my wife."

McCarren winced just as Barrick bolted from his chair.

"What the hell are you—"

Stephens jumped between Barrick and Quinlin.

"Chief," Quinlin said loudly into the phone, "that's conduct unbecoming. My supervising officer is having an affair with my wife. I have proof. That's a violation of regulations. He used a city car to go to my house and screw my wife. That's another violation."

"This is bullshit!" Barrick screamed, reaching frantically around Stephens for the receiver against Quinlin's ear.

Stephens clasped both arms around Barrick in a bear hug and moved him backward across the room, slinging him heavily into a chair against the wall.

"Just shut up," Stephens said. "Honesty's part of the therapy."

The counselor went to his desk and punched the microphone button on his speaker phone, catching the deputy chief in midsentence:

". . . what it takes to make this investigation work."

"This is Jeb's counselor, Jerry Stephens," he said. "For the record, sir, I am absolutely opposed to him leaving the hospital at this point. But if he does, how could he possibly do his job with this conflict-of-interest situation with his supervisor?"

"That's what I was just saying to Quinlin," Chief Abrams said. "Clearing this case is the top priority. It's a hot one, and other people clearly may be in jeopardy. My boss wants a twice-daily briefing on status. However, Quinlin has just made me aware of serious allegations that could reflect on Captain Barrick's professionalism, and I am required by regulation to investigate them. I assure you that Internal Affairs will be notified before end of business today."

Barrick shook his head in disbelief.

"In the interim," the deputy chief said, "I've assured Quinlin that he and McCarren will report directly to me during this investigation. Captain Barrick will have no role whatsoever."

Barrick was out the door before the chief finished his sentence.

Quinlin exhaled deeply and caught Stephens's eyes. The counselor wasn't happy. But Quinlin was relieved, even excited. Was it the thrill of the chase or the satisfaction in knowing that he had just vaporized Barrick's meteoric career? He knew it didn't matter. His mind was already running. He was a cop again. Temporarily, at least.

* * *

Jerry Stephens and Winston Robishawn were in the dayroom when Quinlin and McCarren headed out with Quinlin's gear.

"We've been sitting here trying to figure out how to keep you straight," Stephens said, "against all odds. The pressure's going to be intense on you. The investigation is one thing. Living your life sober is going to be another.

"We thought you could still come back out here and sleep at night, no questions asked. It'd keep you away from the bars, give you a place to decompress."

The offer moved Quinlin, and he shook Stephens's hand, then Coal Tar's.

"I appreciate it, but I can't do that," he said. "I got to make this work on my own."

Quinlin saw Stephens about to jump him. "*With* help from my higher power and the principles I've learned in AA," Quinlin said, remembering the recovering drunk's recitation. "And I'll get to some AA meetings."

Coal Tar handed him a piece of paper with a phone number and an address.

"It's off Central, on Monticello," Coal Tar said. "I got six years' sobriety and, unfortunately, there's no lady right now around my pad. You can bunk with me. Just show up. You need to talk, call me. But don't call me all fucked up. You call *before* you bend your elbow. We straight on that, cowboy?"

Quinlin left the Scout in long-term parking. He needed to know everything McCarren knew and he could get briefed en route to downtown. McCarren could help him get the Scout tomorrow.

The inside of McCarren's squad car should have been familiar ground, with the mike clicks, squelching, and jumble of voices on different frequencies vying to be heard. But the noise was strangely disconcerting, and Quinlin found himself having to concentrate just to hear his partner. The overhead lights on LBJ Expressway, an IHOP sign, the Texaco at the intersection, they all flew by at dizzying speed. Quinlin craned from the passenger seat to see the speedometer. He was surprised to see McCarren was only going sixty-five. Two weeks inside the touchy-feely cocoon, and he was intimidated by the routine pace of his old world.

A couple of miles before the Central exit, he saw a billboard. A team of Clydesdales was pulling a wagon through the snow, with a huge Bud Lite logo. He had been safe at Cedar Ridge. The real world was temptation, and society advertised temptation on bigger-than-life billboards. He felt the fear, not of what someone could do to him, but of what he could do to himself.

Quinlin grabbed the mobile phone off the seat. He had an agenda, a productive one, and he knew he had to stay with it. While McCarren took the Central cutoff south toward downtown, Quinlin dialed Sarah. Three rings, and the recording came on. She had already rerecorded the message, replacing the one with his voice. Now, it was, "*I* am unavailable . . ." Quinlin glanced at his watch; it was almost 10:00 P.M.

"Sarah, this is Jeb," he said in his best attempt to sound neutral. "I'm out of the hospital, and we need to make arrangements for me to pick up my clothes and stuff. Neither of us needs a scene, so just figure out what's best for you and let me know. You can call me at the office. So, uh, well, anyway, just let me know. Hope things are going well for you."

He almost clicked the off button. "I really do," he said, knowing how awkward he sounded.

20

Anne Marie Ingram's murder had changed everything. Before her body was found beyond the meticulously manicured landscape of Cedar Ridge Hospital, Quinlin's and McCarren's theory was that the killer, whoever he or she was, was contained inside the hospital. It was a tedious matter of ferreting out a suspect among forty-two patients, one psychiatrist, a psychologist, four counselors, twelve nurses, four alcohol rehab technicians, and eighteen orderlies, security personnel, and cleaning crew.

The investigation of the hospital staff, assigned with the exception of Bergoff to two junior detectives on the squad, remained the same. The officers were running staff members' backgrounds through computers and looking for any flaw or tidbit that would qualify them as a murder suspect.

The good news was that the number of suspects, at least among patients, had been reduced from forty-two to seven. With Ingram's body being discovered outside the hospital, the killer had to be someone who had had access to the ward, but also the mobility to move beyond it. Seven alcoholics had been discharged from Cedar Ridge since Kristin Williamson's body was discovered and before Ingram's turned up at the mortuary. Quinlin and McCarren kept the file on Bergoff and added the seven discharged drunks to their primary investigation.

The bad news was that the killer was no longer confining the murders to the alcohol treatment ward—which, Quinlin knew, increased the pool of potential victims ad infinitum. The detective also knew that if another body showed up inside the hospital, the killer, more than likely, had to be a staff member. Discharged patients didn't have unlimited access to the hospital.

Making things even more difficult, Quinlin and McCarren didn't know for certain *which* seven of the forty-two patients had been released. Raleigh Waymon, administrator of Cedar Ridge, was a broken record about doctor-patient confidentiality, and he repeatedly refused to tell McCarren the identities of the seven who had been released in the two days following Williamson's death. The hospital's counsel, a medical-malpractice defense lawyer, clearly feared lawsuits from the dead patients' survivors; Daniel Larson, an assistant district attorney, hadn't budged either of them.

Trying to run down all forty-two would be a slow crawl through hell and, Quinlin predicted, no telling how many more corpses would turn up during the interim.

Quinlin phoned Coal Tar and arranged to buy him lunch at Sammie's, a onetime neighborhood grocery store just north of downtown that had been converted into the best barbeque joint in Texas. They carried their trays out onto the patio, which hadn't yet filled up like the main dining room.

The detective surveyed Coal Tar's tray and shook his head incredulously. The plate in the center was piled high with pork ribs and surrounded by smaller satellites of fried okra, red beans, potato salad, cole slaw, a plate of jalapeno peppers and sliced onions, four hot rolls, a piece of coconut cream pie, and three Barq's root beers. The pie, potato salad, and cole slaw were at angles, balanced precariously on the rim of the overburdened tray.

"I figured you for a hernia, carrying all that stuff out here," Quinlin said.

Coal Tar appeared momentarily offended, but continued to douse the ribs with a Coke bottle filled with barbeque sauce. "Man's gotta take care of himself," he said. "My momma told me a man's brain's connected to his stomach. Don't eat right, can't think right."

"Tell you what," Quinlin said, eyeing Coal Tar's stomach, a portion of which lapsed over the edge of the table. "If your brain is proportionate to your gut, you may be the smartest fucker I've ever met."

The black man was in the midst of a mouthful of ribs, but he managed an ominous sideways glare. The detective, meanwhile, picked at his sliced brisket sandwich, enjoying watching the big man eat.

"I remember three of the people who checked out," Quinlin said after a respectful time. "Madeline, Teddy Smith, and Bill Grissom. I need the other four."

The hospital tech was way ahead of Quinlin. He slid a handwritten piece of paper, soiled with a fresh barbeque-sauce fingerprint, across the table.

"I was kinda curious, too," Coal Tar said, "so I took these names off the discharge list, all seven of them. 'Sides, I know there ain't no such thing as a free lunch."

The detective grinned at his friend's foresight. The names were all from Bergoff's advanced counseling group, and all Quinlin knew about them was what he had picked up in the dayroom, during meals, and at AA meetings.

"Anything stand out about these characters, anything that separates them from the pack?"

Coal Tar had just picked another rib clean and was washing down a mouthful of pork with root beer.

"Not really. 'Cept Madeline, of course."

Quinlin's face puzzled.

"She's got an ass that separates her from the *world.*" Coal Tar grinned. " 'Course maybe you had noticed that."

Quinlin tried to remain poker-faced as he ran a napkin over the list of names, folded it, and tucked it in his pocket.

"You gonna see her, aren't you?" Coal Tar was baiting. "Uh-huh, uh-huh. Go ahead and own up, cowboy."

The big man was nodding and laughing his bear laugh, which made his cheeks shake.

"Until I find this asshole, I can't schedule a piss," Quinlin said. "Besides, that's police business. Can't talk about it."

Quinlin hit the coffee machine on his way in, and saw the message light blinking as soon as he sat down. Maybe Sarah was actually entertaining the possibility of surrendering his belongings.

"Jeb, this is Madeline. This is probably nothing, but when I came back from the grocery store and opened my door, a piece of metal fell out. And I, uh, had two hang-ups on my machine. I'm hoping you tried to call and just didn't leave a message. And maybe I'm just freaking out over the Anne Marie thing and being needy. Have I told you how much I hate needy women? But would you call me? Please?"

He checked his watch as he dialed the direct line to Dispatch. Madeline's message was barely ten minutes old. The detective stretched the truth when the dispatcher answered in Communications.

"Burglary in progress with resident inside the house," he told the woman, knowing a unit in Madeline's neighborhood would be dispatched Code 3, with red lights and siren. Otherwise, the unit would respond after three more donuts and two cups of coffee.

Botched burglaries were a dime a dozen in Dallas, occurring about as frequently as pretentious yuppies who zeroed out their bank accounts to lease Lexuses. Still, Anne Marie Ingram, recovering alcoholic, had just been released from Cedar Ridge when she met her demise. Madeline, recovering alcoholic, had just been released, too. Quinlin wasn't interested in playing odds, not with Madeline's life.

He called Tactical Operations and talked to the supervisor, a lieutenant who sounded dubious until Quinlin invoked Deputy Chief Jon Abrams's name.

"You can confirm with the chief," Quinlin said, "but I expect protective surveillance at this address, twenty-four-seven, beginning immediately. You advise before withdrawing it."

He repeated Madeline's address two more times for the TAC lieutenant before he hung up and dialed her number.

Quinlin exhaled deeply at the sound of her voice. She lacked her normal self-assurance, he noticed, but neither did she sound white-knuckled. He tried to sound calm. He told her a police unit was en route and that he had ordered round-the-clock protection for her.

Surprisingly, she didn't argue.

"I'd be there myself," Quinlin said, "but the uniforms are already in the area and can get there quicker. And besides, I'm due at a meeting in fifteen minutes that I can't miss."

Casually, he probed for details, knowing he'd keep her on the phone until the marked unit showed up at her door. The scenario she described sounded like a botched burglary committed, Quinlin surmised, by someone without a lot of experience or someone who had been hurried.

Madeline's machine recorded the two hang-ups at 11:32 A.M. and 12:16 P.M. Calling to see if anyone answered was a common burglar's MO; the second call, probably made from a pay phone within walking distance of the condo, was to reconfirm that no one was home. Madeline said she returned from the store at about 12:35, possibly scaring them before they could finish.

The piece of metal she described falling from her door was

part of a typical burglar's tool, a flexible length of thin metal about an inch wide. Burglars used it to slide the spring-loaded bolt back into the door. It was totally useless on a deadbolt. And even if it hadn't been, Madeline had a high-tech alarm system that she had armed before leaving. Mostly likely rookies or kids, Quinlin figured.

Still, the fact that someone had her new number bothered Quinlin. Hadn't she gotten an unlisted number?

"Well, no," Madeline said, "but I only used my initials on the listing—M. A. Meggers."

Great, Quinlin thought. Every burglar and rapist knows that initials, more often than not, belong to a woman living by herself. Clever as they think they are, there were a lot of single women living with a false sense of security.

"I want you to call the phone company soon as we hang up and change your number to unlisted," he said.

"They're here," Madeline said. Quinlin heard the doorbell ringing in the background.

"Make sure they're the cops before you open the door," he cautioned. "Hey, real quick, you want to have some dinner tonight?"

"I'd be honored," she said.

"You name it."

"Newport's," she said. "Meet you there at eight."

"See you there. Hey, you've got my beep—"

Madeline hung up before he could finish.

21

Dr. Jeremy Aylor's office was on the fourth floor of Central Headquarters, a decent-sized room by DPD standards, with two narrow windows that overlooked a parking lot of white-and-blue police cruisers. The walls were decrepit institutional green like every other office at Central, but several framed family photos on the desk, three diplomas on the wall from the University of Texas, a short, leather couch and two easy chairs, a thriving ficus tree, and other greenery Quinlin couldn't identify made the office comfortable, even warm for a police station.

Granted, it wasn't a conventional place to look for answers in a homicide investigation, but Quinlin also knew there was nothing conventional about the Twelve-Step Murderer. He'd accept help wherever he could find it.

Aylor, a clinical psychologist, had been retained twelve years earlier, originally as a consultant, during one of the darkest chapters in the history of the Dallas Police Department. In barely more than one raw minute, two veteran narcotics detectives and a twenty-four-year-old uniformed female officer were killed trying to serve a search warrant on a drug house in South Dallas. An informant, who swore in an affidavit that he had been in the house during the previous six hours, told officers there were only a man and woman inside and that he saw only one .45-caliber automatic and a nine-millimeter. Not until officers simultaneously slammed through the front and back doors of the shotgun house did they realize their snitch's information was horribly wrong. Inside were six cocaine dealers who cut loose a barrage from MAC-10s and sawed-off shotguns. They were the same drug dealers who had given the so-called informant exactly eight hours to deliver $14,000 in back drug debts he owed them or face an untimely interment in the Trinity River. The drug dealer decided to let the cops pay his debt. Three drug dealers also died in the ensuing gunfight that finally ended eight hours later when cops set fire to the back of the house with tear gas and forced them out.

Aylor was retained in the aftermath to counsel the dead cops' families and the four other officers who were critically wounded in the bloody melee. The city council's Public Safety Committee was so moved by the deaths and destruction that they allocated funds for Aylor to stay on full time. The psychologist's primary job was to counsel cops who killed suspects, saw their partners killed, or who were wounded in duty. Over time, Aylor's job description expanded informally to include cops with drinking and drug problems, cops whose wives buckled under the stress and abandoned them, and "badge-heavy" cops who enjoyed their jobs too much.

Officer Craylon "Mad Dog" Flournoy was the first cop forced to sit on Aylor's couch for being overly exuberant. After six shootings in three years—a record that eclipsed all 2,900 cops at headquarters and four DPD substations—Flournoy's street commander had finally forced him into a psychological evaluation. Aylor's memos were couched in the appropriate psychological terminology, but when Flournoy's captain demanded an understandable definition, Aylor had called the patrolman "a sociopath with a badge" and recommended he be jerked off the streets before he killed again. The civil service board apparently believed Flournoy's explanation that he was a dedicated, aggressive cop who worked the meanest beat in Dallas, and let him keep his badge. Eighteen months later, a television reporter riding with a backup unit for a feature story on drunk drivers saw Flournoy toss a throw-down gun beside the body of a black, unarmed fifteen-year-old.

The shooting splintered the tenuous calm between blacks and whites in Dallas. For three months, the NAACP picketed Central Headquarters every day during the lunch hour. And for six weeks, a group calling itself the New Black Panther Party picketed outside Mad Dog's house with signs and bullhorns. Given Flournoy's propensity for reacting violently, five uniformed officers from the Tactical Squad cordoned off his front yard every day, not knowing whether the violence would come from the black-clad picketers or from the suspended cop inside.

By the time the criminal and civil trials reached the top of the dockets, Mad Dog Flournoy's personnel files, including Aylor's damning psychological evaluation, had been subpoenaed along with the psychologist who wrote it. In both trials, the straightforward Aylor testified that, based on his professional expertise, Flournoy was a menace to society. Flournoy was sentenced to fifteen years in prison for manslaughter, and the City of Dallas shelled out $4.2 million in wrongful death damages to the teenager's survivors. Even cops who agreed with Aylor's bottom line on Flournoy—cops who hadn't fired a single hostile shot in the line of duty in twenty years—went out of their way to dodge Aylor. Overnight, the psychiatrist became a pariah among the professionally cynical people he was committed to help.

Quinlin thought it was strange that Barrick hadn't referred him to Dr. Aylor for an evaluation before forcing him into alcohol treatment. That was a supervisor's MO: Get the shrink's professional concurrence and cover their asses when the cops appealed the inevitable termination with the civil service board.

Was Barrick uncertain about what Aylor would say? Or, more likely, maybe Barrick was in too much of a hurry to get into Sarah's pants to go through the formality.

Quinlin understood the cop's code. There was good reason to close the circle when slime dope dealers made bogus claims of perjury and bribery against cops trying to take them down. Or to back your partner whatever the cost, even with your life. But he also understood there was no reason to blackball Aylor for telling the truth about a cop that even other cops knew was a cowboy who killed first and planted excuses later.

On three previous investigations, Quinlin had dropped off stacks of crime-scene evidence, autopsies, interviews, and offense reports with Aylor. Each time, the psychologist had issued his standard caveat that he was not a trained profiler, and each time he had given Quinlin valuable insights that redirected his investigations. All three cases ultimately were cleared.

Paul McCarren didn't need to be convinced to meet with Aylor, though Quinlin had noticed his partner had been surprised when he suggested the idea.

"Just when I think you're strictly a rubber-hose kind of guy," McCarren grinned, "you come up with something innovative, like seeking professional help."

"I haven't ruled out the rubber hose," Quinlin said, "particularly if Bergoff turns out to be our man."

Dr. Aylor motioned Quinlin and McCarren to the two easy chairs in front of his desk. He poured three cups of black coffee from a coffeemaker on his windowsill, distributed them, and returned to his desk, making idle chitchat about the unseasonably hot weather and the unpredictability of El Niño. The psychologist was tall, maybe six-foot-three, with an angular face and a rapidly receding hairline. Bending his head down to peer over the half-lens reading glasses, Aylor stressed his lack of credentials and noted twice that he was providing "only informal observations." He was pensive for moments at a time, as if he were making sure he had chosen the absolute best words to describe his thoughts.

"There's not much here for us, particularly in the area of cause of death," Dr. Aylor said. "The suspect you're looking for has a unique psychopathy. For example, there's no evidence in the autopsies of sexual assault, but curiously, he actually has some manifestations of a sexual sadist."

McCarren's eyebrows elevated and he turned to his partner. Dr. Aylor didn't want to be interrupted, and he moved quickly to elaborate.

"Sexual sadists strive for domination over their victims. For them, the sexual thrill is dominance and the infliction of pain or suffering. And that thrill is even greater if there is humiliation and degradation. Clearly, there is an attempt on our killer's part, by the messages on the body and the elaborate displaying of the bodies, to humiliate and degrade. That may be as important to him as the actual killing.

"This guy is unusual, it seems, in a couple of respects. First, he has focused his victims on a very specific subgroup of society, alcoholics. This could be because he feels somehow betrayed by this particular group of people. Or, it could be, notwithstanding the fact that he, too, may be an alcoholic, that he feels superior to other alcoholics and has no regard for any of them.

"Secondly, and I find this very interesting, our killer has an additional wrinkle. Humiliation is a common thread among sexual sadists, but it virtually always occurs in a setting in which there is only the killer and the victim. Our suspect goes well beyond that, and it appears his gratification also depends on public degradation for his victims. His acts are retaliatory in nature, it seems. He thinks he's getting even for having been slighted or treated poorly in some manner, which, of course, may have no basis in fact."

"So are you saying this guy's actually getting a 'two-fer'?"

Quinlin asked. "He's getting off sexually on all this, but he's also getting vengeance?"

"His satisfaction is quite intense, possibly even orgasmic. And because he's getting so much gratification from the act of killing, I would imagine he will continue even if he believes this perceived wrong, whatever that may be, has been corrected. I suspect the control he's feeling is pretty heady stuff for him, and he's not going to want to give it up. Can't give it up. Serials never quit on their own."

As Dr. Aylor talked, Quinlin removed the spiral notebook from his breast pocket and scribbled notes. Quickly, the psychologist headed for the bottom line, listing traits and characteristics he believed the killer would have.

"The suspect you're looking for is a narcissist," Dr. Aylor said, "which isn't all that uncommon for a serial. He believes the world revolves around him. He's the axis. He's probably meticulous, both in work and in his dress. I would imagine he is very concerned about his appearance, and probably lives in an upper-class neighborhood and drives a vehicle that he believes exemplifies that grandiose self-image.

"He's concerned about what others think of him, so I would look for him to drive a Mercedes, a Jaguar, definitely something high-end. He's white-collar and, most assuredly, he's exceptionally bright and attentive to detail. His acquaintances probably regard him as aggressive, maybe even arrogant. He's perceived as pushy, maybe even domineering. And obsessive, definitely obsessive."

Quinlin and McCarren eyed each other, and Quinlin wondered if his partner was picturing Bergoff, too.

Their suspect, Dr. Aylor said, possibly was the victim of child sexual abuse or perhaps the child of philandering parents who abused alcohol.

"Whichever the case," Aylor said, "I would look for someone who has a problem with one or both of his parents."

The psychologist scanned the notes on his legal pad.

"Unfortunately," Dr. Aylor said, leaning back in his chair, "you'll see his work again unless he's apprehended. He's very much like the farm dog who sneaks into the hen house. Once he has a taste of blood, he has to go back. Again and again. That's common among serial killers."

Paul McCarren didn't say anything until the elevator doors closed.

"What do you make of all of that?"

"Our killer's an arrogant dick who hates his parents, drives a fancy car, and gets a boner every time he kills somebody," Quinlin said.

"Great," McCarren said. "Simple enough."

The elevator doors were opening.

"Bergoff drives a Mercedes and has a couple of nasty habits," Quinlin said. "Let's go see him in the morning. I'll ask him if he hates his parents, you check his britches."

22

Quinlin arrived early at Newport's, and elected to wait in the small alcove of a lobby. The temperature outside was hovering around a hundred degrees, and he didn't want to sweat through his shirt, not tonight. The sweat, he knew, was as much nervousness as temperature. After worrying all day about what to wear, he had pulled impulsively into the parking lot of a Marshall's on the way to the restaurant. He emerged from the discount clothing store with a blue Bill Blass blazer, the only one they had in a 42 long, and mercifully, not double-breasted with the pointy lapels. Coats in the midst of Texas summers were crazy enough; double-breasted blazers were for fops. He pulled off the sales tags in the front seat of the Scout and pulled the blazer over his blue-and-tan windowpane shirt. Crisp Wrangler Riatas, his newest pair of Tony Lama ostriches and a matching belt, it was the best he could do considering virtually all his wardrobe was being held captive in a house where he was no longer welcome.

Quinlin was skimming the menu when he caught the faint, familiar scent of Contradiction and felt her lips on his neck. When he stood, she turned him by his shoulders and kissed him full on the mouth.

"Gawd, Madeline," he said, "you're more beautiful than I remembered."

Actually stunning, in Ann Taylor black palazzo pants, a white sheer blouse with a white lace camisole, and black, open-toed sandals.

"You must have been drunk," she said. "I am starved. Sobriety makes me hungry."

She squeezed his hand with long, delicate fingers and pulled him toward the hostess. Abruptly, she stopped midway and looked into his eyes.

"Yep," she said. "Just like I remembered. Those blues have gotten you a lot of offers, haven't they, Officer?"

He rolled his eyes. Her foolishness didn't deserve an answer.

Quinlin liked Newport's and was glad Madeline had suggested it. The building previously had been a small regional brewery, and the restaurant was built around the huge brewing vat that still was sunken in the middle of the floor. A brass rail ringed the thirty-foot vat, and tables surrounded the hole on three sides.

Madeline studied the wine list wistfully. With a flourish, she told the waiter: "I'll have iced tea, and bring it in the biggest wineglass you have. Not a puny one, a big one."

"I'll have the same," Quinlin said. "Just a regular glass would be fine."

She settled on a caesar salad, grilled halibut with a light oyster-and-crab sauce, and asparagus, he for a green salad with ranch dressing, a brochette of bacon-wrapped shrimp, and au gratin potatoes. They ate ravenously, laughing about their appetites since they'd been sober, and dipped heavily into the dessert cart, she for chocolate mousse and he for fresh raspberries and cream.

"I'm shaky and scared, but I'm ready to live again," she confided over after-dinner coffee. "I want you to be around, Jeb. Is that something you can handle?"

"I don't think I have a choice," he said. "It may be something I can't live without."

Madeline's left hand was resting on the inside of his left thigh and her right arm was around his shoulder. Her long, thin fingers stroked the back of his neck ever so lightly, and he hoped he didn't have goosebumps. Quinlin's brain was playing point-counterpoint with his privates. It was exactly the dilemma he had hoped to avoid when he twice had declined Madeline's offer to go to her condo after dinner.

"Are you afraid of me, Jeb Quinlin?" she had taunted. "Or, are you afraid of Jeb Quinlin?"

They had laughed at exactly the same time, ending the heavy silence.

"I don't trust either one of us," he had said honestly.

Ultimately, he had acquiesced. He wasn't certain he had a future with Madeline, but he knew he didn't want to jeopardize the potential. And even though the botched break-in at her condo was probably an attempted burglary, pure and simple, he knew going home with her would give him a chance to look the place over and check it for security. In the aftermath of Anne Marie Ingram's murder, he needed a comfort factor about Madeline.

Quinlin followed her BMW from the restaurant in his Scout, wondering with each turn what the next few hours would hold. He couldn't remember his first date, but he was certain there couldn't have been any more pressure than he felt now.

She had put on a cassette of oldies, and while they had listened to "Sea of Love" and other songs that reminded them of better times, they had drunk ice tea with fresh mint and filled four hours with stupid stories about themselves. At some point, Madeline retrieved a thick album of kid pictures that had progressively chronicled her life in braces, basketball uniforms, prom dresses, and graduation gowns.

Quinlin fixed on a basketball picture, one that showed Madeline standing with four other girls, all in red-and-gray uniforms that said LADY COUGARS. Her head was tilted mischievously to one side and she wore a semismile that said she knew a secret.

"I was a junior there," she said. "About fifteen minutes before that picture was taken, the coach told me I was going to be named an all-conference forward. I was pretty proud, but I couldn't tell anybody until the announcement was made."

Jeb flipped a page, then turned back to the basketball picture. Madeline, at seventeen, was mesmerizing. Her body was tall and well proportioned, and her legs were stunning. But she had a child's innocent eyes. The girl-woman juxtaposition intrigued him.

"What are you thinking?" Madeline teased. "You trying to make me self-conscious?"

Actually, he was feeling a pang of irrational sadness, wondering what it would have been like to have known her then, when she was young and innocent and vulnerable. And knowing he would have tried to shield her from the pain of Beau Meggars. Equally irrationally, Quinlin felt genuine contempt for the man who had ended up with her first. She deserved better than she had gotten.

Quinlin lied. "I was just thinking that you must have broken a lot of young hearts," he said.

"Then you'd be wrong," she said. "Matter of fact, I had very few dates in high school. I spent most of my time playing basketball, I was on the swim team, and I studied my butt off. Actually, Mr. Smart-ass, I missed being salutatorian of my class by one-tenth of a point. There wasn't time to date."

"That's because I didn't go to your high school," Quinlin said. "I would have begged and pleaded. You would have gone out with me because you felt sorry for me."

"No, I would have gone out with you because you've got

bedroom eyes and a cute butt." Madeline grinned. "And at that point in our lives, we would have really screwed up, and it all would have been horribly fatal."

Maybe, but Jeb couldn't imagine, even knowing what a dolt he was at seventeen, that he wouldn't have put Madeline on a pedestal and made her ecstatically happy.

Madeline did tit for tat, demanding to examine the few photos he carried in his wallet. Silently studying a snapshot of Sarah in a bikini, one Jeb had taken on their vacation in Hawaii, Madeline was genuinely impressed with her beauty. The photo, a beautiful blond in a provocative pose, momentarily brought them to reality. Fortunately, Madeline didn't let reality last long.

"*This* is the man I've let in my house?" Madeline shrieked, holding up Jeb's driver's license photo. It was a goofy picture of an obviously surprised and wide-eyed cowboy making a pitiful attempt at a grin.

"I had just gotten over pneumonia, okay?" he said defensively. "I was suffering pain that would have killed a lesser man."

She had barely stopped laughing when she looked him intently in the eyes.

"I want to see a picture of you from Vietnam," she said. It was the cold-water plunge that Madeline did when she talked, with no context and no transition. Just stream of consciousness that abruptly took the conversation from levity to seriousness. "Do you have some pictures from Vietnam?"

"No," he said, "I mean, yeah, maybe. Probably buried in some closet somewhere. Why?"

"I want to know everything about you," she said. "And I think about you in Vietnam a lot. I don't know why. Maybe because of your eyes. They've seen so much. I know some of that's the cop thing. But you never talk about Vietnam. And I can't imagine what those eyes have seen. They're beautiful, but they're sad. And deep."

"Darlin'," Quinlin said, deliberately adding to his drawl, "there's not one damned thing about me that's deep. Trust me, what you see is what you get."

"What I see is a man who has gone through more bullshit than I can imagine," Madeline said, her voice turning low and raspy. "And you managed to be a better person for it. I feel goodness every time you touch me. Did you know that?"

Quinlin's mind couldn't conjure a reply. No one had ever talked to him the way Madeline did.

"You ever think of Vietnam?" she asked, refusing to back off.

"Only when it thunders or there's lightning."

She caressed the back of his neck.

"Listen," he said, "I don't want you getting the wrong idea about me. I'm not a hero by any stretch of the imagination. Far from it. I had it a lot better than most and was a lot luckier than most. There's nothing romantic about what I did. In fact, what I did was chickenshit."

Her hand was still on his neck, her nails making him tingly. He knew she didn't understand. He didn't want to explain—he'd never tried to make Sarah understand about the lightning nights—but he heard himself trying now.

"They called us spooks. Like the guys off the *Pueblo*. Except we were on a gunship off North Vietnam, lurking in the middle of the night, trying to pick up the bad guys' communications. Then we'd try to pinpoint where they were coming from. If we could put them down in one place, and they were close enough to the beach, we'd shoot the shit out of them with five- and six-inch deck guns. If they were too far inland, we'd call Yankee Station for F-4s off a carrier. Either way, they never knew what hit them. All they knew was that a bunch of shit came screaming down on them in the middle of the night. Then they died."

"But that was war," she said feebly, sensing how tortured he felt. "It was what you were supposed to do. Why was that chickenshit?"

"Grunts, they had to look at what they did. If they shot somebody, they looked at him, saw him fall, I guess. Not pretty, but decent. Grunts took their chances. It could have just as easily been them who was shot. I never had to look at what I did. I sat off the beach in the fuckin' darkness with earphones on, killing God only knows how many people without ever having to see their faces. God only knows. But a hell of a lot more bodies than grunts ever took care of. And . . ."

Quinlin's voice broke. He lunged forward, pushing his head into his cupped hands. He was embarrassed for her to touch him. He was shaking his head silently, his hands clasped tight over his eyes so no one could see him.

"And what, Jeb?" Her voice was understanding and soothing. He was still shaking his head; she was gently patting his back. "What?"

"Then we'd sneak back into the Gulf before sunrise so they couldn't see us and hit us," he said shakily. "We were cowards, throwing rocks, then running back inside the house to Mom before we could get what was coming to us. Chickenshits."

He was buried in guilt, hearing again the thundering six-inchers and watching the night turn phosphorus-white with ordnance, when he heard her sob. It was so faint, he wasn't certain. He turned to look at her. She was beside him, her shoes off, sitting on one crossed leg and crying.

Now all he wanted was to hold her, no clothes, nothing artificial separating them, just his flesh against hers. No talking, just touching, wherever it led, whatever the consequences. He craved it, and it scared him more than any gun run in Vietnam or any psycho with a gun in a dark alley. He knew how to handle himself when people tried to kill him. He knew he was helpless now, out of his element. Lost. Vulnerable. This was too important. Madeline was too important.

He put his arms around her and kissed her delicately. The kiss was so light that he wondered if he were fantasizing. He shut his eyes and felt his head leaving his body like a helium balloon in a bare breeze.

Her hands went around his shoulders, pulling him down on the couch on top of her. She kissed him harder, and he felt her legs spreading beneath him. His hands moved to her butt, and his mind floated farther. Vaguely he felt her hands between their stomachs, loosening his belt. Or hers?

Abruptly, a startled gasp came from deep in Madeline's throat, and her body went rigid. Quinlin rolled to his left, off the couch, grabbing instinctively for the weapon in the back of his waistband. His hand groped, finding only his back. Moving to one knee, he saw the ominous, black .357 lying on Madeline's leg, where it had fallen when she loosened his belt. Her eyes were wide, and she looked like a scared child with a snake draped on her leg, afraid to move until Dad removed it.

Quickly, Quinlin retrieved the pistol, snapping the cylinder loose and popping out the six rounds into his palm.

"I'm so sorry," he said, putting the pistol on the coffee table and extending his hand. "I didn't think about it. I, uh, I've never had to think about it. That was really stupid on my part."

Madeline exhaled deeply, righting herself on the couch.

"No, I just overreacted," she said, gathering herself. "I've just never been around guns. They frighten me more than I knew."

Embarrassed, Quinlin picked the two tea glasses from the coffee table and took them to the kitchen counter. He returned to the couch and slumped beside her, not looking at her and not knowing what to say.

Finally, it was Madeline who broke the silence.

"This isn't about the gun," she said. "You're afraid, and I don't know why."

"I'm screwing up things," he said, knowing he should have

said goodbye at the restaurant. "It's too important. *You're* too important. To me. It scares me because . . ."

He buried his head in her neck. He didn't want her to see him this way. Twice now, she had. She felt wetness on her neck, and she tightened her hold on him. His mind was out of control, fixing on Sarah, seeing Jerry Stephens, hearing the counselor's warning about avoiding major decisions, and recalling the handsome and confident Beau Meggers in a wedding tuxedo from the photo album.

Quinlin got up from the couch and walked to the window of the den, pushing the drapes aside and looking out. His voice was still shaky, but he knew he had to explain. Silent emotion could be misinterpreted.

"I'm scared because I care about you," he said, keeping his back to her. "More than I should at this point. More than I can say. You make me hope."

"What does that mean?" She wanted him to say it.

"That I love you. That I've got to get it right this time."

Madeline was behind him now, her arms around his waist, her lips on the back of his neck.

"You're putting too much pressure on yourself and on us, too," she said. "Just be yourself. You're a good man, Jeb. I've known it a long, long time, maybe since I first saw you. I love you, too, just for the record.

"But we'll do it your way. Slowly. We'll get it right because it *is* right."

She steered him to the guest bedroom on the second floor, separated from hers by a bathroom.

"I want you with me tonight, even if it's in here," she said, pulling down the covers. "I'm cooking breakfast for you in the morning. Then you'll be begging me to marry you."

Jeb awoke the next morning and smelled Contradiction on the other pillow. The sheets on the other side of the bed were wrinkled and bore her scent. He sniffed his right forearm and caught the scent again. Yes, he was remembering right: She had come to his bed in the night and held him. As he propped himself on one elbow to contemplate the night, he smelled bacon from downstairs.

His Scout had been on her parking lot all night for anyone to see.

23

Five of the seven patients discharged from Cedar Ridge in time to have killed Anne Marie Ingram had arrest records. Three had priors for drunk driving and another for drunkenness in public, not surprising considering they also had extensive histories as drunks. One, however, apparently wasn't a garden-variety drunk, judging from his rap sheet.

Eddie Wayne Sumpkin, according to the computer, had four prior felonies, all violent: aggravated assault on 7/17/85; maiming and attempted capital murder of a police officer, both on 6/19/90; and a brand-new one, another ag assault, just two months earlier, shortly before he would have been admitted to Cedar Ridge.

Sumpkin, Quinlin recalled, was beer-joint trash, about as far from Aylor's bright-and-sophisticated profile as you could register on the food chain. Quinlin remembered Sumpkin bragging at Cedar Ridge about owning his own small trucking company. He hauled fresh produce from the Rio Grande Valley near the Mexico border to wholesalers in Waco, Dallas, and Fort Worth. Sumpkin had sideburns down to his jawbone, an acne-scarred face that looked like it had been carpet-bombed, and a well-cultivated beer belly that shoved his Levis down into a perpetual plumber's butt. In a ward filled with accountants, engineers, and real estate agents, the foul-mouthed, sneering Sumpkin stood out like a street whore in a monastery.

The files in Records showed Sumpkin had gotten probation for beating a man comatose with a pool stick. While he was still on probation, he bit a man's ear off in another barroom brawl, then used a broken beer bottle to carve the cop who arrested him. The attempted capital murder charge was plea-bargained down to aggravated assault, and he did six years in Huntsville. He could have been out in four, according to Texas Department of Criminal Justice records, had he not jammed a shiv, which he fashioned from a bolt on his bunk, into another inmate's stomach.

Sumpkin posted $50,000 bond on the most recent assault, which was yet another beer-joint confrontation on Industrial Boulevard. Sumpkin's attorney, Quinlin figured, had deposited him in Cedar Ridge, hoping to later convince a judge that his client had finally seen the light and taken the cure. Sumpkin was a belligerent and unresponsive patient at Cedar Ridge, according to a phone call from Coal Tar, and he had once been tossed out of Kristin Williamson's room by Flashlight Larry.

Sumpkin's file was one of three that raised questions with Quinlin. The normal course of treatment for alcoholism took twenty-eight days; it was never shorter, but it could be longer if a patient was recycled. Sumpkin was discharged a week short of the normal stay. Toby Smith, according to his file, was in the ward twenty-three days, and Robert Harris had done twenty-five.

McCarren had taken the other four discharge files and was running down the patients to see where they were on the night Anne Marie's body showed up at the funeral home. Quinlin didn't say anything when his partner stuck Madeline's file in his stack of leads to follow, nor did he call Madeline. His relationship with Madeline was personal, and he wasn't going to let it get involved in police business. He tossed Madeline's file out of his stack. He would return it to McCarren; he could check it out if he wanted.

Jerry Stephens was in a session and hadn't returned his call. Stephens would tell him why Sumpkin, Smith, and Harris had been discharged early. While he pondered the possibilities, Quinlin put in his third call to Sarah, getting her recorder again.

He wasn't as polite this time: "Sarah, you're holding my stuff hostage. I would appreciate it, the people I work with would appreciate it, if you would let me get my clothes. If you're trying to dodge a scene, don't sweat it. I'm not even pissed at you anymore. Unless you don't give me my clothes, okay? Call me, dammit."

The phone rang and it was Stephens. Quinlin had just started the conversation when he noticed Barrick standing at his desk.

"I'm interviewing someone here, okay, Captain?" Quinlin said. Things had been tense enough in the bullpen already. He didn't need Barrick hanging on his shoulder. Not to mention the fact that the deputy chief had banned the captain from the case.

"See me when you're through," the captain said tersely. "It's not about the investigation. I, uh, need to talk to you. It's personal."

Quinlin went back to his call. Not surprisingly, Sumpkin had been tossed off the ward for shoving and threatening a rehab tech.

"Too bad it wasn't Winston," Quinlin said. "That would have saved the taxpayers a trial."

Toby Smith's insurance had a $10,000 ceiling, and his benefits ran out.

"Was he bitter about being forced to leave?"

"No way," Stephens said. "You knew Toby. He was a decent guy. I hooked him up with a sponsor, and he's going to try to make it on his own through AA. I think he's got a shot."

Quinlin winced at the reference to a sponsor. He had worked in three meetings in two days, but he had yet to find himself a sponsor. Mercifully, Stephens didn't rag him about it.

Robert Harris, the counselor said, had been caught with booze. Apparently, he had read too many stories about drug smugglers. Flashlight Larry had caught him ripping the lining from his suitcase. Inside were four flattened party balloons, filled with two pints of bourbon.

"Harris made our Who's Who list," Stephens said. "That's one we hadn't seen before. Actually, we normally give them a second chance, but Harris said it was time to leave. No big deal."

Quinlin dialed the number Toby Smith had listed on his patient files, but got no answer, not even a machine. Harris's recording noted, officiously, Quinlin thought, that he wasn't "presently available."

Quinlin drained the last of his coffee, real, one hundred percent Colombian *caffeine* and headed for the address Eddie Wayne Sumpkin had listed on his most recent bond. The streetwise ex-con wasn't the kind that Quinlin wanted to interview on the phone. Sumpkin wasn't sophisticated or smart enough to come out of a hailstorm, and if he had killed the three drunks, he certainly would have left them bloody and mangled, not to mention probably raping Kristin and Anne Marie. Still Quinlin couldn't ignore a suspect with a violent past; checking out Eddie Wayne came under the heading of "due diligence."

Barrick intercepted him before he got to the elevator.

"You heard from Sarah since you been out?" he asked.

"That's a little personal, don't you think, Captain?" Quinlin said. "Why don't you just ask her, seeing as how your relationship with her is currently a lot tighter than mine?"

"I can't find her. She's not at home, and she didn't show up for work yesterday." The captain looked at his watch. "It's nearly ten now, and she's still not at work today. The secretary says she hasn't checked in with anybody."

"Try her mother in Austin," Quinlin said. "It's in information under Douglas Strickland on Greenhaven Road. She's probably tired of both of us and wants to get her head cleared."

Quinlin got into the elevator, but he wasn't as certain as he sounded with the captain. Sarah might dodge both of them, but she would have called her office. Or maybe not. He didn't know Sarah like he used to.

Eddie Wayne Sumpkin was in the back seat of the cruiser, bleeding profusely from his mouth and screaming threats that whistled through a hole previously occupied by two teeth. His hands were cuffed behind his back and, in his fat frenzy, he had worked himself sideways into the floorboard where he floundered and spewed like a beached whale.

He had only himself to blame. Quinlin had asked him three times to account for his time since he had been released from Cedar Ridge. The first two times, the ex-con simply ignored the detective, never taking his eyes off the task in front of him, which was mending the wire mesh on top of the cage that housed Rusty Bandit, his champion fighting cock. It was the third time that got him hurt.

"When I finish this," Eddie Wayne said, eyeing Quinlin sideways, "you still standing there, I'm gonna knock your dick stiff." The thought must have amused the ex-con. "Then," Eddie Wayne said, chuckling, "I'm gonna screw your mamma real good."

"Huh? I didn't hear you."

Eddie Wayne, still hunched over Rusty Bandit's cage, turned sideways, sneering up at the detective. His eyes widened and his face registered shock when he saw Quinlin's fist coming at his face. The blow landed just under his nose, knocking all his two hundred and thirty pounds into the rooster's cage. Quinlin couldn't see everything in the chaos, but when the feathers finally landed and the screeching stopped, the fighting rooster was gone and Eddie Wayne's face looked like he'd been dragged headfirst through barbed wire. Wild-eyed, Eddie Wayne pulled himself out of the pen and lunged at the cop with a pair of needle-nosed pliers he still held in his right hand. Dodging the blind stab of the sharpened pliers, Quinlin slammed Eddie Wayne in the mouth with the side of his Smith & Wesson, returning him to what was left of Rusty Bandit's cage.

Cuffed and crying, Eddie Wayne was screaming threats and obscenities as Quinlin pulled him by the shoulder from the backyard toward the cruiser, trying to keep the trucker's blood off his own clothes. At the corner of the mobile home, a bleached blond with black roots, blue-jean cutoffs, and a red, bulging halter top appeared in front of them.

"You taking Eddie Wayne back to the joint?" she asked.

"That's a fact, yes ma'am," a leery Quinlin said, thinking back to his patrol days when wives routinely turned on cops hauling off their husbands. "I imagine you won't be seeing ol' Eddie Wayne for another five or ten years."

"You sure 'bout that?" she asked evenly.

"If I've got anything to say about it."

She ran for the back door which, Quinlin well knew, was probably trouble. He pushed a balking Eddie Wayne along toward the car, trying to quicken the pace. When Quinlin was still in uniform, a bloodied woman who had called 911 on her husband had hit Quinlin in back of the head with a claw hammer when she saw the love of her life was headed for jail. Quinlin had taken six stitches. He hated domestic disturbance calls worse than armed robberies in progress.

Twenty yards from the safety of his cruiser, Quinlin heard hurried footsteps on the gravel behind them and saw the woman in the red halter running toward them, her bouncing breasts pushing the limits of polyester and her right arm tucked behind her back. He shook his head and imagined a gun.

"Lady," Quinlin said, "I need to warn you. I'm a police—"

The blond made a wide circle around Quinlin, appearing on the other side of his prisoner. Her right hand held a two-foot length of bicycle chain, which she slammed repeated into Eddie Wayne's head. The cuffed prisoner bolted from Quinlin's grasp and ran clumsily toward the cruiser, screaming every time the woman brought the chain down across his head. He stood at the back door, his head bowed against the torrent of blows from the bicycle chain, and screamed like a baby as the blows landed on across his back.

"You rotten bastard!" the woman screamed, never missing a blow. "You think you could come back here and just beat the hell out of me? God *damnnn* you!"

Quinlin lighted up a Marlboro and took the last twenty yards at a leisurely pace. Not all justice, he had long ago discovered, was dispensed in a courtroom. After a decent interval when the scales of justice had probably just about been balanced, the woman still hadn't stopped flailing at Eddie Wayne, and Quinlin had to grab her from behind, trapping both her arms. Eddie Wayne safely tucked in the backseat, Quinlin advised the woman of her right to file domestic battery charges against her husband.

"We're common-law," she said. "That make any difference?"

"No, ma'am, I'd encourage you to file charges," he said. "It'd help show the judge Mr. Sumpkin's propensity for violence, and it could help in making sure he gets the right sentence, if you know what I mean."

The bottle blond hugged the detective before he could get in the car and winked at him as he started the engine.

"You might ought to check on me every once in a while,"

she said as he put it in gear, "if you know what I mean, and I think you do."

Quinlin was content to listen to Eddie Wayne's whining from the backseat until he heard someone trying to reach him on the radio.

"You need to shut up back there," Quinlin yelled. "I can't hear the radio."

The voice on the radio tried again. Quinlin recognized McCarren's voice.

"What's your '20?"

"I-20, about Houston School Road," Quinlin said, "getting ready to turn off on 35 for downtown."

"Meet me at the Farmers Market," McCarren said, squelching badly.

"Can't do it, hoss. I'm transporting Mr. Sumpkin to lockup. Er, negative, make that Parkland, then to lockup."

"Jeb, this is important," McCarren said. "It's urgent. I'll be in the parking lot at Farmers Market in ten minutes. Be there."

Quinlin didn't like his partner's tone. McCarren was steady. If he said urgent, he meant urgent. And whatever it was, he didn't want to put it on the air for everyone to hear.

There was renewed thrashing from the back.

"You sorry muthafucker, you hadn't hit me in the face with that gun, you'd be eating the sonofabitch right now. You're a piece of shit."

"I just figured out something, Eddie Wayne," Quinlin said. "You don't have a drinking problem. You got a human problem. If I've counted right, this assault is number five, more than enough to park your fat ass in Ellis I as an habitual."

"Go for it, muthafucker," Eddie Wayne said. "I got me a lawyer that'll beat your ass good. Then I'm gonna sue the city for you lettin' my ol' lady whip me while I was handcuffed. Plus, ol' Rusty Bandit's running loose outta his cage. That rooster's worth five hundred dollars."

"Naw, that's dead and stinking. That's history. You need to worry about tomorrow. And the way I've reconfigured your mouth, you're gonna be real popular with the guys down at the pen. They gonna call you mamma."

Quinlin saw McCarren leaning on the side of his cruiser when he drove up. Sumpkin was screaming again, and McCarren motioned him to the passenger side of his car and opened the door.

"Jeb, sit down, man, I've got some bad news," the detective said. "It's not pretty."

Quinlin noticed his partner's tie was pulled down and his collar open. He'd never seen that before. The young cop looked through the windshield instead of at his partner.

"So, are you going to talk to me or not?"

McCarren took a deep breath and turned to face him.

"It's Sarah. Somebody, uh, killed her."

There was no expression on Quinlin's face.

"She's dead, Jeb. Sarah's dead."

24

The Moondust, "an elite gentleman's club" according to the purple neon pronouncement out front, occupied the easternmost third of a strip shopping center that was also home to an Arab-owned convenience store and a joint that sold pizza by the slice. The decrepit shopping center faced onto Mockingbird Lane, smack in the middle of the main north-south approach to Love Field, which meant that anyone who patronized the businesses generally had to scream over the roar of 737s on final approach.

Beyond the blacked-out, plate-glass windows of Moondust, seven hard-core patrons, having paid their twenty-dollar cover charge, were sipping ten-dollar, watered-downed drinks when the first show began shortly after ten in the morning.

A semicircular, moveable backdrop with a fake fire station and fireman's pole in the center ground slowly onto the stage while a worn Jerry Lee Lewis tape belted out "Great Balls of Fire." Pulsating red-and-blue strobe lights splashed the set as it moved gradually into full view of the sparse crowd. Not until the set locked in place, and only after the woman at the fireman's pole remained motionless for several seconds did any of the seven men in the semicircle around the stage realize she was dead.

"Hey, there's something wrong with this chick, man! Jeeesus *god*-all-mighty! Look at her face! She ain't moving, man!"

Offstage, the manager heard the commotion, killed the strobes, and hit the overheads. The steady white light sent the patrons scurrying backward as if there were a bomb on the stage. In full light, the petite blond dangled three feet off the floor, her neck in a noose tied to the fireman's pole. Her eyes were locked wide in a perpetual stare, and her body was stiff with rigor, like a flash-frozen deer stupefied by headlights.

Her face was made up garishly, like a Kabuki doll, with ghost-white cheeks, blue eyeshadow, and deep red lipstick, but all the cosmetics and makeup couldn't conceal the beating. Her eyes were puffed and black like a raccoon's, and her lips were swollen twice their size in life. From a distance, she appeared to be wearing blue pasties and a red-white-and-blue G-string. Closer scrutiny, though, revealed the pasties and G-string were body paint. Beneath the body paint on her ample breasts, the areolae were bruised and bore teeth marks. Judging from the razor nicks, her pubic area had been freshly shaved, possibly after her death. The bottoms of her feet had been burned with cigarettes.

Nothing the killer had done, however, was more chilling than the message he scrawled across the woman's back in red lipstick: *Made a list of all persons we had harmed, and became willing to make amends . . .* It was the Eighth Step of Alcoholics Anonymous.

McCarren had been three miles away interviewing Toby Smith when dispatch called. Abrams, the deputy chief, had tossed the call to McCarren not because he was the closest homicide unit, but because the lettering on the unidentified body made him certain the Twelve-Step Murderer had struck again. The uniforms had the crime scene cordoned off and had moved all the witnesses to a corner of the barroom by the time McCarren arrived.

The woman's body was surreal enough from a distance, her feet dangling well off the floor, and McCarren felt his pulse quicken as he approached from the side. Murder was one thing, but defacing a body like this, scrawling it with bright colors, was insane. *Why didn't the bastard just kill the damned woman if he had a problem?* As the young detective made his way to the front of the suspended body, he bore in on detail. Burns, bites, beating. His stomach was turning queasy.

Finally, he focused on the corpse's face. He studied it momentarily and, abruptly, he jolted backwards a half step, a low moan coming from his throat. *Sarah? Jeb's Sarah? Oh, God, no.* He moved to his side, stooping a little to use the good light from the ceiling and making himself concentrate. He couldn't be wrong, not about this. He forced himself up onto the platform and leaned into the lifeless face. His eyes shut involuntarily and his shoulders slumped.

McCarren found himself sitting on the stage; he didn't know how long he'd been there. His legs were still rubbery, but the nausea at the crest of his throat had subsided back down his esophagus, making it manageable. Maybe.

How would he tell Jeb? What would he say? And Jeb. What would he do? McCarren knew he had to take care of business. He was a homicide investigator. There were things to be done, professional things that were important. He arranged them in his mind and forced his body to go along.

The shaken detective talked first to the stripper who was supposed to be on the set, and who was still dressed in her fireman's garb and helmet. She was the only dancer working the early-morning shift, and she had been late to work, not arriving until ten minutes before she was to get on the carousel as it moved on stage. She hadn't finished her makeup when the stage began moving and when she started to jump on, she noticed the body tied to the pole. She was too upset even to yell for the manager, she said, collapsing beside the moveable stage.

Sarah? Sarah wasn't an alcoholic. The MO was recovering drunks, drunks from Cedar Ridge.

McCarren stopped himself. There would time for that later. Now he had to keep his mind on the ball. Nothing was more important than the crime scene. Evidence got moved, lost. Witnesses vanished, died, and forgot. Everything, each detail, had to be logged in his notebook. It was what Quinlin had taught him.

The day manager, the only person working the crowd until noon, said he unlocked the building about nine A.M., but never went backstage. He inventoried the bar stock, retrieved change from the floor safe, and swept out the bar, which the night bartender hadn't done. When he opened the front door at ten A.M., he said, there were seven customers waiting in the parking lot.

McCarren eyed the witnesses huddled in a corner of the bar. He counted six.

"You sure about seven?" he asked.

"Yeah," the manager said, reaching for a small metal box with a slit in the top. "We have to keep our coverage charges separate from the bar money. There's a hundred-forty dollars here—seven dudes, twenty dollars a pop."

The manager remembered the seventh patron easily.

"He asked for soda water," he said. "I told him, 'Don't matter what you drink, fella, it's gonna cost you ten dollars,' and he still wanted soda."

The customer was youngish, maybe twenty-five or thirty, clean-shaven and well dressed.

"Well dressed?"

"Yeah," the manager said, pointing to the other six customers, most of whom wore work clothes and uniforms. "Those guys are more like our regulars. Your guy wore khakis, a starched white shirt, and a blue blazer. Looked like a college man, you know?"

McCarren made a note to check the front and rear parking lots, but he knew he wouldn't find anything.

The detective saw flashes near the body and knew the crime-scene team should be about through with the photos. He found Jay LeFleurs, a field investigator for the ME's office, and pulled him aside.

"What you got here?"

"I'd go with asphyxiation," he said, "probably as a result of the same noose that she's got around her neck now. But death didn't come easy. She was tortured—bitten, burned, you name it. Maybe raped, I don't know yet. She was probably glad to see the noose."

They were staring at the body, saying nothing.

"Shame, too," the ME's man said. "Bet she was a real race-horse in life."

"She was," McCarren said.

The investigator looked surprised.

"You know her?"

"Yeah," the detective said. "If you've got everything you need, could you get her down from there? Please?"

McCarren studied his partner and wondered if he was in shock. He had a persistent vacant stare, but he appeared rational when he spoke. Twice Quinlin had demanded to be taken to SWIFS to see Sarah's body, but his junior partner was unyielding.

"It'd serve no good purpose," McCarren said. "We've got a good crime scene. Let's let the people do their jobs."

In the alternative, Quinlin demanded to know every detail about his wife's death. He listened carefully, trancelike, occasionally stopping McCarren's rundown for an elaboration. He made McCarren repeat the information about the message left on Sarah's body.

"No question, is there?" Quinlin asked, barely audible. "This is my deal. She wasn't a drunk. She was tortured and hanged. This isn't about her. This is about me, Paul."

Then he asked his partner to leave him alone in the interview room.

Quinlin sat by himself in the tiny room in CAPERS, refusing the company of well-intentioned friends, refusing coffee, and refusing the department's chaplain. He emerged an hour and a half later, methodically summoning a handful of players to the conference room. Deputy Chief Jon Abrams, McCarren, Dr. Aylor, and Captain Bill Barrick waited awkwardly while Quinlin shut the door.

"Whatever you're going to do, it can wait," the chief said. "You need to have some personal time. Nothing—"

"The bastard who killed Sarah was in my therapy group at Cedar Ridge," Quinlin said. He spoke evenly in a flat line with no inflection. "He was sitting in the same room with me. It's the only way he could have known to do this. It's symbolism. It's about making me pay."

"I'm not following you," the chief said.

Quinlin was scaring McCarren. His voice was cold and emotionless. It wasn't natural.

"The message on Sarah's body is the Eighth Step in Alcoholics Anonymous. It's about making amends to people we've harmed," Quinlin said. "I did something two years ago that harmed Sarah. She didn't know anything about it, nobody did, but it harmed her. Harmed us. And ultimately got her killed."

He told them about his affair with Holly Doyle, the stripper he met on duty while investigating her sister's murder. He told the story the way he wrote homicide supplements. No rationale, no mitigation, just the sordid facts. The room was silent.

"Before today, the only people I ever told about Holly were the people in my therapy group at Cedar Ridge," Quinlin said.

The detective had everyone's attention.

"This is symbolism," Quinlin continued. "Sarah's body was dumped at the Moondust because that's where Holly worked. She was made up like a stripper," he voice wavered, "because Holly was a stripper.

"I talked in therapy about my old man beating my mother when I was a kid. That's why Sarah was beaten. And if I've followed you, Dr. Aylor, she was tortured because whoever killed her got off sexually on humiliating her."

The psychologist cleared his throat awkwardly.

"I think that's a safe bet," the psychologist said. "He's escalating, just as we discussed. Much more violent, much more direct."

Barrick's eyes were fixed on the table. He was an inflatable man with a slow leak. The room was quiet, and he walked to the door and left.

"The others were alcoholics," Chief Abrams said to nobody in particular. "Why Sarah?"

Quinlin was slumped in his chair at the head of the table. It was Aylor who answered.

"It's not about Sarah. It's about Quinlin. He knows you're out there asking questions, maybe is even watching you. He's smart enough to know it's a matter of time. It's part of the game, and he's just upped the ante to play. It's gratification, but it's vengeance, too. He—"

Loud sobs came from the head of the table.

"I didn't tell her," Quinlin said, his shoulders convulsing. "I didn't make amends. I never told her how sorry I am. That bastard knows. He knows that's important, that I apologize to her for what I did. He knows I can't do it now. Can never apologize. Bless her heart, she . . ."

Sobs overtook him. Dr. Aylor cleared the room.

"He *knows* me, Doc," Quinlin cried. "How can he *know* me?"

* * *

Quinlin drove aimlessly in the Scout for two hours, through the parking lots at Fair Park where he and Sarah had gone to the state fairs, around White Rock Lake, her favorite jogging place, and places he wouldn't remember. Driving was better than going back to the "divorce special." That's what the desk clerk had wryly called it when he had checked in at Southwest Suites. Suites was a stretch. A tiny refrigerator had been tucked beneath the lavatory, and a hotplate had been plugged in on top of the counter next to the yellow-stained sink. These amenities, along with fresh sheets, towels, and maid service once a week, made Southwest Suites, according to the fritzed neon sign out front, "A suite for a day or a lifetime," all for $149 a week. On this day, alone with uncontrollable thoughts in the crackerbox that was his life, he knew he would drink. So he drove with no place to go.

At one point and without any prior intention, he ended up in his own driveway, but he couldn't force himself out of the Scout. It hadn't been his home for more than two weeks. It had always been more Sarah's than his anyway, the way she decorated it and painted whole rooms in the precise colors that matched a teeny stripe in the fabric on a couch or chair. He had reluctantly agreed to paint the outside trim in peach and seafoam only to be surprised at how crisp and clean it looked when he finished. Sarah had an eye for things like that. He saw a neighbor fertilizing his front yard, waving at him. He pulled out of the drive quickly, fleeing without making eye contact or acknowledging the wave. Word would spread in the neighborhood soon enough. He couldn't talk about it.

He drove with the radio off, without thinking. He was supposed to be living his life one day at a time, that's what Stephens told him to do. But what was he supposed to do on *this* day? There was no plan. He meandered, turning right at this corner, left at the next, heading straight through the intersection with the flashing light. It was almost five when he found himself at the Probable Cause.

Billy Earle was off and the barkeep was an off-duty burglary cop whose name he couldn't recall. He took a stool at the end of the bar with his back to the door, something he never did. He was on his fourth round of Bud Lite and double shots of Turkey when he felt the jolt from behind.

"Whoa," he said. He was immediately disoriented; the booze must have lulled him more than he knew.

He felt pressure around his chest, then he was looking at the dark floor sideways. There was juggling and jarring, and then he felt the Texas heat and was blinded by light. His eyes wouldn't adjust. He heard a car door open and felt the sensation of being thrown and landing hard.

"Follow me." It was Coal Tar's voice.

"I know the way." It was Madeline.

25

Now, in Interview Room 2, McCarren put his elbows on the small table and leaned forward, closing the distance between himself and Bergoff.

"We'll try it one more time," the detective said, "and something bad's going to happen to you if I don't hear the truth. And that, by the way, is not a physical threat. See, we already know certain things, Doctor.

"From the top, it's a matter of public record that you're wired wrong. You beat your bufus in front of your wife. You've got a documentably bad habit of writing stuff in lipstick. You were in the room to hear Willard Beane confess to molesting his grandson. Now, Willard's dead. You forced Kristin Williamson to admit she was a slut. Kristin's dead. Poor, pathetic Anne Marie, you finally buckled her, too. Anne Marie's dead. You heard Quinlin admit to having an affair with a stripper and not telling his wife. Now Sarah's dead. Sir, I think this is what we call a trend.

"And not just dead, Doctor. Oh, hell no. These people were humiliated in death the same way they humiliated themselves in life. Their honesty killed them. So, for the final time, exactly where have you been during the last forty-eight hours?"

It was Bergoff's turn and he wasn't playing, staring into his lap.

"You go smug on me again, sir, and I'm going to a judge and tell him everything I've just said. He'll be impressed with this little trend, and he'll give me a search warrant. Then, with the authority of the great state of Texas, Quinlin and I will personally disassemble everything in your home, your office, and your Mercedes down to the last nail and bolt. And in the process, I wouldn't be surprised if all this didn't find its way into the newspaper. Now, you tell me, Slick, what's it going to be?"

"I was in Albuquerque," Bergoff said. He was barely audible, and his eyes stayed on his lap. "Three days. I returned late last night. I stayed at the Airport Hilton; I flew Southwest. There'll be a record."

"What were you doing in Albuquerque?"

The psychiatrist readjusted himself in the chair.

"I was at a seminar on aberrant sexual behavior."

"Good," McCarren said. "Then your name should be on the program."

"I wasn't there as a presenter. I was in the audience."

Bergoff's voice was getting fainter and fainter, and the detective leaned closer to hear.

"Check with the Board of Medical Examiners," Bergoff said. "It's part of my probation. My attendance was mandatory."

Antabuse, the way Jerry Stephens explained it, was an insurance policy against drinking. Or, if Quinlin wasn't totally committed to staying sober, Antabuse would become his worst nightmare.

"Hangovers won't even come close to what Antabuse will do to you," Stephens said.

Disulfiram, the generic chemical name for Antabuse, was a failure at its original purpose, which reportedly was unclogging sewers in London. In the mid-1930s, disulfiram was used in the manufacture of rubber. In 1948, Antabuse, the pharmaceutical trade name for disulfiram, was introduced as an aversion medication to keep people from drinking. It was wickedly efficient.

A single daily dose of 250 milligrams orally was inert in the bloodstream. But the chemical was so sensitive to alcohol that, even mixed with the minuscule amount of alcohol absorbed through skin pores from aftershave, it produced a throbbing headache, respiratory difficulty, and nausea.

Quinlin didn't have to imagine what a straight shot of Turkey would do.

"I didn't recommend Antabuse when you left because you hadn't completed treatment," Stephens said. "It's dangerous. You can't cheat Antabuse, Jeb. There's no margin for forgiveness. But given what's happened in the last twenty-four hours, I don't think you have much choice."

Quinlin had spent the night at Cedar Ridge in a vacant room. McCarren, he learned, had gone straight from the emotional meeting Quinlin had convened after Sarah's death to a phone and called Coal Tar, recommending a mandatory AA meeting. Coal Tar and Madeline one-upped McCarren. They abducted Quinlin from the Probable Cause and locked him up.

"Yeah," Quinlin said. "I'll take it. I need to be able to do what I need to do."

An MD on the staff had already written the prescription. Stephens shoved a bottle of octagonal white pills at him and cautioned him to wait another forty-eight hours before taking his first dose.

"Your body needs to purge your little screw-up from last night," Stephens said. "Follow the instructions there to the letter."

26

Eddie Wayne Sumpkin was too stupid to be the Twelve-Step Murderer. Besides, Quinlin had found Department of Transportation log books in the cab of Sumpkin's Peterbilt that showed he had picked up a load of spinach and tomatoes near the Mexican border and hauled it to the Winn-Dixie distribution center in Fort Worth during the timeframe when Anne Marie Ingram, according to the ME's office, would have been killed. Not that being cleared of the murders was going to keep Sumpkin out of a return engagement at the Texas Department of Criminal Justice. Had it just been the one-sided battle with Quinlin, the detective would have settled for revoking Eddie Wayne's parole. But Lana Marie, Eddie Wayne's common-law wife and mother of his three kids, had heeded Quinlin's advice, showing up at headquarters the afternoon he was arrested and filing a lengthy domestic abuse report.

When the report was forwarded to Quinlin two days later, the homicide detective noted that Eddie Wayne had beaten her severely enough to hospitalize her four times in five years. The bastard was as violent as Quinlin's old man. God only knew what he had done to the kids. Lana Marie's abuse complaints were old, and she hadn't called the police but once. Besides, the allegations might end up before a judge who wouldn't take them seriously. Quinlin scooted his chair to the computer on his desk and slowly typed out a complaint that charged Eddie Wayne with attempted capital murder of a police officer. Beside the blank that said *weapon*, Quinlin typed in *needle-nosed pliers*. With Sumpkin's priors, Quinlin figured the new charge, even plea-bargained by a whiplash defense lawyer and a give-a-shit junior prosecutor, would be worth a minimum fifteen years behind bars.

"Whatever works," Quinlin muttered to himself. He called Victim Services, and gave a social worker the information on Lana Marie. She didn't appear to work, had three kids to raise, and was losing her source of income. She'd need some help. Victim Services would line her up with the AFDC people, and at least give her some financial help with the kids.

Quinlin had more trouble giving up on Bergoff as a suspect. He took McCarren through the hoops about his questioning of the psychiatrist, challenging his junior partner on every detail of Bergoff's story about being in New Mexico.

"I don't give a damn if his name was on the flight manifest, the hotel register, and the register at the pervert seminar," Quinlin had yelled. "He could have paid some fuckin' wino to use his name and go for him. Happens all the time. I've seen it."

"Not only do you have to have a photo ID to get on the plane, Jeb," McCarren had explained, "but you've got to show your driver's license to get credit for the seminar. It's a Probation Board requirement. I'm telling you, they saw Jerkoff's face before they logged him on the register. He wasn't in Dallas."

Quinlin knew he had made a mistake, mixing personal feelings in an investigation. He had his own reasons for despising Bergoff. He was an exploitative, arrogant asshole who had more kinks than Don King's hair. Which didn't necessarily make him a murderer. It just made Quinlin *want* him to be a murderer.

Quinlin apologized to McCarren.

Toby Smith, a meek, perpetually nervous dog groomer released the same day as Eddie Wayne, was ruled out as a suspect, too. McCarren discovered that when Smith, who ran his own small business, had run out of insurance coverage, he had chosen to visit his sister in Brownsville, in the Rio Grande Valley. Not coincidentally, McCarren learned, Smith's brother-in-law was a Baptist minister. Smith was so frightened about potentially falling off the wagon that he intentionally put himself in the least likely place to drink.

Quinlin was trying to ensure his own sobriety. He knew he had to stay busy. Idle time, self-pity, and guilt were a dead-end trip to a bottle of Wild Turkey. Sarah's funeral in Austin wasn't to take place for two more days, pending the arrival of her brother, a navy lieutenant commander who was flying in from Japan. Sarah must have told her parents about the divorce. Quinlin had left a message on their recorder with the numbers of his office and his "suite" at the Empty Arms, but they hadn't returned the call. What else, he wondered, had she told them?

One day at a time. Stay busy. Keep on keepin' on. Stay calm.

He called Madeline at home. If there wasn't a uniformed cop in front of her condo, some TAC lieutenant's head was going to roll. Yes, Madeline assured him, there was a cop out front. In fact, there had been two cars at one point.

"Can you imagine what the neighbors must be thinking?" she said, aiming for levity.

"Yeah, that you're a cop groupie."

"That could happen, Officer."

"I, uh, appreciate what you and Coal Tar did last night," he said. His embarrassment was total. He had disappointed himself and, curiously, he felt like he had let Madeline down. He was disappointing everyone, including his partner.

"I can't imagine what's going through your mind," she said. "This is a delicate time for me, too. I'm here for you, I know that. I want to help you. But I don't know what you need. Or want. I'm so, so sorry for Sarah. And for you. Are you holding up? What can I . . ."

"I don't know, Madeline," he said. "It's like every once in a while, for just a few minutes, it doesn't seem possible that she's dead. It's so unreal that I can't picture it. From left field. I was worrying about you, and I never even thought about Sarah. I mean . . ."

"Well, why should you?" Madeline said. "This guy was killing alcoholics. Sarah wasn't like the rest. How would you have known?"

"The guy's a psycho, I know that now," he said. "There're no bounds. He has no bounds. Where he might go or what he might do. He's too screwed up to plot. Just means there's not one damned thing we can rule out. We have to consider everything. Anything."

Silence took over the line.

"Jeb, let me just tell you this," she said. "I'm here, if you need me, whenever you need me. I'll be here."

"I don't know what I need," he said feebly. "I know I want you. It's just that . . ."

"That's for later," she said, "After you take care of business. There'll be time for that."

"Still?" he asked. "You sure?"

"Like you said, I don't think I have a choice," she said, hanging up the phone.

The detective turned to the last of the files for the three patients who were discharged early.

He remembered Robert Blaine Harris, Jr., though he didn't know him well. Harris had been in his therapy group, but only briefly before he was transferred to the advanced group. Harris was a pretty-boy, Quinlin remembered that. Well dressed, smug, quiet. In Quinlin's first day out of detox, while he was killing time in the dayroom awaiting a room assignment, it was

Harris who had failed to log out for his afternoon furlough. He'd caught hell for it, too; the dubious nurse had forced him to take a urinalysis.

Surely Harris had passed that UA or he would have been tossed then, or at least recycled. Quinlin turned to the lab section in Harris's file. That urinalysis from two weeks earlier was, in fact, part of his file. It had been clean. Quinlin flipped through the rest of the UAs, glancing at a calender on his desk. Harris hadn't had a furlough since then, and Quinlin surmised it was because he had been late reporting back to the hospital from his previous furlough.

This was a guy tossed out for smuggling booze into the ward and, according to his urinalysis reports, he was clean, even in a random test two days before he was caught with booze. Harris went to all the trouble to smuggle booze into his room, but didn't drink it? Or hadn't gotten to it?

Quinlin had skimmed the file earlier. What else, he wondered, had he missed? He knew he had to get his mind off Sarah and concentrate. He started at the beginning of Harris's file and went page by page. The admittance sheet listed Harris as barely twenty-three; under his employment, Harris had written "investor." Quinlin figured investor meant that Harris lived off daddy's money. He knew he was right when he got to the space for insurance information. It was marked *prepaid in full.* Twenty-eight days in the jitter joint totaled about fifteen thousand, a substantial amount of change for a guy barely twenty-three.

Harris had left the emergency notification section blank. In the family history data, he listed his mother as deceased, but he showed his father, Robert Blaine Harris, Sr., with an address on Armstrong Parkway in Highland Park. So in the event that Junior suffered an alcoholic seizure that left him a cucumber, he didn't give a damn whether anyone notified Daddy? Or maybe Daddy, like a lot of relatives of drunks, had simply run out of patience with his errant son and disowned him. Still, someone had picked up the tab for Junior's treatment. There was probably a story there, Quinlin figured.

Quinlin motioned McCarren off the phone, and they headed for Junior's condominium. The high-rise condo overlooked Turtle Creek in Highland Park, the genteel home to Dallas's deepest pockets, and was less than a mile from Daddy's house, proving, Quinlin quipped, that apples really don't fall far from the tree. The traffic out of downtown was stop-and-start. When Quinlin finally got to the front of the long line of idling traffic, he cursed a DART bus which was parked in a right-hand lane. The driver had flicked on his emergency blinkers, leaned his seat as far back as it would go, and looked to be asleep.

"Bastard must be ahead of schedule," Quinlin muttered. "Or on coffee break."

"Maybe he's broken down," McCarren suggested.

Quinlin wasn't in the mood for explanations that didn't include negligence or malfeasance, not when it came to the city's mass transit department, which he cursed on a daily basis.

"Naw, he's just fucking off," Quinlin said. "At least if he's asleep, he's not running over people in red lights."

Once out of the central business district, the traffic lightened and the scenery changed as they neared Highland Park. The bus fumes and mirrored office buildings were replaced by yellow and gold carpets of zinnias planted alongside Turtle Creek and multimillion-dollar mansions.

"How'd you like to wake up to this every morning?" McCarren asked.

Quinlin recounted a story in the *Register & News* in which Highland Park's most influential residents were privately in a snit because Jerry Jones, the millionaire owner of the Dallas Cowboys, had built an addition onto his Spanish-style stucco mansion. They didn't object to the expansion per se, according to the story, but the pink was "too garish."

"It might be an acceptable color in Arkansas," one anonymous resident was quoted, "but in Highland Park, it's simply inappropriate for the surroundings."

"What you figure an aesthetic faux pas like that would do to a neighbor's property value?" McCarren asked. "Drop it $500,000? Maybe a million? See, even the big guys have it tough."

"Bet I could learn to live with it," Quinlin said, remembering the Shetland-sized mouse that had scampered across his naked foot that morning at Sweaty Suites. Sarah's lawyer had had the decency to phone, explaining that her divorce petition was now "moot" and that he could return to his house if he chose. He chose not to. He wasn't having that much success staying sober anyway. Sarah's ghosts, he knew, sure as hell wouldn't help.

Young Robert Harris's neighbors at One Regency Park, according to a database Quinlin ran on the computer, included a former Republican governor and oilman, a smattering of CEOs, and several old-line families whose money was so old *they* probably couldn't remember its origin.

The detectives parked the white Ford in the circular drive beneath the burgundy awning, and a doorman encountered them before they could get inside the lobby.

Mr. Harris did, in fact, live in 16-D—the "penthouse," the doorman called it—but he was "not available."

"What does that mean?" Quinlin asked with a semigrin.

"It means, sir, that Mr. Harris is not presently accepting visitors," the doorman said, eyeing the Crown Victoria haughtily.

McCarren produced his badge from his breast pocket.

"Accept this," he said. "Is he up there or not?"

The doorman didn't appear overly impressed with the badge. "Mr. Harris has been ill and in the hospital," he said. "He is on an extended vacation, recuperating."

The doorman had his eye on a red Jaguar convertible pulling

up the incline into the drive.

"We have valet parking, of course, and you're going to have to move your car."

"When'd he leave?" Quinlin asked.

"Yesterday, if I recall correctly."

The doorman grimaced at the brunette in the Jag and held his palms up helplessly.

"When's he coming back?"

"I don't have that information."

Quinlin smiled at the perturbed brunette and waved cordially.

"Who would know?" Quinlin asked, still smiling.

"I'm sure I wouldn't know, sir."

Quinlin produced a business card with a silver DPD shield embossed on it. "When he comes back, or if you hear from him, have him call me at this number."

"Hope it starts this time," McCarren said, nodding toward the Ford and winking at his partner. "Sure screwed us up this morning."

"I wouldn't worry too much," Quinlin said, pointing at the Jag. "She'll give us a jump if we need it."

It took only four minutes to get to the senior Robert Harris's mansion, which sat on a full acre of some of the highest-priced residential property in Dallas County. The house was a two-story English Tudor made of hand-cut Austin stone with an archway over the side driveway that connected with servant quarters. It lay far back from Armstrong Parkway, beyond a circular drive that was probably an eighth of a mile and bordered by red begonias. The grounds were manicured like putting greens and enclosed by a black wrought-iron fence. Fortunately, the double gate into the circular drive was open.

The doorbell was a series of chimes that lasted a good ten seconds.

"Maybe," McCarren said, "Daddy got tired of Junior being

a sot—no reflection intended—and cut him off."

"I prefer the term *lush*," Quinlin said.

A man about sixty, wearing a gray suit, finally opened the door.

Seeing Mr. Harris, he allowed, would be quite impossible.

"Mr. Harris died two weeks ago," he said.

Quinlin identified himself and showed his badge.

"How did he die, if you don't mind my asking?"

"I understand it was a heart attack, though Mr. Blackstock would certainly know more about that than I."

Averill Blackstock was a name partner in a small but prestigious downtown law firm. He had handled the business and legal affairs of Robert Harris, Sr., for nearly four decades, a period of time in which his client had gone from wildcatter "without a pot to piss in," he said, to one of the wealthiest independent royalty producers in the Southwest.

Blackstock was cooperative and chatty, an old-school Texas lawyer who still maintained straightforwardness—particularly since his client was dead and beyond the reach of anything a couple of homicide cops could be asking about. The lawyer also, Quinlin noticed with envy, wore a pair of black anteater Lucchese cowboy boots worth about $1,200.

"Bob had more money than some small countries." Blackstock grinned, shaking his head. "Not that you'd know it from talking to him and not that it smoothed any of his rough edges. He was tough and mean like the old-time wildcatters, and he cussed like a sailor on liberty."

"Was he a drinking man?" Quinlin asked.

"Johnnie Walker Black by the barrel-loads," Blackstock said, looking at the detective curiously. "Why'd you ask?"

"Just wondering," Quinlin said. "How'd he get along with Robert Junior?"

Blackstock's face turned serious, and he rolled his chair back from the desk and folded his hands over his stomach.

"So this is about young Robert, huh?" the lawyer asked. He waited a decent interval and neither detective volunteered a response. "Well, it would be fair to say father and son got along like a couple of starved buzzards. You have to understand that my client grew up dirt-poor in the Great Depression, no money, not much schooling to speak of. But he was a hard worker, ambitious, and had a lot of natural common sense. He started out a roughneck. He didn't always play by the rules, he cut a few corners here and there, I suspect. But at some point, he hocked everything he owned, borrowed every dollar he could get his hands on, and started drilling oil wells. And he was damned good at it. At the time of his death, he was worth about six-hundred-seventy-five million, give or take.

"He had Robert late in life, not a life, by the way, that was particularly harmonious. By fifteen, young Robert had problems in school, primarily because he had a drinking problem. I figure Bob probably forgave him for that, considering he was a walking still himself. What the young boy didn't have was any ambition or drive. And I don't think his father could forgive him for that. It's fair to say that Bob regarded his son as a spoiled rich kid. How do you think they got along?"

The detectives digested the information.

"As a matter of fact," Blackstock said, "I defended father against son a couple of years ago, when young Robert turned twenty-one. It's public record; you'd find it anyway."

The oilman had created a trust for his only child the first week of his life. It was happier times, and Robert Senior, proud enough to have given his name to the boy, wanted to ensure his son would never face the tribulations he had. Three percent of every barrel of crude went into the account. The trust was payable in full at age seventeen if his father was deceased, at age twenty-one if his father was still alive.

"Pure and simple," Blackstock said. "Junior came after his trust money, which by then had reached about seventy-five million after taxes, and we tried to break the trust. There had been certain events, family things, that had made Daddy reconsider his charity. I told Bob that trusts were damned near impossible to penetrate, but he was hell-bent. We lost, just like I told him we would. Young Robert walked off with his trust money, free and clear.

"To my knowledge," the lawyer said, "it was the last time they saw each other, there in the courtroom."

"Could Junior have killed Daddy?" Quinlin asked.

The question was off-the-wall, and it caught his partner and the lawyer off guard. The lawyer recovered quickly.

"I'm figuring you know something I don't or you wouldn't ask that question," Blackstock said. "Tell you the truth, it wouldn't surprise me in the least. Young Robert, well, he's kind of different, I guess you'd say, like he doesn't have any emotion about things. Cold, you know? But killing his father? Honestly, I never really thought about it. But proving it, now that'd be a horse of a different color."

Robert Harris, Sr., was seventy-two and drank like a horse, according to his lawyer of forty years. But he also had physicals every six months, and routinely was pronounced to have the body of a sixty year old. He'd never had heart trouble in his life.

"Yet the doctor tells me that's all he can figure," Blackstock said, "a heart attack."

The old lawyer ruminated over something, started to speak, and apparently thought better of it. Then he broke his own silence.

"I don't want to play poker with you boys," he said. "You obviously have some interest in young Robert. I haven't asked. Don't really need to know. 'Sides that, I don't have anything to give you in that regard except something I can't prove."

He pressed the intercom on his phone and told his secretary to make a copy of Robert Junior's affidavit in the trust case.

Then he explained to Quinlin and McCarren that while his client was dead, he nonetheless felt a moral obligation to continue to act in his best interests. That included, he said, not dragging his reputation through a mud puddle.

"You'll leave here with some allegations that Junior made under oath," he said. "Frankly, it wouldn't surprise me if some of it were true. 'Course, that's not what I told the judge when I was fighting to keep it out of the trial. It could explain some things. I hope you'll be discreet in your use of it.

"The other thing is, and you'll think this is the meanderings of a suspicious old man, but the hospital gave me the clothing and belongings that my client was wearing when he died. There was something there that just didn't add up, not about the Bob I knew."

Blackstock wasn't moving quickly enough for Quinlin.

"You sure got my attention," the detective said. "What was it?"

"Keep in mind, my client drank from the moment he got up until he went to sleep. Johnnie Walker Black was his only good friend. Well, supposedly he had this card in his shirt pocket, the kind that they give out at AA meetings."

Quinlin glanced at his partner. McCarren had picked up on it, too.

"You know a man over forty years," Blackstock said. "I know Robert B. Harris, Sr., would just as soon have a dead rat in his pocket as an AA card."

Quinlin retrieved Junior's sworn affidavit and three volumes of his testimony in the trust case from Blackstock's secretary on the way out.

While McCarren drove, Quinlin filed an attempt to locate on the license plate for young Harris's black Porsche convertible.

"This is an attempt to locate," Quinlin emphasized. "*Do not* apprehend, but advise location immediately."

"I know what you're thinking," McCarren said. "The AA card is the best thing we've got. But if Daddy died more than two weeks ago, Junior would have still been locked in the hospital."

"I wouldn't bet the farm on that," Quinlin said.

27

Jeb Quinlin cursed Southwest Suites. Again. The tired, tan two-story lay in the midst of a cluster of worn-out motels along Airport Freeway in Irving, halfway between downtown Dallas and the southern entrance to D/FW Airport. In their original incarnations, the motels had been Holiday Inns, Ramadas, Rodeways, and La Quintas. But thirty years of depreciation and decay had driven the national chains farther west toward the airport, where they erected high rises with bubbling fountains and in-room messaging systems. Independents with stretched financing and nonexistent maintenance took over the rooms that already had absorbed generations of traveling strangers' sweat, body odor, and God only knew what else. Quinlin tried to check his imagination as he walked barefoot across the stained green carpet.

His room was around the corner from a cinder-block enclosure that contained a Coke machine, a candy machine, and an ancient icemaker that sounded like a scrap-iron truck on rough road. On Tuesday and Thursday mornings, between 4:00 and 4:30, a forklift truck emptied the Dumpster across the alley, slamming it to the ground with the intensity of an Airbus falling from five thousand feet.

Quinlin didn't return to his room until he was dead tired

and ready to sleep. At first light in the morning, he didn't linger between the sheets. He shaved and showered as fast as he could and fled to the parking lot for the Scout. It was a stellar day if his journey didn't include a barefooted encounter with Steroid, world's largest roach.

Customarily, Quinlin made a U-turn beneath the eight lanes of Airport Freeway and headed halfway up the block on the frontage road to a Diamond Shamrock convenience store. An engaging Ethiopian woman, whose name tag said she was *Nurit*, had quickly snapped to his routine. She had three packs of Marlboro Lights waiting on the counter by the time he appeared with his sixteen-ounce black coffee. Balancing the hot coffee and a Marlboro he lighted in the parking lot, he tried to fight two lanes of oncoming traffic for the inside frontage lane and a green light at the intersection. With luck, he could hit the entrance lane to Texas 183 and be downtown in twenty-five minutes.

On this morning, seven minutes before 8:00 A.M., he made it only to the middle lane, and when the driver in front of him abruptly slammed on her brakes for a yellow light, Quinlin jammed the brakes hard on the Scout, sloshing coffee on his khakis and stopping only inches from her rear bumper. He was dabbing at the coffee with a Kleenex and cursing when he saw the glint in the tiny convex mirror to his left.

A dark-complexioned man with a pockmarked face was leaning halfway out the car's passenger window. Quinlin's eyes moved curiously to the Scout's larger outside mirror. Was the man trying to tell him something? He figured he must have a low tire. Quinlin was reaching for the window crank when he saw the muzzle. He watched in the left mirror as the car eased up beside him. Instinctively, Quinlin tossed the coffee cup into the passenger floorboard and lunged between the seat and the dash. He heard himself groan as he jabbed his ribs into the shift for four-wheel drive.

The blast deafened him, and shards of glass made spitting noises as they hit the opposite window. Flying glass stung his face and left arm. There was a second or more of falling glass and then four more blasts in rapid succession. The last shot was low, ripping through the upper part of the driver's door. Quinlin felt air swoosh over his left ear and heard the impact on the door above his head and shattering glass from the passenger window.

He was breathing hard and hugging the floorboard as tightly as he could. Time to get small. He lay still, waiting for the next round. A couple of inches lower, and he was a dead man. Instead, he heard the high pitch of winding RPMs. He pushed himself from the floorboard with his right arm, peering over the dash in time to catch the black quarter-panel of a Lexus coupe rounding the corner of the underpass.

His right palm stung badly, and he realized he was propping himself up on a floorboard of broken glass. The white filter and ash of the Marlboro was still between his fingers.

"You'd be dead if you hadn't been in the Scout," Paul McCarren said. "It's a lot higher than a Lexus. If you'd been eyeball-to-eyeball with the bastard, you wouldn't have to worry about bleeding."

"*Two* bastards. He had to have a driver."

Quinlin was sitting on the back of the Mobile Care Unit, flinching as a paramedic used tiny forceps to pick glass from his face. His shirt was drenched in blood, but the wounds were superficial. The only real damage was the right side of his rib cage where he'd fallen into the shifter for the four-wheel drive. He figured he'd cracked a rib.

"Irving Memorial is about twelve blocks from here," the paramedic said, renewing his suggestion. "They can get this glass out a lot better than I can, and you need an X-ray on those ribs. Plus, you may be about a pint low. Take maybe thirty minutes."

"Naw, it feels like you got the big pieces out already," Quinlin said. "But I'd appreciate it if you could wrap my ribs real tight. That'd help."

McCarren knew better than to argue. He was pacing and thinking out loud, stream of conscious.

"How do you know that Harris wouldn't hire somebody to kill you? It's not like he doesn't have the money. We asked a lot of questions in a lot of places yesterday. You're the one who keeps telling me how smart he is. Why not?"

"Ninety-nine percent of serials work by themselves," Quinlin said. It was another tidbit, this one from an FBI seminar he'd attended five years earlier. "And because he's an ideologue or whatever you call 'em. A fanatic. Harris wouldn't pay somebody to do something he gets his rocks off on. All this bullshit, these killings, are a crusade with him. It's his holy war."

"So the zit-face with the MAC-10 just doesn't like the way you change lanes?"

Quinlin shot his partner a go-to-hell look.

"Gimme your cell phone, Mac. I got a pretty good idea of what's going on here, and it ain't Harris."

Quinlin dialed Madeline's number.

"Madeline, darlin'," he said calmly. "I'm just curious. When's the last time you heard from Beau?"

"You did?" Quinlin asked, looking down at his beeper.

"Yeah," he said, checking it, "the message is here. I, uh, guess I just didn't hear it go off."

Beau Meggers, according to Madeline, had called her about 8:00 A.M. from his jet. He was so irate he barely made sense. Less than twenty-four hours after the divorce was finalized and her $2.5-million check drawn on the Meggers Group had cleared her bank, the IRS froze Meggers's bank accounts. He had gotten a call from a banker in San Diego a night earlier, saying the IRS had showed up in his office; agents of the IRS Criminal Investigation Division had locked up Meggers's account and seized all the records associated with it. It had been too late to check with the other banks, but when Meggers had phoned a bank this morning in White Plains, he had heard the same version from the East Coast.

"Where is he?" Quinlin asked.

"He didn't say, just that he was on the jet," Madeline said. "But, Jeb, he was crazy, saying that something bad was about to happen to my boyfriend. He cursed me, accused me of jumping in the bed with cops to ruin him. Said it was supposed to be a message to me. He went crazy, screaming at me about testifying against him. You've got to be careful, Jeb. He knows who you are. I guess he had me followed. There's no telling what he might try.

"Oh, and he said it was out of his hands, whatever that means."

Quinlin knew exactly what it meant. Meggers was drawing heat from the criminal guys at the IRS, but it probably wasn't nearly as hot as the heat from the South Americans. The impounded funds were *their* money. Madeline and her little plan had jammed up her ex-husband big-time with both parties, one of which wanted to put him in prison and the other of which undoubtedly was intent on making him die slowly.

"The feds could fuck up a crowbar," Quinlin said. "I don't want you there. I'll come get you and move you to a hotel somewhere. Put you on a plane to—"

"No, I can't," she said. "The IRS brought a box of bank files over last night. I'm going through them, trying to identify the illegal accounts and all the wire transfers. They're sending a messenger for them later. It's part of our deal. I've got to finish.

"Besides, your uniformed cop is still out front," she said, trying to reassure him. "I saw him ten minutes ago sitting in his car. I'm fine. It's you he's threat—"

"I'm fine," he said. "If you hear from him again, find out where he is. And let me know immediately. And as soon as you're finished with that fed stuff, I want you out of there. You hear me? I'll call you later. And *be careful.*"

McCarren looked quizzical.

"This isn't about Harris," Quinlin told him.

His partner continued to stare intently.

"It's about Madeline and her ex-husband, okay?"

"You mean a domestic deal? You got shot at because you're—"

"Don't be a jerk," Quinlin said. "Her ex-husband's tangled up with a bunch of drug smugglers and Madeline's caught in the middle. I'll explain on the way downtown."

McCarren motioned at the Scout as they headed for his Ford. The truck looked like it had marginally survived Beirut. The side glasses were blown out along with two-thirds of the windshield, the outside mirror was shattered, the driver's door had a bullet hole in it, and the floorboard was puddled with Quinlin's blood.

"Guess the silver lining is that you've finally got to get a new set of wheels," the young detective said.

Quinlin raised an eyebrow and yelped in pain.

"Get real," he said.

28

Quinlin wasn't cavalier about not going to the hospital. In fact, his ribs screamed internally every time he took a breath or turned his torso. Denying medical attention was rooted in time management. And staying sober. He knew doctors would have admitted him, not in some genuine concern for his well-being, but to protect the City of Dallas against an in-the-line-of-duty medical claim. Cops were notorious for cheating the customary twenty-year period for pensions by claiming early medical retirements. The city knew it was a scam and began hospitalizing cops for hangnails, just to build the medical record against potential fraudulent claims.

Getting laid up in the hospital would mean Robert Harris, Jr., would continue unabated and on the loose, probably whacking a few other drunks, and Madeline, meanwhile, would have to fend for herself in the ambush between the feds and her cheesedick ex-husband. Propped on his butt in a hospital bed, he knew, would only add to the stress. And stress would only add to his wanting a drink, and by the time the snowball reached the bottom of the hill, it would be a genuine, by God, avalanche of boozy temptation. Besides, he'd had his fill of hospitals.

Once in the office, and between inquiries from colleagues

about the fresh spatter wounds on his face, Quinlin dutifully wrote up his report on the attempted capital murder of a police officer. He typed his name as the complainant and listed the suspects as unknown. The paperwork was a waste of time. He had a vague description of the shooter, no description of the driver, no plate number for the Lexus, and no idea of the whereabouts of Beau Meggers, if, in fact, it was even Beau who had ordered the botched hit. Quinlin doubted Meggers had the stones to take someone out; it sounded more like the South Americans acting on their own. The detective vowed to never again berate victims who didn't know anything.

For no good reason other than harassment, Quinlin sent McCarren to the corporate offices of the Meggers Group to ask questions about their missing boss. Quinlin was certain his partner wouldn't come up with anything, but if Meggers had a snitch on his staff that he checked in with, the snitch would undoubtedly pass along the fact that a homicide cop was asking questions about him. Meggers was a mope playing over his head, and Quinlin figured the combined pressure of the IRS, the South Americans, and DPD Homicide would make his sphincter slam shut like a cellar door.

Quinlin was tired of answering questions and catching curious stares in the bullpen. He had to concentrate. The shooting, as badly as it pissed him off, was a diversion. There he was a peripheral player in a game that didn't really involve him. Which wasn't to say he wouldn't deal with Beau Meggers when the time came. But his job was to catch a serial killer. He had to keep his eye on the ball. He forwarded his calls to an empty sergeant's office, gathered the stack of documents Averill Blackstock had given him, Robert Harris, Jr.'s, file from Cedar Ridge, and sequestered himself in the sergeant's office.

Except for trips to refill his coffee, Quinlin stayed in the small office until he had skimmed all three volumes of Robert Harris's trust case and read his twenty-three-page affidavit line by line. He had just finished when McCarren made it back to the office.

"Other than the fact that Meggers has been porking two of his assistants, I came up dry," McCarren said. "And you know how I found that out? One pointed out the other one. Ol' Beau must be quite a trophy.

"I also have a very strong feeling that I wouldn't care if the South Americans found him before we do. I think we would admire the efficiency of their justice."

"Junior killed Daddy, no question," Quinlin said, loading a fresh packet of coffee into the maker and changing the subject. "There's a note in Harris's file, a memo from a nurse to Bergoff, that says Junior had an afternoon furlough, didn't sign out on the log and came back early.

"I actually remember it. My first hour out of detox. I saw Harris at the nurses' station when he came in. I just couldn't remember the date. That date, my young friend, would be the same date that appears on Daddy's death certificate."

"You got to love coincidence."

"Of course, it doesn't mean jack," Quinlin said, "except to prove he had opportunity. It also means he's whacked five, not four."

"*However* he's doing it," McCarren said. "I stopped off at the ME's. I've never seen Berryman so humble. He's calling this 'the case of his career.' He's taking it personal."

"By the way, we owe Averill Blackstock, Esquire, the biggest steak in Dallas. The answer to *why* Harris is killing is in the affidavit. Stevie Wonder could see it. I know why Blackstock didn't want a jury looking at it."

According to the transcript, the judge had agreed with Blackstock and ruled Robert Harris, Jr.'s, affidavit irrelevant and inadmissible in the trust case against his father. It was a self-serving document, Quinlin understood that, but it was revealing nonetheless. Millions of dollars, one of the most exclusive addresses in Texas, a summer retreat in Colorado, and a Gulfstream jet, and none of it had spared the Harris family from the same kinds of turbulence that wrecked families on food stamps.

More than once, Quinlin found himself swallowing around a lump in his throat as he paged through young Harris's affidavit. Their social classes were light-years apart, to be sure, but Quinlin and Harris shared a stunningly similar and sorry past. At times reading the document, Quinlin saw Harris as a child; sometimes he saw himself. The detective empathized, but always he weighed Harris's childhood tribulations against the backdrop of the innocent people he killed. The detective was transfixed reading the affidavit, watching the psychosis build in a total stranger until the man became unhinged nearly a decade later and tortured and murdered innocent Sarah, who couldn't have had a clue why a man she had never known was killing her ever so slowly.

Harris's affidavit was a tragic psychological autopsy, but it didn't change fact. Facts frequently were pathetic, particularly in Quinlin's business, but they didn't change bottom lines. Facts only mitigated or explained. Five people, Quinlin was convinced, had died at Harris's hands. However he did it. Now, at least, Quinlin thought he understood why.

By young Harris's account in the affidavit, his millionaire father was not only a drunk, but a vicious one. For as long as Junior could remember, his father had beaten his mother, Dora. As he grew older, he attempted to intercede in his mother's behalf, only to be beaten, too. The younger Harris recounted a litany of broken bones, bloody noses, and bruises growing up.

"But whatever he did to me was mild compared to what he did to my mother," Harris swore in his statement. "On many occasions, the maid or some other member of the staff drove my mother to our doctor, Dr. Cranson, for emergency care. I recall three times in which she was actually hospitalized. On one of those occasions, the doctor even called the police, but they never did anything. My father was far too influential in Highland Park for anyone to charge him with domestic assault."

Highland Park had its own small police department and, Quinlin knew, officers weren't known for their aggressive enforcement, particularly against the power brokers who paid their salaries. In some ways, the police department was merely an extension of their constituents' servant staffs. While homeowners were on extended European vacations, according to a friend who once worked in the Highland Park department, cops were expected to visit the houses daily, not only to check security systems, but to fill swimming pools and make sure the lawn sprinklers had been turned on by the automatic timers. And on any given day, a minority or a blue-collar white in a pickup truck was guaranteed to be stopped for some infraction. The joke among Dallas cops was that the only way a Mexican or black could safely navigate Highland Park streets without being arrested was to have a lawnmower in the back of his truck.

Over time, according to Junior's affidavit, Dora Harris seldom ventured from the mansion. In consummate irony, Quinlin thought, she elected to soothe her wounds with the same elixir that created them—alcohol. Twice, Junior recalled, once immediately before her death, his mother had been hospitalized at Timbermeadow, an exclusive, private mental hospital that also treated alcoholics. She underwent intensive therapy and was given prescriptions, he said, but neither visit apparently was successful.

Mother and son kept the horror of their trauma to themselves, and Quinlin figured the abuse probably became their unspoken bond. The detective knew firsthand; he had invoked the secrecy himself as an abused child. Once, when he was in the second grade, he had confided to a friend that his father got drunk and beat him. The boy not only avoided him like he was a leper, he told other kids in the class, and Jeb was taunted and teased during recesses about his father. Even as he read Junior's affidavit, he was embarrassed at how vividly he still felt the pain. All he ever wanted was to be *normal.* It didn't seem even to a kid to be asking too much.

Later, as a uniformed patrolman, Quinlin had almost daily doses of domestic battles. In virtually every case, mother and child lied about how they suffered injuries, and they almost never filed charges. Deep in his mind's eye he saw a seven-year-old boy, his face covered with blood and his eyes puffy, who refused to say his drunk father beat him. "I got to stay here," the boy told Quinlin. "You get to go. I wish I was lucky like you."

According to Harris's account, he stole his first swallow of booze from his father's bar at age nine. He was drinking steadily by eleven, and by the seventh grade, he was in counseling for alcoholism. Two weeks short of his sixteenth birthday, he was expelled from St. Matthew's, a preppy private school, after an instructor noticed he was disoriented and discovered a flask of bourbon in his book bag.

"I find it more than a little hypocritical and ironic," the younger Harris wrote, "that my father of all people would tell the headmaster that he didn't understand why I had a problem with alcohol. I inherited his impaired genes, and it was predestined that I would be an alcoholic."

Impaired genes? It was curious phraseology, Quinlin thought. *Predestined.* They were obvious references to a growing body of research that showed alcoholism as an inherited trait, similar, Quinlin supposed, to the genetic tendency toward being left-handed with red hair and freckles. *I inherited his impaired genes.* It was a simple, declaratory sentence, actually neutral in its meaning. But coupled with *predestined that I would be an alcoholic*, Quinlin could see the anger and resentment on the page. And blame. He highlighted the sentence with his yellow marker and read on:

> There wasn't a day of my life that he didn't expose me to alcohol. The Southwind jet had a full-sized bar, and his Suburban had a wood-grained console stocked with Johnnie Walker Black and a small, refrigerated ice chest. It is difficult to remember my father without a drink in his hand, and certainly never without the smell of scotch on his breath.
>
> His drinking ruined our lives. He was physically abusive to my mother and me, but his mental cruelty was probably worse. He had several girlfriends, and one of them, Gwendolyn, he put up in a condominium less than a mile from our house. He flaunted her to my mother on many occasions, and one of my mother's best friends lived in the same condominium complex, and saw them together frequently. Of course, the friend told my mother.

Quinlin figured he didn't have to have a doctorate in psychology to figure the contempt Harris would have had for a promiscuous woman like Kristin Williamson. If even half of the self-serving affidavit Robert Harris, Jr., had drafted about his father was true, Quinlin knew there was more than a little motivation for murder. He had seen people killed for their Air Nikes and gold wheel rims, and for shooting the finger at a tailgater or just simply because they were standing on the wrong corner at the wrong time.

The years of violence and dysfunction within the Harris mansion erupted cataclysmically in the predawn hours of a July morning in 1991. Junior was almost sixteen, by his sworn account, having been expelled only a few days earlier from St. Matthew's, and grounded by his father pending a decision on his punishment. Among the possibilities were a military school in New Mexico and a Catholic boarding school in New Jersey. "He actually didn't care," young Harris wrote, "as long as I wasn't around any more. Mother insisted that I wasn't going anywhere. She wanted to enroll me in public school and get me more counseling for my drinking."

Junior went out the back door. It was an uneventful escape; his mother, a week out of Timbermeadow, and father were screaming at each other in the study. Junior went four houses down to a seventeen-year-old friend's who had a car. They drove to South Dallas and paid a black man fifty dollars to buy them a bottle of Jack Daniel's. By young Harris's account, he returned home at 3:00 A.M. "too blitzed to care if I got caught." His father intercepted him at the back door and pulled him into the breakfast dining room.

"He told me that Mother had just fallen down the stairs and was dead," his affidavit said. "He said I needed to say that I saw her stumble and fall. He said it would look better if I said I saw it instead of him, considering that the police had been called previously about him beating Mother. He swore to me that she really did fall and that he had been in his bedroom when he heard her fall."

In a poignant portion of the statement, Harris had written: "It was the only time in my life that my father acted like he needed me."

The teenager recited his father's story, claiming that he had witnessed his mother's fatal fall. Certainly an accident was conceivable; she had a documented drinking problem and had only returned home recently from treatment. Too, there had been a violent confrontation with her husband over their son's schooling, more than enough stress to knock her off the wagon.

Quinlin imagined how the kid—intoxicated, disheveled, lying, and scared—would have appeared to investigators. He wouldn't have been a witness, but a suspect.

Young Harris was taken to Highland Park's police station, ostensibly to give a statement about his mother's tragic accident. The youngster knew something was wrong when they drew a syringe of blood from his forearm and locked him in a juvenile detention cell all night. Early the next morning, his father appeared at the station with a criminal defense lawyer, introduced the two and dismissed himself. From outward appearances, he was the dutiful father attempting to shield his son.

"I asked the lawyer why they kept me all night," the younger Harris said in his affidavit. "He told me my mother had bruises on her throat. She had been choked before she was shoved down the stairs. There were other bruises that they said couldn't have come from a fall. It wasn't an accident. It was a homicide. And the lawyer said the police knew I was lying."

From the questions the detectives asked, in the presence of the lawyer his father had retained for him, it was clear to young Harris that his father had left him open to blame. Only later would the boy learn that his father had actually framed him for a murder he committed. Masterfully, his father not only had concocted a story that removed him from the crime scene, he left his only son standing in the middle of it. The elder Harris claimed to have been ill with a stomach virus and had gone to bed early. He heard his wife scream, he said, and rushed out of his bedroom. He looked over the second-floor railing to see her body on the marble-tiled floor beneath him. Robert Junior, he claimed, was standing emotionless at the railing, looking down at his mother. As if he hadn't betrayed his son enough by putting him at the crime scene, he obligingly provided police a motive. Earlier in the evening, Harris Sr. told police, his wife and son had had a violent battle over *her* decision to send him off to military school.

Realizing too late that he was about to take the fall for his father, the teenager changed his story and told the truth to a pair of a status-quo Highland Park detectives and a defense lawyer paid handsomely by one of the wealthiest oilmen in the country. The detectives perfunctorily interviewed the parents of young Robert's alibi, the seventeen-year-old with whom he had been drinking, but they had claimed their son was at home all night. Interviewing their son, they said, would be quite impossible; he had left on a two-month ski tour in the Swiss Alps.

In Texas, juvenile crime is handled as a civil action. Hearings and trials are conducted in closed court, and the cases are sealed from public view. Quinlin imagined how the scenario would have played out behind closed doors: The prominent defense attorney would have portrayed the younger Harris as a "troubled teenager," lamented his documented history of alcoholism and incorrigibleness, and begged the court's lenience because of his incapacitated state.

Texas judges run for reelection every four years, and creating influential enemies doesn't build political longevity. Quinlin figured the judge would have been predisposed to accept the senior Harris's magnanimous offer to hospitalize his son, at his own expense, in a private mental institution in Austin. Young Harris was kept there three and a half years, based on a commitment order by the State of Texas.

McCarren was incredulous when Quinlin finished the story.

"Daddy wins all the way around," the young detective said. "He gets rid of a wife he's tired of beating, gets to play full-time with his girlfriend, zeroes out the problem child, and sets up the stage to screw the boy out of his inheritance. This guy's father of the fuckin' year. I would have killed the bastard, too."

"Yeah, it would have been a public service," Quinlin said. "*If* he'd just stopped there."

29

Four hours after Quinlin expanded his attempt-to-locate bulletin to include the midcities and Fort Worth, a diligent patrolman for the D/FW Airport Department of Public Safety found Robert Harris's black turbocharged Porsche 928 parked in the south remote lot of the airport. The electronic monitor at the gate showed the Porsche had entered the lot at 10:58 P.M. a night earlier.

Dumping the Porsche, Quinlin knew, was a significant development. Harris knew Quinlin was onto him. There was no love lost between Harris and Blackstock; his father's longtime lawyer wouldn't have tipped him. The doorman at the condo? Maybe the man in the gray suit at his father's house. Or maybe Harris had been watching *him*. He didn't think so. By habit, Quinlin watched his rearview mirror as much as the windshield, a fact that only recently had saved his life.

Something had made Harris rabbit. With his money, he could have gone anywhere. Or had he split? Maybe he had just rented another car, a possibility that scared Quinlin. That would mean he hadn't completed his agenda. He was volatile now, more frenzied, just as Dr. Aylor had predicted he would be. Poor Sarah had proved that.

Quinlin took the airlines, starting with those that had international departures. McCarren started on the car rental agencies, calling their security officers with Harris's driver's license number and physical description.

Only twenty minutes into his his list, McCarren yelled, "I got it!

"Harris rented a white Ford Taurus from Hertz last night at 11:23 P.M. He's got it for a week."

Quinlin called Communications with the plate number, Harris's license information, and his physical description. He hung up the phone and muttered that virtually every car in company fleets was white and how Taurus was the biggest seller in Dallas, surpassing even the Honda Accord.

"How'd you know that?" McCarren asked. "Where do you get this stuff?"

"Just a little tidbit from a vast repertoire of useless knowledge," Quinlin said. "Actually, I read the business pages."

The irony, Quinlin also knew, was that he didn't even have enough probable cause to issue an arrest bulletin; it had to be an attempt to locate, which most patrol units regarded as seriously as a prowler call.

Harris had opportunity: He was on furlough when his father died; he was in the hospital when Willard and Kristin were found on the ward, and he had been discharged and on the streets when Anne Marie and Sarah were killed. He had motive: The affidavit more than linked his background of booze and betrayal to the cryptic messages left on the bodies. But everything Quinlin knew was circumstantial; there wasn't an iota of physical evidence to justify searching his car or condo, much less arrest him. The district attorney, professionally obtuse and personally condescending, had been crystal clear on that.

"And you want me to give you a warrant because this Harris guy is some kind of sociopath?" the DA asked cynically. "And that makes him different, how, from say two hundred fifty thousand or so other people registered to vote in this town?"

"You know goddamned well why I'm asking for a warrant," Quinlin had said. "And if you weren't so worried about win—"

"Fuck you," the prosecutor had said. "You got nothing to put your guy with the dead drunks or with the shots fired at you."

"Not all the victims were fuckin' drunks."

"Well, bring me a thumbprint, a license-plate number from a murder scene, a thread, even a fuckin' hair off your boy and I'll give you your warrant. And until you do, I'm making sure Abrams keeps you out of the building."

Quinlin was pacing now, which only aggravated the pain in his ribs. He was reasonably trying to contemplate the unreasonable reactions of a psychotic killer. His hands tingled, he was sweaty and lightheaded, and his legs were rubbery. A drink would steady him. Not a binge, too much depended on him for that. Just one. A shot of straight Turkey to burn off the haze so he could get his bearings.

The reverie of Turkey was gone, and he realized he was staring out the window at Gold's Gym across Main. He was having a BUD, just like Stephens told him he would. Like everything else in AA, BUD was an acronym. He was Building Up to Drink. The symptoms were there: frustration and fatigue, stress, and he couldn't remember the last time he ate.

He headed down the hall, dodging a handcuffed suspect who lurched off-balance in a shove from the uniformed cop behind him.

"Sorry," the cop said. "He thought he'd just stay downstairs in the car."

Quinlin went to the vending machine, retrieved a stone-cold pimento cheese sandwich, a package of Fritos, and a decaffeinated Sprite. He spread them over his desk. It was the first time he had actually had time for a deep breath. The ribs were killing him. He couldn't remember to breathe shallowly until it was already too late. But the BUD genuinely troubled him, and he wondered how close he had come to the wagon running over him.

He called Madeline, told her he needed an AA meeting badly, and asked if he could pick her up for a five o'clock meeting. He decided to wait until her saw her in person to tell her about the shooting. It wasn't like he could keep it from her. His face looked like an acupuncturists' convention had practiced on it.

His mind jolted, and as he cradled the receiver between his ear and neck, he reached into the lap drawer and retrieved a brown prescription bottle. Finally, he could take his first shot of Antabuse.

Madeline said she was still up to her ears in financial documents. The IRS had received more faxes of records from banks throughout the country and had delivered them to her condo. More faxes were on the way, the last batch, the feds promised.

Quinlin rolled his eyes. Right.

"I'm actually helping them make some connections," Madeline said. "A lot of this stuff is coming back to me. But I'm going to be up all night going over this crap. You go ahead to a meeting today, sounds like you need one. But how about a noon meeting tomorrow? You familiar with the term 'afternoon delight,' Officer?"

It was vintage Madeline, saying something off the wall that she knew would make him blush.

"I don't know how many brain cells I've killed, but the ones for imagination still work," he said. "I can figure it out."

They talked about Robert Harris, Jr., and he told her about finding the Porsche. He'd also gotten a uniformed officer for his mother's house. Sarah had been killed for no reason other than her relationship to him. He wasn't going to risk another loved one.

"Peek out the window every once in a while," he told Madeline. "Make sure the cop isn't asleep. Or OD'd on doughnuts.

And you don't open the door for *anyone*, including messengers, unless the cop says it's cool, okay?"

"This is a poll, Detective Quinlin," she said, sounding cavalier again. "When's the last time you made love sober?"

"I don't remember the last time I made love, period."

"Well, that's too long," Madeline said, hanging up.

Quinlin nibbled at the cold pimento sandwich while he read the directions for Antabuse that were taped to the bottle. He needed to avoid anything that was made with alcohol: sauces, vinegar, cough mixtures, aftershave, even Tabasco, which was going to be a real problem. He doused everything with hot sauce.

Quinlin assumed Stephens had embellished the chemical's effects to scare him. But here it was in black and white. Antabuse was odorless and tasteless, innocuous and inert. It rode innocently along in the bloodstream *until* it encountered the faintest hint of alcohol. At that point, the way Quinlin read the directions, the ensuing concoction created the equivalent of rat poison.

It was impossible for a drunk to cheat the diabolical chemical. Apparently as little as a few milligrams of Antabuse mixed with a lot of alcohol triggered a violent reaction. Conversely, a substantial amount of Antabuse mixed with just a swallow of alcohol created an equally violent reaction.

Quinlin shook one of the octagonal, white pills into his hand. Stephens had given him the 500-milligram tablets, even though Quinlin had read that an average dose was 250 milligrams. Showed what Stephens though about his problem. One a day, it said on the label. He tossed the tab in his mouth and chased it with Sprite. His eyes moved to the larger, bold type at the bottom of the instructions: *In severe reactions, patient may experience respiratory depression, cardiovascular collapse, myocardial infarction, acute congestive heart failure, unconsciousness, and death.*

The detective was in midswallow, and he was so excited that gagged, sending the Sprite through his nose and burning like hell. He sloshed the drink returning it to his desk.

"I'll be goddamned," he yelled, coughing.

Congestive heart failure. It was what Dr. Berryman had found in the deaths of Beane, Williamson, and Ingram. And maybe Sarah.

Quinlin called the ME's office and demanded to be transferred to Dr. Berryman who, at the moment, was staring futilely through a microscope at tissue from one of Sarah's kidneys.

"Doctor, is Antabuse on your toxicological scans? Is it something you test for?"

"You mean the antidrinking medicine?" Berryman said. "Well, no. There's forty-seven different substances, but Antabuse isn't—"

"Well, *can* you test for Antabuse?" Quinlin asked.

"I don't know, to be honest," the forensic pathologist said. "I've never had to try. What's going on?"

"Maybe nothing. And I don't have any evidence yet, but I think Antabuse could be our killer. What'd you call it? Our mechanism of death?"

30

The room was beginning to fill with regulars. They held their disposable coffee cups in their left hands, reserving their rights to shake hands and slap an occasional shoulder or jab a rib. The old-timers, a few with twenty-five and thirty years' sobriety, had customary places of honor at center left. Everyone else at Dallas North AA fell in around them, as if whatever intangible, sober traits the revered old guys had mastered would miraculously rub off on them.

They awed Quinlin, the old guys. When the meeting started and they would go around introducing themselves, he would have to say, "I'm Jeb. I'm an alcoholic. I've been sober three days." Not years. *Days.* Actually seventy-one *hours.* They would all say, in their rote, singsong unison, "Hi, Jeb."

He would feel their eyes, maybe catch a knowing smile out of the corner of his eye. But he wouldn't look at them. A day after he had botched it at the Probable Cause, he had confessed to the four rounds of Turkey and Bud Lite. A few of the old guys sought him out afterward, each with their own piece of advice.

"Work the program," they had said. "One day at a time," they said. "Keep it simple, stupid," they said. He despised the clichés. They were what made AA work. He couldn't argue their success, but he hated hearing the same crap every time he turned around. The clichés minimized the severity of his state. He was shaky, under more pressure than he'd ever been in his life, and vulnerable. In twelve-step vernacular, he was a "dry drunk," which meant that while he wasn't actually drinking, he was still thinking like a drunk and consumed with fantasies of alcohol.

What he was, Quinlin thought, was a fuckin' cop trying his damnedest to stay sober *and* catch a raging sociopath before he killed again. *Work the program.* Bullshit. It was like telling a man holding by his fingernails to a seventh-story ledge to "hold on." Well, duh, *how?*

He envied them, despised actually a few of the more sanctimonious ones, and wondered if he'd ever even get to say *year.* Twenty-five years for him was about as likely as getting the right six numbers in the lottery.

Quinlin was in the lobby dodging the pregame warm-up. Hugging, he surmised, apparently was as critical to staying sober as humiliating yourself in front of strangers. He hated the ritual. Not to mention the fact that he knew the real recovering alcoholics, the old pros, would look at his face and assume he'd stumbled again and gotten his ass kicked in a beer joint brawl. He wasn't in the mood for knowing grins.

He saw the Cedar Ridge drunks as they filed in. They were awkward and hesitant, like cats dropped into new surroundings, and they stopped at the last row and slid in sideways, keeping their eyes on the floor. True to habit, Coal Tar dragged up the rear like a prison bull. Quinlin grabbed him and steered the big man to a deserted row halfway up, motioning him into a chair.

Coal Tar jerked his arm dramatically from Quinlin's grasp as he dropped into the chair, assuming mock indignation.

"You been shaving with a brick or what?" he said, catching Quinlin's face. "Jeeesus, you look like shit."

"Harris is our man and he's on the run," Quinlin said. "I need you to help me. His file doesn't show any prescription for Antabuse. I've got to show he had access. There're two possibilities."

"Good evening," said the leader at the front of the room. "My name's Mark. I am an alcoholic."

"Hi, Mark." The room was in unison, like a scout meeting.

"Alcoholics Anonymous is a fellowship of men and women who share their experience, strength, and hope with each other that they may solve their common problem and help others to recover from alcoholism. The only requirement . . ."

"Harris spent three years in a psychiatric hospital in Austin before he ever got to Cedar Ridge," Quinlin said in an urgent whisper. "And he mentioned in an affidavit that his mother—she was a drunk, too—had been given 'medication' at Timbermeadow. I think that means Antabuse. Couldn't be anything else, could it?"

". . . Rarely have we seen a person fail who has thoroughly followed our path." Mark was into "How It Works," a part of the AA ritual that began every meeting.

"Is there any way you can find out," Quinlin whispered, "if he or his mother had a prescription for Antabuse? Some professional inquiry or something? *Any*thing?"

Coal Tar's forehead wrinkled in thought, and he held up a big index finger, silencing Quinlin as he contemplated the question.

Madeline Meggers considered herself fortunate to have found the condo on Rio Rancho Drive. It was a chic tri-level in a cluster of condos that filled both sides of a tree-lined block on the edge of University Park. Her neighbors, who appeared to be lawyers, CPAs, and stockbrokers, were nice enough, but, most important, they went their own way. The condo was close to the walking trails of Dallas Country Club, where Madeline fully intended to use Beau's membership—if, of course, the IRS didn't take that, too. And she had been mulling a master's degree, maybe in fine arts, at Southern Methodist University, which was only five minutes away. Keeping her mind and body busy, according to her counselor, only increased her odds of winning the booze battle.

The condo was spacious—2,400 square feet over three levels—and had two baths, two bedrooms, and a study. She knew when she signed the lease that it was too large just for her. But she also knew that she would be spending time with Jeb Quinlin. She was aware of the admonition about recovering drunks not making major life decisions in the first year of sobriety. But she also already knew that the good-natured detective had more character and decency than Beau Meggers had had on his best day. She admired him and respected him. And his easy, scarred grin made her wonder how a man who had seen what he had seen, been where he'd been, still had room for compassion. They could help each other make it. She wasn't stupid. She vowed to play out the relationship over time.

The condo, Madeline knew, was more than a new place to live. It was a symbol. Every moment she had been there had been a sober moment. There wasn't a bottle of Chablis in the house, no hangovers and no blackouts. No bad vibes. As she had told her counselor on the phone, "I've arrived from hell."

Except for the reams of financial records scattered over her dining room table. They were irrefutable proof of how perverted her former husband's ambition had truly become. Reading the documents hadn't been easy for Madeline, who hadn't hesitated to sign the IRS agreement to testify against him at trial. She wondered, scanning the illicit accounts filled with drug proceeds, if Beau had changed or if he had always been a thief. Could she have been that wrong about someone she lived with, someone with whom she had been intimate? An IRS agent had told her that he could be sentenced to sixty years in prison if convicted, and she wondered how she'd feel when it happened. Another set of documents to go over, a day with a federal prosecutor and a forensic accountant, and the saga would be behind her. The final vestiges of hell.

The phone rang at 5:15 P.M. It was the police officer Quinlin had stationed out front.

"Ms. Meggers, there's a man down in front to see you," the officer said. "Says his name is Chamberlain. Hold on a second. A Mr. Ray Chamberlain."

"Is he from the IRS?"

"Just a second," the officer said, talking to someone in the background. "Yeah, he's from the IRS. Could you come down to the car and sign the log authorizing him to come up?"

She peeked through the security hole in the door. The clump of azaleas obscured part of her view, but she could see the officer sitting in his squad car. He was talking to someone through the window.

Madeline smiled. Quinlin's concern for her safety wasn't only reassuring, it was sweet. In the midst of her chaos with Beau, the slow-talking detective was the anchor that moored her. She vowed to wean him off the Marlboro Lights, then slid off the night latch, unlocked the deadbolt, and headed down the steps to the parking lot.

The man wore blue slacks and a starched white shirt. His back was to her, with his left arm on top of the roof of the patrol car, and he was talking through the window to the cop, who was laughing.

"You got some papers for me?" she said as she approached.

In one uninterrupted motion, the man's hand flashed from his right pocket. Madeline saw a reflection off something silver as his hand sliced through the window of the car. In the windshield, she saw the cop's eyes widen in horror, then a torrent of red.

The cop fell toward the seat in slow motion. As he disappeared below the dash, his face was puzzled, surprised, and his mouth moved, unleashing more red.

The blood froze her, and immediately the man had her blouse with his fist, the knife pushing into her stomach.

"Our stories disclose in a general way what we used to be like, what happened, and what we are like now." It was the AA premise, tried and true for more than sixty years, that recovering drunks learn from each other's hard falls and recoveries. Periodically, they told their life stories, or "drunkalogues," at meetings in the hope someone might find a nugget to use in his or her own battle with the bottle.

As splintered as his thoughts were, with Harris on the loose and no clue what he was up to, Quinlin was nonetheless mesmerized, and scared, by Mark's story. Mark was a salesman, thrown constantly into situations in which clients expected to be wined and dined in return for big accounts.

Mark said he had three years' sobriety "this time." Before he fell off the wagon, he had been one of hundreds of thousands of AA success stories. Previously, he had gone without a drink twelve years before having dinner with a client and, as he explained, selling "my soul and my sobriety for twenty-four thousand dollars in commissions."

He'd only had three drinks that night.

"I handled the booze, I did my job, and I made a hell of a lot of money. And I left the restaurant with some stinking thinking. I had been able to shut it down after three drinks and, therefore," he said, grinning at his own stupidity, "I clearly wasn't an alcoholic."

The crowd laughed knowingly.

Over the next three months, everything that had meaning in Mark's life toppled like chain-reaction dominoes. He became a "low-bottom drunk" who swigged himself straight into the gutter. In brutal detail, which he laced with painful self-deprecating humor, he had an affair with his best client's secretary, lost the account, lost his job, was drinking a quart and a half of Absolut a day, lost his wife and children, and shot himself in the guts with a .38.

"I couldn't even commit suicide right," Mark said bitterly. "All I did was hurt myself real bad. *Real* bad."

Quinlin fidgeted and leaned next to Coal Tar: "If he doesn't hurry up and get to the happy ending pretty damned quick, I'm walking before I eat my own gun."

Suddenly the sound of Quinlin's beeper was incessant, and by the time he grabbed it and punched the button to silence it, Mark and the rest of the drunks were staring at him. Quinlin felt his face redden. He was embarrassed. And when he stole a glance at their faces, he was inexplicably mad. They looked perturbed, like they were monks in some goddamned monastery, and he was some outsider who had just proven himself ungodly. Their chants were holy, and he had interrupted their ritual. "Fuck you," he wanted to yell. "You're a roomful of drunks! Just like me." The beeper went off again while he was holding it.

"Fuck it," he said, standing from his seat and heading down the aisle for the phone in the lobby. He cursed with each step and was too wound up to see Coal Tar, his brow wrinkled in concern, following behind.

The number on the digital display looked familiar, but Quinlin couldn't place it; 9-7-7. It was one of the downtown exchanges. It only rang once before a man picked up.

"Clint?" Quinlin asked. "Clint Harper? Hey, what's the—"

"Jeb, listen to me." The reporter's voice was no-nonsense. "I just got a call from a guy who saw my story on the Twelve-Step Murders. Gave me an address and says I need to check the trunk of a BMW if I want the real story. Gave me a plate number, too. Could be a crank, but he . . ."

Coal Tar saw Quinlin's face turn hard.

"What's the address?" Quinlin asked.

"Rio Rancho Drive," Harper said. "It's—"

"I know where it is! It's Madeline's condo!" he yelled, dropping the receiver.

Quinlin bolted through the double glass doors into the parking lot with Coal Tar on his heels. The cruiser was already rolling when the big black man threw his ample butt into the seat, bracing himself on the inside of the roof while he tried to shut the door.

"Something's happened to Madeline," the detective said. "The motherfucker has done something to Madeline!"

He grabbed the magnetized flashing red light from the floorboard and stuck it through the window onto the roof of the car, slamming Coal Tar back in the seat as he floored the accelerator. He steered with his left hand, holding the radio microphone in his right.

"David 16, Base," he said.

"Base, go ahead David 16."

"This is an emergency. Contact the marked unit on protective surveillance at 3161 Rio Rancho Drive," Quinlin yelled, "and have him contact me ASAP on the CAPERS frequency."

He repeated the information and dropped the microphone onto the seat, grabbing the cell phone. He dialed McCarren's pager number, heard the beep, and plugged his own number in. McCarren should still be on stakeout at Harris's condo.

Traffic on Interstate 35 South abruptly turned to a parking lot in front of Quinlin's Crown Victoria, gridlocked by perpetual construction. Quinlin swerved onto the right shoulder, glancing the right rear bumper of a bronze Infiniti J-30.

"Stupid fuck," he muttered.

Communications called back on the radio.

"David 16, we are unable to raise the unit on Rio Rancho,"

the dispatcher said. "I am sending a beat unit to that location, Code 3. Will advise."

"Roger, Base. Speed it up, and roll another unit. I'll be there in five minutes."

Five minutes? Coal Tar grunted, but checked himself.

The shoulder of the interstate was pitted and rough, bouncing the Ford on its shocks. Quinlin accelerated, spraying gray dust and gravel onto the idled traffic. He cursed, periodically gesturing wildly at motorists edging their way onto the right side. At sixty and with Quinlin still hugging the shoulder, the big passenger closed his eyes, put his hands on the dash, and braced himself.

McCarren had been monitoring the frequency and called on the radio instead of the cell phone.

"Where's Harris?" Quinlin asked.

"No sign of him. I pushed the doorman and he swears Harris hasn't been around."

"We're en route to Madeline's," Quinlin said. "Meet me. We've got a problem."

Except for a uniformed officers' once-through to make sure Madeline wasn't dead inside, the patrolmen had stayed outside by the cruiser and Officer Richard Tranthem's body. The cruiser was cordoned off, and a line of blue held a group of curious onlookers on the grass beyond the sidewalk.

Quinlin paused at the open driver's window of the blue and white Ford. The officer looked young, maybe twenty-five, and was slumped in the middle of the seat on his right side. The detective figured he probably bled to death from the gaping wound across his throat before his body came to rest. His left hand was on his hip, and a wide gold wedding ring on his third finger. Somewhere, Quinlin knew, someone wearing blue was consoling a wife, maybe a mother and a child. He had performed the ritual himself, and he felt a buildup of nausea high in his stomach.

Madeline's door was closed but unlocked, and the unarmed electronic security system bleeped when he opened the door. Coal Tar stood inside the entryway while Quinlin ran from room to room and up, then down, the stairs. The condo was undisturbed and orderly, except for the dining room where financial records were scattered over the table. The Braun coffeemaker was on, and there were four cups of coffee in the decanter. A one-gallon water sprinkler, half full, was on the parquet floor in the dining room, next to a ficus tree.

Coal Tar watched Quinlin finish sweeping through the condo, and then stop. The detective was standing at the base of the stairs leading from the foyer. He was motionless and dazed. Silent.

Quinlin jolted when he heard his name yelled from outside. He went to the doorway and saw Clint Harper, a uniformed cop restraining him by his shoulder beyond the yellow tape.

"Damn," Quinlin said, just then remembering what Harper had told him on the phone. "Madeline's car. We've got to find Madeline's car.

"Let him through," Quinlin yelled at the cop.

"The BMW's in the parking lot around the corner," Harper said. "I've already spotted it. It's got the right plates."

The parking spaces weren't reserved, Quinlin noticed as he and the reporter ran around the building. Parking was first-come, first-serve. The spaces in front of Madeline's condo must have been taken when she last drove up.

"We'll have to chisel it," Quinlin said, staring across the lot at the trunk of Madeline's BMW 740i. Two uniformed officers ran to their patrol cars for tire irons.

"There's blood all over the sidewalk," Quinlin said to no one in particular. The crimson trail led diagonally across the walk from the trunk into the freshly cut lawn. He followed the path quickly past an iron-fenced swimming pool to an inset at the corner of the building. Inside the unlocked cedar gate were stacks of pool chemicals and long-handled skimmers. The cement floor was puddled with blood. Tossed on a can of chlorine was a bloody shirt, a pair of pants, and a rag, all of which were drenched in blood. There was little doubt what he'd find in the trunk. The question was who. He ran for the BMW.

His mind raced with his feet. Harris was into symbolism. In his psychosis, would it be perverted logic to stuff Madeline, who complained in group sessions about her husband's greed, into the trunk of her $75,000 car?

"Get Crime Scene around the corner," he yelled. "Somebody's lost a hell of a lot of blood around there." He noticed he didn't say *died*. He couldn't. Not yet.

Coal Tar stood a few feet away, trying to stay out of the way of the small cluster of cops gathered around the back of Madeline's BMW 740i. He watched Quinlin rubbing his right hand over his forehead, glancing periodically over his shoulder at the parking lot to check on the status of the tire irons. Quinlin was clearly scared, Coal Tar thought, and the detective paced a semicircle behind the car, rubbing his forehead.

"Want me to pop it?" one of the uniforms volunteered.

"No, I got it," Quinlin said, grabbing the tire iron.

The detective took a deep breath and exhaled. It was something he had to do himself. He wedged the iron between the frame of the car and the bottom lip of the trunk and pulled up. It was solid and didn't give easily. Quinlin heard the trunk lock pop on the third try, and the lid rose slowly on its own.

All he saw was blood, more blood than he'd seen as a cop. Not in twenty-five years, not since Vietnam. Blood obscured everything.

"Let me get the photographer," a voice in the back said.

"No," Quinlin said, not looking back. "There's no time."

"I'll get some gloves from the car," the voice said.

Quinlin didn't wait. He focused on mass, and made out what appeared to be a white shirt, but the head was twisted beneath the body toward the front of the trunk. Slowly, he bent over the trunk and leaned into it, pulling gently on what he believed was a shoulder. As he pulled the body upright, the head came with it, and he saw sideburns, long black sideburns on a man's profile, and his body sighed involuntarily.

"Who is it, can you tell?"

"Not anybody I know," Quinlin said.

The man appeared to be Hispanic, but with all the blood, Quinlin couldn't be certain. His throat was slit ear to ear. Quinlin pulled him nearer to the edge of the trunk and, as he was about to roll the body over the lip of the frame, he spotted another torso beneath the corpse.

"There're two!" Quinlin yelled, feeling the tension again. "There's another one under him!"

Quickly now, he rolled the first body onto the parking lot. It was emotional Russian roulette. The other corpse was face-down. It had caught all the bloody seepage from the man on top, and it was barely distinguishable as a body. The detective's hands were already covered with blood, and he reached for the far side of the lump and rolled it slowly toward him.

He cringed at the thought of it being Madeline, and he clamped his eyes shut and prepared himself. The corpse was a man. But not until Quinlin rolled him out of the trunk into good light did he recognize him. He was the pock-marked asshole with the MAC-10 who had come precariously close to killing him a day earlier.

Paul McCarren had joined the cluster of cops behind Madeline's car. He pushed his way to Quinlin. His senior partner was covered in blood to his elbows, and the first corpse had bloodied the front of his khakis when he rolled him out.

"So where's Madeline?" McCarren asked. "We still don't know?"

Quinlin lowered himself to the curb. Impervious to the

blood on his hands, he leaned his head into his palms. He was shaking badly.

"I can't think, Paul," he said. "I don't know. I don't know how this bloodbath happened. And I don't know where the fuck Madeline is. Or even . . ."

He breathed deeply to keep from crying. Coal Tar had found a water hose, which he turned on to a trickle and dragged to the curb.

"Stand up and lean your arms out here," the big man said, grabbing Quinlin by the shoulder. He was a hospital technician. He knew the danger of AIDS from blood.

He sprayed Quinlin's hands and arms, rubbing away the blood with his own hands under the flow of the water. Though it was more symbolic than effective.

"I don't want their shit on you," Coal Tar said simply.

31

An hour after Quinlin's arrival, the 3100-block of Rio Rancho Drive was under police siege. Three separate crime-scene units were on the ground, one scouring Patrolman Dick Tranthem's cruiser, another going through Madeline's condo room by room, floor by floor, and yet another that had cordoned off her BMW and the pool storage area. The summer sun was deep behind the trees, and a Dallas Police van stood by with portable floodlights. A medical examiner's van had already left with the dead officer, and another was about to leave with the two Hispanics, neither of whom carried ID. Deputy Chief Jon Abrams, having visited the scene and left, had pulled six detectives from CAPERS, and they were canvassing Madeline's neighbors and everyone else they could find. A team from Tactical was scouring the Dumpsters, shrubbery, and the banks of White Rock Creek, which meandered behind Madeline's condo, for the murder weapon.

Meanwhile, a small army of curious residents was clustered in the lawn beside Madeline's condo. Save for an occasional car burglary, the neighborhood was virtually crime free. Multiple murders and a kidnapping had electrified the tenants with fear. There was talk of alarm systems, and a few of the white collars talked about getting gun permits. Pushing the yellow line in front of Madeline's condo was a throng of reporters and minicams with cords that snaked across the parking lot and into vans with signs that said LIVE ON FIVE and EYEWITNESS NEWS. The sergeant in charge of media relations was on scene and promised hourly updates. "Problem is," Sergeant Tim Chandler was telling reporters, "we just haven't put all the pieces together yet.

"What we do know is that we have three homicides and one apparent abduction. One of the deceased is a Dallas police officer, whose name is being withheld pending notification of his next of kin. We hope to provide that information for you shortly. Additionally, we have two dead, unidentified Hispanic males who were found in the trunk of a car approximately one hundred and ten feet west of the police officer's. All three of the victims died of apparent stab wounds to the throat. See the medical examiner for official confirmation.

"A thirty-seven-year-old white female who is a resident here is also believed to have been kidnapped during this, ah, episode. At this time, we are not releasing her name. We don't want to jeopardize our investigation. Motive is unknown. I'll see you in an hour, and hopefully I'll have more for you."

Murphy Griffin, the manicured and shellacked on-screen star of *Live on Five*, had seen Clint Harper on the other side of the yellow tape. Not only was he not pleased about a competitor getting better access, he also knew the *Register & News*'s Pulitzer Prize winner didn't cover homicides, no matter how big they were. Harper's only recent story was about the drunk murders. Griffin played his hunch.

"Sergeant Chandler," Griffin yelled. "This connected to the Twelve-Step Murders?"

"We're not certain. That's all for now."

Three minutes later, the tease on Channel 5 was "The Twelve-Step Murderer apparently has struck again. A Dallas police officer and two others are dead at an exclusive North

Dallas apartment complex. A woman is missing. Details are moments away."

Crime Scene released the first floor to Quinlin as soon as they finished photographing and dusting. The brass had come and gone, and Quinlin pulled an extension phone to the dining room table. Periodically, he checked his message machine or called headquarters. They were futile exercises that kept him busy. Coal Tar had taken the liberty of emptying the coffee decanter and brewing a fresh pot. Madeline's dining room had become, by default, an impromptu emergency-operations center. Coal Tar, McCarren, and Harper sat around the table, as did a late, unwelcome arrival, an IRS Criminal Division agent named William Gladstone.

Gladstone, the investigator assigned to the Meggers case, had showed up after an IRS flunky had appeared at Madeline's condo with a briefcase of new faxes, saw the commotion, and phoned his office. Had Coal Tar and McCarren not stepped between them, Quinlin almost certainly would have knocked the federal agent on his butt.

"How can you not think that the fuckin' Colombians aren't going to come after their money, genius?" Quinlin had yelled. "You told Madeline's lawyer that you'd arrest Meggers's buddy, the consultant, and make them think he had rolled over on them. But that didn't happen, did it?"

"We couldn't find him," the IRS agent said lamely. "He must have gotten a tip or something."

"Like Beau Meggers, who's flying his little jet to Belize or some other bumfuck country where you'll never find him? So you just go ahead, freeze the Colombians' money, no problem. You're a popdick, you know that? Look around you. You happy?"

Periodically, a detective appeared with an update. Quinlin wasn't surprised when the door-to-door team came up empty.

Despite the fact that people should have been coming home from work, no one had seen anything. It was a yuppie neighborhood. White collars worked their own hours. A lot of them had to be young and single, and they stopped off for drinks, had business dinners, shopped, had dates, played racquetball, and worked out at spas after work. Condo-dwellers were erratic. It wasn't like investigating a crime in suburbia where you could set clocks by commuters, car pools, and Little League practices. And where you had Neighborhood Crime Watches and a handful of retired geezers who knew the whole block's business.

A TAC officer found a black Lexus coupe similar to the one used in Quinlin's shooting in a parking lot across the street from Madeline's condo. The Lexus had a Meggers Group parking decal on the windshield, and the plates checked to a leasing company. It would be morning before they could check the leasing company in New Jersey, but it almost certainly was leased by Meggers's company.

The scenario was taking shape, but it was built on speculation. Madeline was next on Harris's list, and he must have been watching her. The Colombians took a shot at Quinlin, probably to scare Madeline into backing off her deal with the IRS. But they still couldn't get their hands on the money or Meggers, so in typical drug-world strategy, they went for vengeance: Madeline.

"Man, it must have been a circus in that parking lot," McCarren said. "A psychopath and two Colombian guns stumbling over themselves trying to get to the same doorstep first. It works for me, but I still don't know how Harris lures two thugs into a storage room, slits their throats, and buries them in a trunk."

"Harris is far from stupid," Quinlin said, breaking his long silence. "He spotted them first. And he had to have a gun. It's the only way he would have the leverage to get them back there.

Once he got them there, cutting their throats wasn't that hard.

"The fucker's uncanny. He changes clothes, dips a rag in the pool, and gives himself a sponge bath.

"And figure this," Quinlin said, his voice turning hard. "He stuffs the boys in the trunk *after* he grabs Madeline. Had to. He had the keys to her trunk. No, he doesn't leave them in the storage bin. He's so goddamned meticulous and driven that he spends another ten minutes at the crime scene in broad daylight. He wants the stiffs found in Madeline's car. It's another statement. That's why he called Clint. He's proud of his little feat. It's the bow on his package."

"How'd he keep Madeline quiet while he was hauling the bodies?" McCarren asked.

"Maybe he tied her up," Quinlin said. "Or . . ." He couldn't continue.

Madeline's phone rang just as Quinlin was waving off the fourth or fifth suggestion that he get something to eat. He knew when he answered that his hunch had paid off.

"I knew I'd find you there, Quinlin," the voice said. "Gosh, I bet you're weary, huh? You've had a busy few days, checking in on Madeline, hitting a few AA meetings. And let's not forget my doorman. And Morton, Dad's assistant, and his ever-devious but effective lawyer, Averill Blackstock."

Harris had watched their every move, a realization that unnerved Quinlin.

Harris's voice was surreally casual, as if he were chitchatting before confirming a luncheon appointment with an old friend. Quinlin thought he heard Madeline in the background, but he couldn't make her out. He also thought he heard traffic noise. He checked the suction cup on the receiver that led to a small tape recorder.

"I knew you'd call," Quinlin said, gauging his words. "You're a narcissist, and this is your greatest coup thus far. I knew you'd want the credit."

Harris laughed.

"I never underestimate you, my drunken friend," he said. "But if you're trying to engage me to stay on the phone, don't waste your time. This is a cell phone. The only trace you'll get is to the nearest mobile transmitter. I'm afraid it won't help you."

"So how did you get rid of the Colombians? I'm impressed."

"Just a detail," Harris said.

Abruptly, his small talk turned dark and foreboding.

"We both know this has to end," Harris said, "and obviously, it must end tragically for one of us. Which one will it be?"

"That's true," Quinlin said, "but it doesn't have to involve Madeline. Why not—"

"Quinlin, tell me," Harris said, getting into the game, "you're a man of diverse interests. You ever read the Bible? Like the verse that goes, 'God made only water, but man made wine'?"

Harris's inflection was different. There was a pause, and Quinlin thought he heard paper crinkling. Harris cleared his throat.

" 'On the final day, when the king was feeling high, half drunk from wine, he told the seven eunuchs who were his personal aides . . . to bring Queen Vashti to him with the royal crown upon her head so that all the men could gaze upon her beauty, for she was a very beautiful woman.' "

The line went dead.

32

Manhunts are adrenaline-pumpers, those uncommon opportunities that break the patrolman's monotony of loud parties, drunken husbands and crying wives, prowlers, suspicious persons, and public drunks. The physiological edge in a manhunt is even sharper when it's a high-profile case; commitment and individual ego, measured sometimes in promotions, commendations, or even photographs in newspapers, are strong stimulants. But when the fugitive is a cop-killer, duty becomes a mission.

Old bulls near retirement, slackers, whiners, *everyone* in blue takes a fallen colleague personally. It's an axiom they may not repeat in front of their partners, but they feel it inside: There but for the grace of God go I. The fraternity mobilizes. Off-duty cops show up at substations, helicopters get launched, and cops from adjacent jurisdictions volunteer.

Mike Marshall, an off-duty patrol sergeant, heard about Dick Tranthem's murder on the radio on his way out of town. Tranthem was assigned to a different district, but Marshall aborted the family camping trip and had his wife and sons drop him off at Central. He tucked his spare .38 snub-nosed Smith & Wesson into the waistband of his cutoffs, checked in with the patrol captain, and took the only marked unit left in the parking lot, a Chevrolet Impala that had been red-lined for preventive maintenance.

Marshall headed southwest of downtown to the Mixmaster where I-35 and I-30 intersected in a concrete maze of overpasses, underpasses, frontage roads, and exits. He'd been in patrol thirteen years, and he reacted with habit. And common sense. The Mixmaster was the busiest exchange in North Texas.

The sergeant meandered through the interchange four times, making lazy-eights onto frontage roads and retracing his routes. White Tauruses were a dime a dozen, and he saw three in less than fifteen minutes. The tags were wrong on one, and the other two, whose tags he couldn't make out from the oncoming lanes, were driven by a black woman and a guy whose car was packed with kids in red caps, apparently headed for a Texas Rangers game in Arlington.

Marshall wound north on I-35 and exited onto Woodall-Rogers, the loop that connected I-35 with U.S. 75 to the east. He met two DPD units in less than a mile. Other cops were street-savvy, too, and Marshall knew he was duplicating their efforts. He twisted around, heading north on Harry Hines, a six-lane, divided boulevard that ran past Parkland Memorial Hospital and the sprawling University of Texas Health Sciences complex.

There was another white Taurus, headed south, almost hidden behind a Roadway eighteen-wheeler. Marshall slowed and spun his head sideways, staring momentarily into the last rays of the setting sun. He missed the letters on the plate, but the numbers were 591. He glanced at the sheet on the seat; it was a direct hit on the Hertz rental.

The sergeant was in midblock, and he wheeled the Impala into the six-inch median that separated the north-south lanes. He heard a crunching sound on the undercarriage, and the engine went dead. He twisted the ignition key frantically with no success, cursed, and grabbed the microphone.

"Charles 32. Suspect white Taurus in officer's death is headed southbound on Harry Hines from Motor Street. Suspect vehicle is driven by a white female accompanied by a white male on passenger side. Unable to pursue because of, uh, uh, because of mechanical problems."

The mike was still keyed. Everyone on the net heard the sergeant's frustration: "Dog-ass piece of *shit!*"

Quinlin knew his thoughts were frayed, and he wrestled with himself to remain functional. He asked a patrol sergeant to check on the officer stationed outside his mother's house. Harris had hit all around him. Sarah, and now Madeline. He had to know his mother was all right. At one point, when Quinlin was requesting a couple of detectives to continue the stakeout on Harris's penthouse, he ended up on the phone with Captain Barrick. "Hang in," his former supervisor had said, "you're doing fine." He had sounded like he meant it.

Though Harris had been vague in his phone call with Quinlin, the call had finally given the detective the probable cause he needed for an arrest warrant and a search warrant. While Quinlin had phoned in the bulletin to arrest Robert Harris, McCarren had headed downtown to type up the affidavit in support of a search of Harris's penthouse. Clint Harper had gone with him. The veteran reporter had already phoned in a story for the early State Edition; he wanted to be with McCarren when the cops searched Harris's apartment. The detail inside a serial killer's penthouse would be stunning in follow-ups.

"C'mon," Quinlin said as he walked toward Madeline's front door. Coal Tar had tried to be a wallflower, hanging on the periphery and out of the way where he could still keep an eye on Quinlin, who he feared would implode any second from the stress.

"Where we going?"

"I can't stay here," the cop said. "A man your size probably ought to eat a little something. We'll stop off, grab a bite. Then we'll meet up with McCarren and Harper at Harris's. We've got to do *some*thing."

They had just pulled away from Madeline's condo when Quinlin brought up his conversation with Harris. He had played the recording back two or three times for everyone in the room, trying to get everyone else's ideas on the bizarre message.

"What you think that trash meant?" he asked, resurrecting the discussion yet again.

"I don't know about the first part," Coal Tar said. "But I think the second verse is biblical. Guess the beautiful queen had to be Madeline. Water and wine. I mean, the man's hell-bent against liquor and people who use it. He's lost his shit big-time."

The part that bothered Quinlin was the reference to the queen with the royal crown, something about holding her up for everyone to see. Each of Harris's killings had been more public, more degrading and dramatic than the last. Killing three people who obviously weren't a part of his "master plan" for killing drunks had only showed his frenzy. And his message had definitely said "on the final day." Even Harris had said the game was about to end. If Quinlin couldn't stop it, he knew, the finale wouldn't be pretty.

Quinlin was headed west on Inwood Road, almost to Northwest Highway, when Sergeant Marshall's sighting of the white Taurus moved across the frequency. Quinlin activated the flashing red light, hit the siren, and careened left onto Northwest, slamming Coal Tar hard against the door.

He weaved in and out of traffic, cursing and waving at puzzled motorists, until he got to I-35 and swung south, toward downtown. Landmarks were blurring past Coal Tar's window; the exit to D/FW Airport, Mary Kay Cosmetics, Mobil, then the straightaway with Dallas's skyline filling the windshield. Coal Tar craned to see the speedometer. The needle was buried out of sight in the right side of the dash.

The radio squelched and crackled; every officer's report was negative on the Taurus. To the left of the expressway, somewhere south of Parkland, a police helicopter was flying a grid. Dusk was settling in, and a conga line of red-and-gold Southwest 737s was readying for final approach to Love Field, the inner-city airport.

Quinlin deliberately passed the exits that led to the Parkland medical complex. Right now, that part of Dallas probably had a higher concentration of cops than doctors. He'd go south and double back, picking the fringes.

"Shit, look!" Quinlin yelled. Coal Tar, who had been watching the helicopter, couldn't look at anything. Quinlin's scream had scared hell out of him, making him believe they were about to run through the rear of a truck. Just as Coal Tar dared to open his eyes, Quinlin locked down the brakes. Only the three-inch-wide shoulder strap kept Coal Tar's three hundred pounds from hurling through the windshield. When Coal Tar finally collected himself, he could see Quinlin pointing at the billboard on the far side of the interstate.

The billboard was a distinctive Dallas landmark sitting atop a five-hundred-foot-tall hill—a geographic anomaly in a city surrounded by prairie. On an average day, one hundred ninety-two thousand cars passed beneath it on Interstate 35, the asphalt artery that bisects middle America and connects Canada and Mexico. Lighted from top and bottom, the billboard rose more than one hundred thirty feet from the hilltop, making it visible from either direction on the interstate.

Its focal point, the single element that made motorists rubberneck, was a thirty-five-foot waterfall that cascaded down over man-made, Gunite rocks. The water collected in an eight-foot pool, and hidden pumps recirculated it through pipes concealed in the back, forming the continuous waterfall.

"Right there, goddammit!" Quinlin was yelling. "See it? Look at the sign. Wine, water, the queen with the crown? He was telling us what he was going to do. Look!"

In gigantic type to the left of the waterfall, the sign read CROWN REGAL, BLENDED WHISKEY SMOOTH ENOUGH FOR KINGS. Quinlin scanned the area around the sign and saw nothing. He was five hundred yards away, and he wasn't sure he could see anyone if they were there. Trees and brush surrounded the base of the sign, and he sure as hell couldn't see behind the sign.

At the last second, Quinlin swerved onto the Continental exit. His speed was too fast, and he lost control before he got the Ford righted on the frontage road. He ran the red light at the intersection and made a U-turn under I-35 and headed back north toward the billboard.

He slowed and veered right, off the shoulder of the interstate and down a steep embankment. He took the cruiser over two sets of railroad tracks to a gravel road that snaked along the base of the hill. He stopped directly beneath the sign and jumped from the seat. As he rounded the front of the car, he saw there was no hope. The base of the hill was craggy rock, with dense brush and briars growing out of its crevices. It was a good fifty feet just to get to a landing where he could get footing. He cursed loudly. The billboard had to be accessible to service crews. Staring at the rocky base of the hill, Quinlin knew the access had to be from behind the sign. He leapt back in the car.

He followed the gravel road and finally hit pavement at Oak Lawn, which he took to Harry Hines where the Taurus had been spotted a good thirty minutes earlier. Quinlin headed south into the deepening shadows of downtown. It was a three-mile U-turn to get to the back side of the hill.

"You think that's the way?" Coal Tar said, pointing to a street sign that said Goat Hill Road.

Quinlin steered hard right, overshooting the pavement and dropping the left tires in a shallow drainage ditch before he righted the Crown Victoria. A third of the way up the hill the asphalt turned to gravel, and he could see the road disappearing into the treeline ahead of him. He shoved hard on the accelerator to force the cruiser up the thirty-degree incline and cursed the sound of tires spewing gravel.

They were into the treeline, rounding the last bend, when he spotted the Taurus. It was parked near the crest of the hill and it appeared abandoned. Under normal circumstances, Quinlin instinctively would have radioed his discovery. But now he bailed out of the car and moved quickly up the hill, cursing the gravel that crunched beneath his boots. He moved to the weeds alongside the road, and pulled his .357 Smith & Wesson from the holster.

At the crest, he saw Madeline and Harris at the back side of the billboard. Dusk had settled in, and floodlights from the front of the board bathed its corners. Madeline was in jeans and a red, short-sleeved shirt, sitting on a caliche rock, her hands bound in front. Her knees were up tight against her chest, and Quinlin figured it was as close to a fetal position as she could get and still sit upright. Her eyes widened when she saw him, but she checked her impulse to cry out. Her brow wrinkled in concern, and she nodded her head to her left at Harris.

Quinlin's eyes moved over her, looking for blood or injuries. Thank God, he thought, she seemed all right.

Harris had seen him, too, and moved like a startled deer toward Madeline. Quinlin pulled his arm shoulder-high and drew a bead with the revolver, but Harris was already too close to Madeline to risk a shot. Harris grabbed Madeline by her collar and pulled her to her feet. He stuck the point of a ten-inch knife lengthwise against her jugular and eyed Quinlin defiantly.

The detective held the revolver out in front of him with both hands, and continued to ease closer. His focus was Harris, but his eyes moved quickly on either side. He saw an opened plastic tool box. A huge pulley with an inch-thick nylon rope lay on the ground. A foot away was a leather harness with metal eyelets—the kind window washers wore on high-rises.

Quinlin imagined Madeline's body suspended over the waterfall, hanging grotesquely on the billboard for strangers to gawk at as they drove seventy miles an hour down the interstate. Anger raged inside him. He didn't have time to think about it. Harris was exerting control.

"I know you saw the three unfortunate young men outside Madeline's condo," Harris said, positioning himself directly behind her.

Quinlin fixed on Madeline's eyes. They were striking even in fear. And vulnerable. He wanted to hold her.

"So there really can't be any doubt in your mind that I have the capacity to do it again," Harris said. "Drunks like it simple, Quinlin. That's what they tell us, isn't it? This should be simple enough: You save Madeline's life by dropping the gun; you kill her by continuing to walk toward me.

"How does it go, Quinlin? 'Those who do not recover are people who cannot or will not completely give themselves to this simple program. . . .' "

The line was from "How It Works," the preamble that led off every AA meeting.

"There's another line," Quinlin said. "I'm new at this, but it goes something like, 'There are those, too, who suffer from mental disorders, but many of them do recover if they have the capacity to be honest.' "

Too late Quinlin knew he'd made a mistake one-upping Harris. Madeline's abductor pulled her head backward and pressured the knife against her neck. Quinlin had already seen what a slashed carotid and jugular looked like. Harris was a psychopath, only marginally in control. He'd kill her in a heartbeat. Quinlin threw the .357 three feet in front of him.

Harris moved Madeline toward the gun, still staying behind her. He was composed again, arrogant.

"See Quinlin, it truly is a simple program."

It was then that Quinlin saw the big man in hospital whites emerge at the edge of the billboard. Coal Tar moved quickly, undoubtedly the way he had as a defensive end stalking a quarterback. He fell in behind, then crept almost beside Harris. Coal Tar was huge, but Quinlin was amazed by his agility. With his left hand, Coal Tar came down hard on Harris's forearm, slapping the knife from Madeline's throat. The blow knocked Harris off balance, but he managed to cling to Madeline with his left hand. Before he could use the knife, a black fist slammed below Harris's right ear like a sledgehammer, knocking him to one knee.

Coal Tar grabbed Madeline from Harris's grip so violently that the big man lost his footing on the rocks, his momentum pulling Madeline backward with him. The hill jutted sharply inward beside the billboard. They screamed at the same time, and Coal Tar disappeared down the drop-off. Quinlin saw Madeline grabbing frantically, finally grasping the base of a small oak sapling with her tied hands.

Harris still had the knife in his right hand, but Quinlin was on him just as he reached the .357. The detective slammed the revolver with the back of his fist, knocking it a good five feet away. Harris was up on his feet, retreating around the corner of the billboard to the front. He leapt onto the rock base, the floodlights capturing him full, and began sprinting to the other end. Quinlin stopped long enough to retrieve his revolver, losing precious ground. He was three feet behind Harris by the time he reached the base of the billboard.

They were at the center of the billboard and the heavy spray from the crashing waterfall saturated them. Quinlin felt his right boot slip on the slick rock, but he regained his footing. Harris was younger and agile, and the distance between them was growing. Quinlin, his injured ribs screaming again, knew he was as close as he was going to get. He sucked in a deep breath of air and flung himself at Harris's legs. He fell hard on his elbows onto the three-foot-wide rock retaining wall. He could feel kicking and thrashing, and he knew he had Harris's pants leg.

The fall scrambled the detective's senses, and he felt a sharp pain in his ribs. The lights from the billboard were blinding, and he saw little black dots when he opened his eyes. It was summer, but the spray from the waterfall was surprisingly cold. He felt himself shaking. Vaguely, he thought he heard a helicopter. And the knife. Where was Harris's knife?

Paul McCarren had to prowl deserted halls before he found someone to authorize the search warrant for Robert Harris's penthouse. Not until he and Clint Harper finally were headed to Harris's did they hear the radio traffic about the sighting of the Taurus. It was clear from traffic that the search was still underway, but no one was mentioning a location. Finally, as McCarren was about to request a 10–20, a uniformed unit advised his supervisor that he was at Harry Hines and Wycliff. The detective put the accelerator on the floor and headed for I-35, the quickest route.

"We must be getting close," Harper said only moments after McCarren had pulled onto the interstate. He pointed to his right at a hovering police helicopter whose floodlights illuminated the hillside where the billboard stood. "I wonder if they've got Harris or if they're just looking."

"I'll take Oak Lawn," McCarren said. "That'll put us in the general area."

The whine of acceleration momentarily drowned the radio.

"... but can't get to them. You need to roll an ambulance and backups."

"10-4, rolling an ambulance and backups."

"Roger that, Base, and tell them they'll have to come from, uh, Hines. From up here, it looks like they can't get there any other way."

The transmission was from the helicopter. They must have put Harris down on the ground.

"He said *them*," McCarren said. "He must still have Madeline."

The detective swerved around a slow-moving car into an inside lane.

"Look!" Harper yelled. "There under the sign. See?"

The floodlights silhouetted two writhing bodies on the base of the billboard.

"Looks like a hell of a fight," Harper said.

McCarren cursed and wheeled back into the outside lane. He slowed gradually to keep the car in back from rear-ending him, and he aimed the Ford down the embankment off the interstate.

"I don't have a clue how to get there," he said, bouncing behind the wheel, "but this looks as good as any."

Quinlin heard the shoe crack his nose even before he felt the pain. The sickening sound of splintered bone gave way to intense, radiating pain that he felt all the way to the back of his head. Still he managed to keep his grip on Harris's pant leg.

He pulled himself hand over hand on Harris's pants and shirt until he was straddling him. Quinlin's eyes wouldn't focus, but he felt Harris's nose and mouth with his left hand. He swung blindly with his right, twice, and he could feel the blows landing on bone. His chest wasn't cooperating and he was gasping, trying to suck in air when he felt the prone body beneath him roll sideways under his left leg. He heard the splash in the reservoir five feet below.

Harris was in the pool; he could wait. Quinlin lay facedown on the retaining wall, staring at the wet rock and breathing hard, trying to adjust his eyes to the intense light. His head was swirling, as if he was in a fifty-five-gallon drum rolling downhill.

Abruptly, he was frozen by a guttural scream, and he felt white-hot pain shoot through his left shoulder. He was lightheaded, and his breathing went shallow and trembly. He tried to think, but his mind wouldn't focus.

Quinlin heard more thrashing in the pool, and deep inside his shoulder he felt twisting and jarring. It was the knife. Harris had slammed the knife into his shoulder socket and now the bastard was trying to dislodge it, rocking the handle backward and forward, trying to extract it from bone and gristle.

Another blow from the knife and Quinlin knew he'd be dead. He sucked in as much air as his lungs could contain. He pushed himself forward with the toes of his boots and his outstretched right hand. He screamed with pain and thought he was losing consciousness. He heard Harris curse, and he could tell the knife wasn't jiggling in his shoulder anymore. Slowly, the cop braced himself with his right hand and pushed himself into a sitting position.

He told himself to concentrate on one task at a time. He was dizzy and unsteady, and he knew he had lost blood. His right hand wobbled with the Smith & Wesson, and he tried to steady his aim with his left. Harris's back was facing him as he crawled from the reservoir up the rocks into the waterfall.

Quinlin heard familiar voices below him, and he knew they belonged to Coal Tar and Madeline. *One task at a time.* He cursed the bouncing light that he realized now was attached to a helicopter above him. The searchlight was why his eyes wouldn't adjust. He saw Robert Harris standing above him now, on a ledge halfway up the waterfall.

Harris was defiant, as if there had been a child's race to the top of the mountain, and he alone had made it. Quinlin squinted and moved the revolver upward, toward the ledge. He realized he couldn't raise his left arm, which hung limply at his side. *The knife. The knife was still lodged in his shoulder*. Looking down the barrel, he was surprised how young Harris appeared. Handsome, clean-shaven, too young, too innocent to have killed.

Quinlin's mind was in overload, too consumed with pain and survival to be rational. Fleetingly, he saw a seven-year-old boy, bruised and lacerated, sitting on a curb as he drove away in a cruiser. For a nanosecond, he saw himself, his little arms trying to fend off another drunken blow by his father. He was nearly delirious.

The pistol was shaking again in his right hand. Their eyes locked and didn't flinch. Sarah would have seen those eyes, maybe the absolute last thing she ever saw. Had they been charming when he first approached her, catching her off guard and susceptible? How had they looked when he was painting her breasts? Obviously, the young patrol officer hadn't seen danger in Harris's eyes. He was still in the front seat, his gun snapped in the holster. Madeline had seen the horror in those eyes, too. Quinlin couldn't envision what must have gone through her mind when she saw the harness and the rope. That she was about to be stripped and killed just like Sarah, Anne Marie, and Kristin?

Quinlin adjusted his wobbly aim, bringing the revolver down to the midpoint of Harris's chest for a body shot. He flexed his right index finger through the trigger guard, and felt the metal against the second digit of his finger.

The pistol was as steady as it was going to be.

"Don't do it, Jeb!" It was Madeline. "I'm okay. He can't ever hurt anybody again. Jeb. Don't do it! He *wants* you to kill him."

The cop's eyes stayed on Harris. He was grinning, and his

hair was wet and over his forehead, like he had just bobbed up in the pool in his father's backyard.

Harris sensed Quinlin wasn't going to shoot. He ripped his shirt open, his eyes never leaving the cop's. A silver metal flask was taped to his ribs. He tore the tape loose and unscrewed the top.

Quinlin's mind wasn't computing. A flask?

Harris held out the flask in a toast, and yelled over the sound of rushing water:

"First you take a drink, then the drink takes a drink, then the drink takes you."

He put the flask to his lips and held it there until he drained it.

His face flushed crimson and the muscles at his jaws contorted grotesquely. He fell to his knees, bracing himself with one hand and grabbing his chest with the other. His torso heaved, and yellowish fluid trickled, then spewed from his mouth. Still he was staring. He jolted forward on the small landing like he'd been shocked. He landed limp.

The surging water washed him from the ledge, carrying him down the waterfall.

Quinlin sensed his body was moving, but he wasn't controlling it. He was hazy and shaking. And cold. He'd never been this cold. Someone was ripping his shirt, he could hear it and feel it. The rock was rough on his face, and he tried to move, to be comfortable. He couldn't. Then pain seared through his shoulder, and he could feel himself drifting.

"We'll have to leave the knife for Parkland," a voice said. "It's wedged. Don't want any more damage. But we've got to stop the bleeding somehow."

Quinlin was living now in splotches. Seeing, hearing, then gone. Dark, oblivious, quiet. Then back again.

He felt his head being tilted backward. Something rigid over his nose and an elastic slap at the back of his head. He heard a *whoosh*, and there was a jolting blast of cold air in his nostrils. He'd never been this cold. Couldn't somebody just give him a blanket? *Something?* He felt a sting inside his forearm and he tried to look, but he couldn't get his face off the rock.

"CareFlight's no good." It was the voice he heard earlier. "It's not flat enough around here. The MCU is closer. We can have him at Parkland in five minutes."

"The fuckin' hemorrhaging is out of control." Another voice. "We gotta get him out of here *now!*"

Quinlin heard it, but didn't react. He wondered what it meant that he wasn't scared.

He was being jostled, and pain shot like a laser through his shoulder and ribs. The rock was gone from his face and someone had his head, turning it sideways. Coal Tar was above him. He felt straps being cinched up across his back and legs. He knew he was on a gurney. A blanket would . . .

"Goddammit, don't drop him!" McCarren?

Quinlin felt a sudden sensation of falling, and he knew he was going downhill. He could hear the gravel crunching beneath their feet. He saw the white wash from the floodlight on the back of the mobile care unit. He could feel himself being hoisted, and he was bathed in intense light. He was facedown, and under the high-intensity light, he could make out the tiny fibers in the cotton sheet.

Now he was scared. His eyes watered and he couldn't swallow.

The touch was light, and at first he thought he was hallucinating. The faint, familiar scent, what'd she call it, Contradiction? It was there again, fingertips on the back of his neck, moving, caressing, consoling.

He felt lips lightly on his ear. A tiny kiss and a hoarse whisper:

"So, Officer. Have you ever done it on a gurney?"

Quinlin felt motion, and he knew he was moving forward.

READ ON FOR AN EXCERPT FROM
HOWARD SWINDLE'S NEXT BOOK

DOIN' DIRTY

COMING SOON IN HARDCOVER
FROM ST. MARTIN'S MINOTAUR

1

Jeb Quinlin had done the best he could to put Brett Holman in prison for the rest of his life. Now, as he stepped down from the witness stand, he wasn't sure he'd done enough. Quinlin had testified about Holman's prints being found on the murder weapon, offered proof that he had bought the Smith & Wesson .380 from a sporting goods store a week before the murder, and destroyed Holman's only alibi witness, a bottle blonde who wasn't nearly as eager to commit perjury after Quinlin had threatened her with a guaranteed ten years at Gatesville for the vial of cocaine in her purse.

Still, juries were dice-rolls. They liked things neat and nice, with no loose ends. Hell, life was a loose end. Not black, not white, just a bunch of diffuse gray which, often as not, obscured the truth like fog on a rock. Juries wanted motives, and Quinlin hadn't given them one. He knew why Brett Holman had rung Gerald Richardson's doorbell, then shot him three times in the face and chest when he opened the door. But *knowing* something to be true and *proving* it was a horse of a different color. The OJ trial had taught him that, along with several judicial abortions of his own.

On his way out of the courtroom, Quinlin spotted a seat on the aisle and impulsively slid in. The stack of paperwork on his desk could wait a half hour. Pluck Watkins was the prosecution's next witness, and Quinlin figured Pluck would be worth hanging around for, particularly if he was sober. Pluck could give the jury the motive. If they believed him.

Pluck Watkins had been the Richardsons' gardener. Quinlin had found him just two days before trial, and even when he had, he wasn't sure about Pluck's abilities as a witness. The old man was nearly seventy, stooped and grayed, and spoke with a near-indiscernible black dialect. Worse, Pluck was a career wino. Drunk, he spoke his own language.

Pluck had been trimming hedges in the Richardsons' backyard when he happened to glance through the windows into Loretta Richardson's bedroom, catching the lady of the house and an equally nude Brett Holman doing the horizontal mambo.

Now, on the witness stand, Quinlin noticed, Pluck was nervous and edgy, which probably meant he was at least quasi-sober.

"You're appearing here to testify voluntarily, aren't you, Mr. Watkins?" the prosecutor asked.

"Not 'zactly, no suh," the old man said earnestly.

"What do you mean, 'not exactly'?"

"Well suh, that *dee*tective, Quinfield. . . ."

"You mean, Quinlin?"

"Yas suh," Pluck said, "he told me he'd put my sorry ass *under* the jail if I wudn't sober and tell the truth."

Quinlin felt his face turning red. He hoped Pluck stopped there, not volunteering that the detective had also promised him a bottle of Thunderbird if he showed up sober and did a good job on the stand. The assistant district attorney grinned and waited for the light laughter to end before moving along. Quinlin sensed the jury liked the old man, who clearly was trying to do his best despite his alien surroundings. The prosecutor led him though the questioning, which put Pluck in the

Richardsons' backyard with his hedge trimmers and, by happenstance, glancing through the window of the master bedroom.

"When you saw Mrs. Richardson and Mr. Holman in the Richardson bedroom, how were they attired?" the prosecutor was asking Pluck.

The old drunk looked at him quizzically, but didn't say anything.

"Come on, Mr. Watkins," the assistant district attorney said, annoyed. "Don't be bashful. You can tell the jury. How were they attired?"

The old man's forehead wrinkled and he stared distantly at the ceiling.

Finally, the judge interceded. "Mr. Watkins, I can hold you in contempt and put you in jail if you don't answer," he said. "Now, answer the state's question. How were Mrs. Richardson and Mr. Holman attired?"

"Well suh," Pluck said finally, "they wasn't a-tired. They was a-fuckin'."

The jury gave Brett Holman life.

As it winds its way south from Dallas, Houston School Road moseys through flat, indistinguishable farmland. South of Loop 635, decades of farm machinery and neglect by county commissioners has turned the asphalt into a quilt of pits, ruts and patches. Day or night, Jan Baynum knew the stretch of road by heart, veering over the center stripe by rote to dodge a pit, swerving to the sloping shoulder to avoid a rut. She'd made the same trip five days a week for more than fifteen years from her home in Lancaster to Baylor Medical Center in downtown Dallas.

On this night, the registered nurse was woefully late. It was 3:30 A.M. before she finally left the hospital, forced to stay late because every bed in the sixth-floor cancer ward had been full and her counterpart on the overnight shift had phoned in sick. Administering chemotherapy was exacting work, made even more difficult if the shift was short-handed; she had volunteered to stay over.

Jan Baynum would later put the time at about 3:55 A.M. when, just as she neared a curve in the road, she saw a pair of taillights appear almost spontaneously, as if they had just swerved onto the road from the ditch. Instinctively she touched the brakes entering the curve. That's when she saw the little sports car beside the road. As her car was almost beside the vehicle, the splash of her headlights swept the silver sportster, and she thought she saw someone slumped against the driver's side glass. The taillights that had appeared so abruptly in front of her had already disappeared into the darkness.

She was a woman by herself, in pitch-black darkness on a lonely road, but the more she drove the more she knew she had to go back. She was a registered nurse after all, and someone could need help. She turned around and went back.

She stopped on the opposite shoulder of the two-lane road, leaving her engine running and her headlights on. She removed her cell phone and dialed 9-1-1, but didn't push the send key. The phone was primed if she needed it; the push of one button would summon help. Cautiously, she approached the car and tapped on the side window. She could see the side of a man's head and his ear. When he didn't move, she opened the door gently, reaching quickly over the top of the glass to keep the man from slumping out of the car.

She put her fingers on his jugular vein, but found no pulse. She couldn't see it in the dark, but she smelled the vomit. Jan Baynum pushed the send key on her phone and walked back across the road to her car to wait for the police.

She collected her wits. She almost forgot about the taillights that had appeared from nowhere and then vanished so quickly.

* * *

The early-morning smells invigorated Quinlin, made him happy to be alive and up early before the sun moved things ahead on its own agenda. For some reason, the clock moved more quickly in the light than the dark. The smell of brewing coffee gurgling in the pot on the counter mixed with the freshness of sourdough bread toasting in the oven, all of which was overpowered by the aroma of bacon crackling in the microwave.

And there was Madeline, meandering obliviously through the logged kitchen and great room in nothing but a white Dallas Cowboys jersey and a pair of black panties, making it tough for him to concentrate on the five eggs scrambling in the skillet. Physical attraction was one thing. Lust, after all, was a dilemma with a twenty-minute solution. But whatever the intangible trait that lay beyond her skin-deep beauty, Quinlin knew, that was the real reason Madeline had become habit-forming.

She took her customary position at the back window, peering intently through the faltering, pre-dawn darkness at the deer feeders twenty-five yards from the back of the ranch house. Deer moved early, and once they had discovered the corn in the two galvanized feeders, the backyard of Quinlin's house had become a regular stop. The ritual also became an anticipated treat for Madeline and Quinlin, who ate their breakfast in the nook at the back windows, watching the deer gouge and butt each other for their turn at the yellow corn in the troughs.

"Jeb, he's back!" Madeline yelled, just as he was spooning the scrambled eggs from the iron frying pan onto the serving plate. "Get over here quick before you miss him!"

Quinlin dumped the eggs onto the platter and moved quickly to the telescope at the back of the great room. The sun hadn't yet made its grand debut, but it was already diluting the darkness the way a hefty splash of cream lightens black coffee. He could see the right side of the buck's rack, then a portion of his muzzle through the cross-hairs. He squinted over the amplified glass to orient himself. The deer in the distant dawn was sturdy and big, his muzzle maybe even reaching Jeb's shoulders.

"Let me see," Madeline said, pushing Quinlin from his vantage point behind the telescope. "God, he's so beautiful. Can you imagine how many people have tried to put him on their walls? He's just majestic."

The buck didn't have a lock on majestic. Not with Madeline bent over the telescope, the Cowboy jersey clumped at her waist, leaving nothing to cover the black panties. It was sensory overload, with Jeb looking over her shoulder at the spectacular deer, then glancing down at a rounded butt that couldn't be contained.

"This ol' boy's bound to be pretty good at staying alive," Quinlin said, still in his coarse, pre-coffee rasp. "He's a trophy, all right. How many white deer do you see anyway? I need to nail him before he gets away again."

He moved to the tripod with his Canon Rebel already mounted and loaded with the fastest film he could find. He hoped for enough light as he focused the zoom lens and hit the motor drive. He had reserved a special place for Whitey's picture above the mantle on the native rock fireplace. The motor drive roared, clicking off all thirty-six frames in only seconds.

As if the white buck instinctively sensed the intrusion, he meandered off behind a clump of blackjack oaks, taking the three does with him.

"You'd have missed Whitey if you hadn't finally listened to me," Quinlin said, grinning. "Told you it'd be worth your while to spend another night. But no, you just had to get back to town. So tell me, Ms. Meggers, how many sights like this do you see from *your* back door?"

"Whitey's the only reason I've been hanging out here," she

said, acting indifferently. "Now that we've got him on film, guess I'm fresh out of reasons for living like a part-time hill-billy."

"I think you mean red-neck," Quinlin said. "There's a difference. Socially and politically. Tell you what, leave your car out here and drive in with me this morning. While we're in Dallas, we'll get a doctor to look at that arm, too."

"What arm?" Madeline asked, clearly clueless.

"The one that I'm apparently twisting against your will."

2

Detective John Dabney appeared in the squad room with a cup of vending machine coffee and carrying a large transparent plastic evidence bag with someone's personal belongings. Carefully, he put his coffee on the edge of his desk, and dumped the contents of the plastic bag unceremoniously onto a stack of unfiled police reports. Wallet, a BMW monogrammed key ring with six keys, a Yale class ring, and small change. The young detective opened the wallet, spent several seconds counting, and announced to no one in particular: "Not your normal corpse-beside-the-road. BMW Z-3 convertible, a cool three hundred fifty-seven dollars in knock-around cash, and dressed like Jeb's stockbroker."

Quinlin let the jab, an obvious reference to his new ranch and pickup truck and probably his girlfriend's money, slide.

"Where'd you find him?" Quinlin inquired from two desks away. It was early for the day watch, and the two homicide detectives had the Crimes Against Persons bullpen to themselves except for a night shift detective named Simmons, who was dozing with his feet on his desk.

"Early this morning, on the shoulder beside Houston School Road," Dabney said. "Another ten, fifteen feet and he'd have belonged to Lancaster."

Quinlin grinned, remembering his rookie year as a detective. Gus Branson, a legendary old homicide detective, was two weeks from retirement. Branson's remarkable claim to fame was that he had cleared every case he'd ever been assigned, though word in the squad room was that some of his cases were about as shaky as the old man's grip had become in the last few years.

Quinlin, in only his second week out of uniforms, watched incredulously one night as Branson dragged a corpse by its collar across four lanes of Coit Road where he dropped it in a parking lot on the westernmost reaches of the City of Richardson's jurisdiction.

"Richardson never gets any murders," Branson said, dodging a pickup on his return across Coit. "Hell, the body's been dumped anyway. Doesn't matter where it lands. They'll probably be proud to get one. Give 'em something to do."

"I'm figuring Mr. Carlisle here as a medical," Dabney said, bringing Quinlin current. "Not a mark on him. Vomited all over himself. The JP ordered an autopsy, but it's gonna be a heart or something. The good—and should I say well-heeled—die young."

Quinlin went back to his coffee and newspaper. An advertisement left him shaking his head and muttering. The quad-cab, four-wheel-drive Dodge pickup he'd bought three months earlier to replace his bullet-riddled International Scout was fifteen hundred dollars cheaper at a dealership in Denton. He pulled the felt-point pen from his pocket and did the math, knowing he was going to be even more pissed. Thirty-eight miles north to Denton, fifteen hundred dollars. Yep, $39.47 a mile, that's what it broke down to, one-way. Could have saved some money on that trip.

"Uh oh," the younger detective said ominously. He was holding a small laminated orange card in the air when Quinlin looked up.

"It's a DPS press card, Jeb," Dabney said. "Says our stiff's a staff writer for *The Register & News*. Somebody named Richmond Carlisle. Ever hear of him?"

"No, but it doesn't matter," Quinlin said. "You better hope like hell it's a medical, else you just got your ass dropped in the grease. The media takes it personally when something traumatic happens to one of its own. Page One. Politically sensitive. Count on it."

Within the hour, Deputy Chief Jon Abrams, Dallas' chief of detectives, walked into CAPERS, grabbed a red marker and wrote Richmond Carlisle's name on the eraseable board under the heading *Quinlin/McCarren*. Dabney, less than three months in plainclothes, was quietly relieved; Quinlin wasn't excited, but neither was he surprised.

Clint Harper answered on the first ring, producing a sigh of relief from Quinlin. Nearly every other time he'd tried to reach *The Register & News*' highest-profile reporter, he had been out of town on assignment.

"They finally take your American Express card away from you?" Quinlin asked. "What you doing in town?"

"Naw, the editors are in a big circle-jerk trying to figure out what my next assignment's gonna be. The executive editor apparently thinks I don't hum the company chorus. He thinks that I take too long to produce too little, so he's lobbying for me covering the SPCA or some other sacred cow of his. Meanwhile, I'm just hanging loose, waiting on a puff of smoke from the Brain Trust."

"Guess the aura from the Pulitzer's long gone, huh?" Quinlin said to no response. "Tell you what, Clint, this isn't all social. Do me a favor. Go to your Human Resources, find out who Richmond Carlisle's next of kin is, and let me pick you up in front of the building in five minutes. We've got a problem. I'll run it down for you, what little I know at this point, but the bottom line is, your Mr. Carlisle's met his last deadline."

"Foul play?"

"Probably not, but we're not sure right now."

"Wouldn't rule out accidental suffocation, if I were you," Harper said.

"What you talking about?"

"Accidental because Carlisle's got more than a healthy respect for himself, and suffocation because he's always got his nose up some editor's ass."

Quinlin laughed: "Take it you're not gonna be a pallbearer?"

"All of Richmond Carlisle's pallbearers are gonna be strangers."

Quinlin led the way, and headed to a booth at the back of the Farmers Market Grill. The café, a time-worn institution on the city's southern and frayed edge, was in a lethargic time warp between breakfast and lunch, and about a quarter of the tables were filled with malingering coffee drinkers. A curious odor of coffee and collard greens hung heavy in the air. The detective caught the waitress's eye, held up two fingers and slid into the side facing the door. Old habit. Quinlin didn't sit with his back to any door.

"I called our friend at the medical examiner's office and asked him to pull out all the stops on your buddy," Quinlin said. "Berryman said he'd do the autopsy himself, which makes me feel a lot better."

Quinlin had also phoned Richmond Carlisle's next-of-kin information to his partner, Paul McCarren, who would put in the call to Carlisle's folks in Manhattan. Death notification was one of cops' worse jobs. That's why they invented junior partners. Quinlin had handled his share of horrible news over the years. There was still the issue of notifying the dead man's employer, *The Register & News*, which Quinlin dreaded like a salt-water enema. A reporter's death—even if it ultimately turned out to be a natural causes—was guaranteed to become what Quinlin called a "head-shack" case, one that would get the attention of headquarters and all the brass that inhabited it.

In Richmond Carlisle's case, *Register* editors undoubtedly would make phone calls to chiefs' private lines to express their "concern." There would be mutual consternation between the powerbrokers who controlled the city's only printing presses and the politically-appointed police brass. Air was thin at those heights, and gravity would take over. Shit would roll downhill and become avalanches, which was where Quinlin always found himself in politically sensitive cases—up to his armpits in sewage.

The waitress appeared with two white cups and a small, copper-colored thermos of coffee. Judging from her twang, she was from some widespot in Deep East Texas, where she'd apparently got about twenty pounds too familiar with biscuits and gravy. She was a peroxide blonde with big hair, and her cowgirl butt was enshrouded in a pair of Wranglers so tight they had to have been sprayed on.

"Don't reckon y'all want to bother with the menu, huh?"

"No," Harper said, anticipating her concern, "but if you'll let us borrow your booth here for a little while, we'll make it up in the tip. That fair, hon'?"

She rolled her eyes in a seeing-is-believing look, did a pert about-face and strutted her cowgirl butt to the waitress station, where she turned abruptly to make sure she still had an audience. She wasn't disappointed, catching Harper's eyes locked on her most prominent asset.

"Don't want to upset your natural-causes fantasy about Richmond," Harper said, sucking flame from a Bic into a Marlboro Light, "but he was way over his head in some pretty heavy stuff when he croaked. Maybe just coincidence; maybe not."

"I'll let you enthrall me with the details if you'll let me bum one of those Marlboro Lights first," the detective said, looking around guiltily. "Madeline doesn't have to know anything about this. Staying off the booze is one thing; redlining *everything* in my life is another."

"You're preaching to the choir," Harper said, passing the disposable lighter and a Marlboro across the table. "If I had to give up smokes right now, I'd be drinking again by nightfall. I've got to have *a* vice. Otherwise I'd be as boring as you, Jeb."

"It's true," Quinlin said. "I'm a damned choirboy. Don't know why anybody would even want to associate with me. I wouldn't, truth be known."

Harper didn't mince words; it was one of the hallmarks of their longstanding relationship. They shot straight with each other, not having to read into the record the routine caveats about, "Don't quote me on this," or, "I'll lose my job if anyone finds out where this is coming from." The precautions were taken for granted over years and, occasionally—but only when absolutely necessary—were protected by flat-out lies, even to lieutenants and editors. The relationship meant not only that Harper and Quinlin were professional colleagues, but that they drank and chased together in the not-so-old days.

"Richmond Carlisle was a *prima donna* without portfolio," Harper said. "He talked the talk, but he was lame on the walk. Bottom line, he was an Ivy-League golden boy who ingratiated himself to our executive editor, sucked up to get good assignments, almost always investigative stories, and virtually, at least in my opinion, almost always missed the bullseye. He was one of those who wanted to use *The Register & Dispatch* as a stepping stone to get to the hallowed *New York Times*. Mommy and Daddy have some stroke with Brewster; I hear they own a substantial chunk of stock in the paper. So when Junior graduated with honors from Yale, he landed in our newsroom like he was Pulitzer's bloodline. He's a pompous asshole. Was, I guess.

"Anyway," Harper said, "young Carlisle was meddling in a couple of things that could have gotten him in trouble. You read the stories a few weeks back about Bumpy Rhodes?"

"About Bumpy not having enough collateral to write all the bail bonds he's got outstanding?" Quinlin said. "Yeah, you guys cost him a cool half-million dollars and got his inside man at the sheriff's department fired, right?"

"Well, that was Richmond Carlisle's handiwork," Harper said. "Probably the best stuff he's done since he's been here. It was a throw-down series, all based on public record, and I hear the courthouse reporter actually got the tip. Carlisle just checked it out and it fell together. But it created some problems for Bumpy with the Bail Bond Board."

"Bumpy ended up naked, holding his crank on that one," Quinlin said. "And Bumpy's never been real fond of that posture."

"Yeah, but is Bumpy going to risk a thriving business just to get even with a schmuck reporter over a story that's already run?" Harper asked. "Been my experience that the real danger is *before* the story runs, not after. That's when you can get some ribs broken. Afterwards, well, that only brings the heat on you, and you're already in the floodlights anyway. And Bumpy knows he doesn't need any exposure."

Quinlin knew Delbert "Bumpy" Rhodes mostly by reputation. And Rhodes' reputation in law enforcement circles was about as stellar as the Nightstalker's. Quinlin knew a detective in Robbery & Theft who caught Bumpy taking food stamps and child welfare payments from the wife of a man who had absconded on one of his bonds. Bumpy, all two hundred seventy-five pounds of him, was puffed up and indignant, claiming it wasn't theft at all, just merely an "escrow account of sorts," until the fugitive turned himself in on the outstanding

$100,000 bond. Rhodes returned the welfare proceeds and a grand jury declined to indict.

"Did Bumpy threaten Carlisle?" Quinlin asked.

"Bumpy threatens everyone," Harper said. "Probably did, but I can't see him following through, not with a reporter."

"You said Carlisle was working on a couple of things," Quinlin said. "What else?"

"Well," Harper said, "coming from where you come from, you're gonna know who he was messing with when he ended up with a tag on his toe. And you're gonna know why I told the executive editor he was full of shit if he thought I was going to babysit Richmond through the investigation. That's why he thinks I'm not a company guy, I guess. I don't know what the lead was, or where it came from, for that matter, Junior was being really cagey about what he had and where he got it. But Junior was screwing around with Clinton Colter and his boys."

Quinlin swallowed the mouthful of coffee and let out a low whistle. "The Colters," he finally said. "That's about as strong as it gets in this state. What, he couldn't find any crap on the governor?"

"It would have been easier," Harper said, "and probably a hell of a lot safer. That's why I think Berryman might find more than a congenital heart problem or a stroke. I tried to tell them that. . . ."

Quinlin was lost in thought. Yeah, he was intimately familiar with the Colters, or at least had been as a teenager growing up in Comanche Gap, where the Colters still headquartered their statewide business conglomerate. He had gone to school with Buck and Wade, Clinton Colter's two sons. Even been to the famous Pan Permian Headquarters Ranch on several occasions when school classes would have barbecues and swimming parties at the Colters' Olympic-sized pool and cabana. What he had seen was opulence beyond a young country boy's imagination. Jeb was the son of a divorced mother who scraped by working the overnight shift mopping floors and emptying bed-pans at a nursing home. But at the Colters, Mexican butlers moved among the students and teachers offering cabrito, tamales and fajitas from trays that were gorged with exotic food, some of which Jeb couldn't even pronounce.

Supposedly, Clinton Colter's main house was an exact replica of the governor's mansion in Austin. Two hundred yards away, a huge aircraft hangar sat beside an asphalt runway used exclusively by the Colters' Beech King-Aire. It was undoubtedly a Lear Jet by now, Quinlin imagined. That was thirty years ago. Rumor was rampant in Comanche Gap about how ol' man Colter came up with his untold millions, and vague speculation was that it wasn't all that legitimate. A younger Jeb Quinlin dismissed much of what he heard as envy and wishful thinking. Sul Ross County was, for the most part, a relatively poor ranching county and it was understandable, he thought, that its residents would resent wealth in the midst of their bareknuckled, hardscrabble lives.

"Can you find out for sure what kind of lead Richmond had?" Quinlin asked.

"It'll be tough since I bowed out," Harper said. "Particularly now that he's dead. But one of the many reasons I refused to participate is that the smug bastard wouldn't say. Just 'impeccable sources.' Well, that didn't cut it with me. That's not the way I play the game. A reporter doesn't trust me enough to tell me where his information's coming from, I don't trust him enough to work with him."

Quinlin was momentarily lost in thought. The sound of breaking plates brought him back. Across the room, East Texas was red with embarrassment, standing in the debris of broken dishes.

"Figure I'll drive out and visit the scene when I leave here," Quinlin said, "just to get the lay of the land. Our rookie assumed he was investigating a medical, and I get the feeling that the only thing Crime Scene did was take pictures. Between you and me, that could come back to bite us in the ass."

The detective eyed his watch; it was 11:30. "*After* I get something to eat," Quinlin added. In the almost year since he'd been sober, he'd been eating anything that didn't bite him first. He ordered a chicken-fried steak, mashed potatoes with cream gravy, pinto beans, collard greens, cornbread and homemade coconut cream pie. Harper opted for a cheeseburger and fries.

"You keep eating like this, you gonna make Bumpy Rhodes look like a runt," the reporter said.

"Doubt it," Quinlin said. "I got good metabolism. It's the only good side-effect from being Type-A, and damned sure the only decent trait I inherited from my old man."

Before they headed for the crime scene, Harper pitched a ten-dollar bill on the table for East Texas's tip, noticed her eyeing him, and nodded to her on the way to the cash register.

"You know," Harper said, falling in behind Quinlin, "take fifteen or twenty pounds off that cowgirl, and you might be surprised."

"Wouldn't be enough," Quinlin said. "She'd have to lose the double-bubble, too."

"You talkin' about the gum or the hair?"